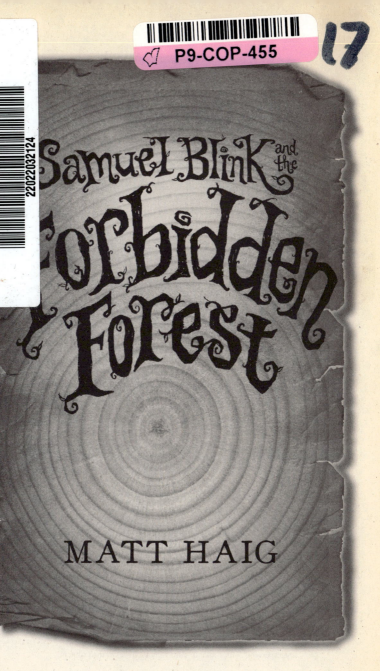

# Samuel Blink and the Forbidden Forest

## MATT HAIG

PUFFIN BOOKS

PUFFIN BOOKS

Published by the Penguin Group

Penguin Young Readers Group, 345 Hudson Street, New York, New York 10014, U.S.A.

Penguin Group (Canada), 90 Eglinton Avenue East, Suite 700, Toronto, Ontario, Canada M4P 2Y3
(a division of Pearson Penguin Canada Inc.)

Penguin Books Ltd, 80 Strand, London WC2R 0RL, England

Penguin Ireland, 25 St Stephen's Green, Dublin 2, Ireland (a division of Penguin Books Ltd)

Penguin Group (Australia), 250 Camberwell Road, Camberwell, Victoria 3124, Australia
(a division of Pearson Australia Group Pty Ltd)

Penguin Books India Pvt Ltd, 11 Community Centre, Panchsheel Park, New Delhi - 110 017, India

Penguin Group (NZ), 67 Apollo Drive, Rosedale, North Shore 0632, New Zealand
(a division of Pearson New Zealand Ltd)

Penguin Books (South Africa) (Pty) Ltd, 24 Sturdee Avenue,
Rosebank, Johannesburg 2196, South Africa

Registered Offices: Penguin Books Ltd, 80 Strand, London WC2R 0RL, England

First published in Great Britain as *Shadow Forest* by Random House UK, 2007
First published in the United States of America by G. P. Putnam's Sons,
a division of Penguin Young Readers Group, 2007
Published by Puffin Books, a division of Penguin Young Readers Group, 2008

3  5  7  9  10  8  6  4

THE LIBRARY OF CONGRESS HAS CATALOGED THE G. P. PUTNAM'S SONS EDITION AS FOLLOWS:

Haig, Matt, date.
Samuel Blink and the forbidden forest / Matt Haig.
p.  cm.
Summary: Accompanied by his aunt's Norwegian elkhound, Ibsen, twelve-year-old Samuel
ventures into a weird forest filled with strange and dangerous creatures to rescue his younger
sister, Martha, who has been mute since their parents' recent death.
ISBN 978-0-399-24739-2 (hc)
[1. Brothers and sisters—Fiction. 2. Magic—Fiction. 3. Imaginary creatures—Fiction.
4. Norwegian elkhound—Fiction. 5. Dogs—Fiction. 6. Orphans—Fiction. 7. Norway—Fiction.]
I. Title.
PZ7.H12597Sam 2007  [Fic]—dc22  2006024827

Puffin Books ISBN 978-0-14-241191-9

Set in Apolline
Design by Katrina Damkoehler

Printed in the United States of America

*For Andrea*

# CONTENTS

# Part II

# Part III

*There is a place you must never enter. It is a place where evil has many faces, and where creatures of myth and legend live and breathe. And kill. It is a place beyond dreams or nightmares—a place that has so far been too feared to be called anything at all. Now, in this book, I will explain the unexplained, and give fear a name that suits it well. That name shall be Shadow Forest, and it will plant terror in your hearts.*

*—Professor Horatio Tanglewood*

*The humans and other creatures you will meet in this book*

# THE HUMANS

## The Blinks:

*Samuel Blink*—A twelve-year-old boy, with worse luck than most, who has never considered himself to be a hero. Which is a shame, as he'd really make quite a good one.

*Martha Blink*—Samuel's younger sister, who thinks she's in a musical. She's not. She's in the back of her parents' car singing annoying songs in Samuel's ear. Well, it is her birthday.

*Liv Blink*—Mother of Martha and Samuel. Thinks Martha's singing isn't annoying at all, unlike her husband's driving.

*Peter Blink*—Father of Martha and Samuel. Angry driver. Going to be lucky if he makes it through the first chapter.

## The Norwegians:

*Aunt Eda*—Liv Blink's Norwegian sister. Samuel and Martha Blink's aunt. Former Olympic javelin thrower. Owner of a happiness lamp, ten pairs of long johns, a house near Shadow Forest, and a hairy chin. She misses her husband, Uncle Henrik, who disappeared in the forest ten years ago.

*Uncle Henrik*—Ssssh! Don't mention Uncle Henrik when Aunt Eda's around. She'll probably start crying.

*Oskar*—A grocer in the village of Flåm, with a soft spot for bow ties and tall women (especially Aunt Eda).

*Fredrick*—Oskar's son, who likes to play on his calculator. Don't worry too much about him—he's only in two chapters.

*Old Tor*—He's old. And . . . er . . . he's called Tor. He paints pictures of mountains and fjords. And the occasional two-headed troll.

## Other Humans:

*Professor Horatio Tanglewood (aka the Changemaker)*—An evil Englishman who lives in a wooden palace in the middle of Shadow Forest, which he rules under the name of the Changemaker. He wrote a book called *The Creatures of Shadow Forest* and keeps the pickled heads of his enemies in jars. His favorite music in the world is the sound of a child screaming. He is currently working on his autobiography.

*The author*—Goes by the rather boring name of "Matt Haig," although he was in fact christened Zerebubul Osrich Winterbottom the Third. He rudely interrupts the story on two occasions, just when you're getting into it. He once bumped into Professor Horatio Tanglewood in his local library. The Professor asked to borrow his pen but never gave it back.

## The Dog:

*Ibsen*—A Norwegian elkhound, owned by Aunt Eda. Loves brown cheese, sleep, and human children. Hates the forest.

# THE CREATURES
# OF SHADOW FOREST

## The Witches:

*The Shadow Witch*—Uses the power of shadows to transform herself and other forest dwellers. Lives with her master, Professor Horatio Tanglewood, in his wooden palace. She breathes shadow clouds, and usually turns herself into a cat when she leaves the forest.

*The Snow Witch*—The Shadow Witch's sister, who used to cast weather spells. Currently in an underground prison with weakened powers, she faces certain death. She has known better times.

## Huldres:

*Vjpp*—A thoroughly cruel prison guard who, like all huldres, fears daylight and lives underground. In case you're wondering how to pronounce his name, you can't. It's impossible.

*Grentul*—A slightly less cruel prison guard who is extremely loyal to Professor Tanglewood (known to huldres as the Changemaker). He dreams of the old days, when huldres weren't scared of the sun.

## Trolls:

*Troll-the-Left and Troll-the-Right*—Two heads of the same troll, who hate each other's guts (which, technically speaking, they share).

*Troll-Father, Troll-Mother, Troll-Son, Troll-Daughter*—A friendly family of trolls who have only one eye among them.

# Other Creatures:

*The Tomtegubb*—A golden, barrel-shaped creature who wears bright-colored clothes and sings happy tunes, even when he knows there is nothing to be happy about.

*The Truth Pixie*—A pixie living in a log cabin on the Eastern region of Shadow Forest who poisons passing visitors and finds it impossible to lie. (If he invites you to dinner, have a good excuse ready.)

*The Slemp*—A giant furry creature, combining the physical aspects of a bear and a lion, with a belly comfier than any pillow. He spends most of his life asleep, dreaming of berries. Can gobble a human head in one bite.

*Gray-Tail the Rabbit*—An old rabbit who has convinced the others in his pen that Thubula, the rabbit God, is going to save them all. In fact, they're probably going to end up in a troll casserole.

*Calooshes*—Even more stupid than rabbits, Calooshes are tall, three-headed birds who run around the forest squawking and falling into holes.

# Part I

# On the Way to the Really Big Surprise

The tree trunks lying on the back of the truck were stacked up like a pyramid, and fastened with three gray straps. One of the straps was a bit too loose and caused the trunks to vibrate as if they were restless, or as if they were trying to escape and make it back to the forest.

The truck overtook the car at a reckless speed.

"Have you seen anything like it?" Samuel's dad, Peter, was saying. "What a maniac!"

Samuel's dad thought every driver apart from himself was a maniac, and truck drivers were the biggest maniacs of the lot.

"Great," he said as the giant vehicle began to slow down, hogging both lanes. "Now we'll never get there."

"There's no hurry," said Samuel's mum, who was called Liv.

Samuel didn't know where they were going, but he knew he didn't want to spend another minute having to listen to his sister's singing. Well, *singing* was hardly the word for it. *Cat-strangling* was a more accurate description of the sound.

"Mum, tell Martha to stop making that horrible noise."

His mum tutted. "It's not horrible noise. It's beautiful singing."

This was a lie. One of the million parent lies Samuel had grown used to during his twelve years on the planet. But he knew he wouldn't get any support today. After all, it was Martha's birthday—a fact indicated by the two pins on her sweater saying I AM 10 and 10 TODAY.

The singing got louder. Samuel's head vibrated like the logs as he rested it against the car window, and stared out at the fast blur of grass on the side of the motorway.

"Dad," he said, asking the second-in-command parent. "Tell Martha."

His dad ignored him. He was too busy grumbling. "This is ridiculous! Why bother passing us if you're going to then go slower?!"

Martha twisted around in her seat belt and sang really loud in Samuel's ear:

*"I'm your baby girl,*
*And you could be my world—"*

Ugh! Samuel thought he was going to be sick. He hated his sister's singing at the best of times, but especially when he was tired. He'd only had two hours' sleep the night before, because he was having his usual nightmare. A nightmare about strange gray-skinned monsters with tails and eyes that never blinked. He'd woken in a cold sweat and couldn't get back to sleep.

"They should make murderers have to listen to you as punishment," he told Martha.

"Shut up, Smell-uel. You're just jealous."

And then she started again, singing bits of silly girly love songs. He knew she would sing all day. After all, she sang every day. It was like Martha's whole life was one big long song. As if she was trapped in one of those rubbish musicals she always watched on TV.

Samuel went back to looking out of the window and prayed for Martha to be quiet.

*Quiet as a log.*

Even when she said something normal, she turned it into a song, going high and low to make each word a different note.

So instead of just asking, "Where are we going?," she sang:

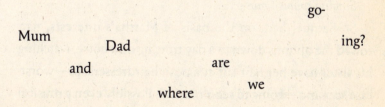

To which their mum said, "You don't want us to spoil the big surprise, do you?"

"Yes," sang Martha.

"Well, you'll find out soon," said her mum.

"Not if we stay stuck behind this truck," said her dad.

Samuel wondered what the big surprise was going to be. He hoped it was a trip to a theme park, like it had been for his last birthday. A loop-the-loop roller coaster would stop Martha singing, if only for a short while. He had gone on a ride with his dad called the Catapult that went so fast you couldn't move your face. Samuel had loved every high-speed second of it, and his dad had pretended to feel the same way until he had to rush to the toilet and throw up his lunch (parent lie number 910,682).

But Samuel suspected that the big surprise was going to be something far more boring than a theme park. He thought of all the rubbish things Martha liked doing.

*Horse-riding . . .*

*Doing hairstyles . . .*

*Spending her pocket money on rubbish music . . .*

*Listening to rubbish music . . .*

*Singing rubbish music . . .*

So Samuel had, on the basis of Martha's interests, narrowed the options down to a day trotting on a horse, watching his sister have her hair cut at a posh hairdressers, or—worst-case scenario—going to see a musical. Possibly even a musical about a hairdresser who becomes a show-jumper and sings to her horse.

Samuel smiled at the unique version of hell he had created in his mind.

*Beeeeep!*

The daydream of people singing on horses ended with the sound of his dad blasting the car horn at the truck.

"This is ludicrous," his dad said, switching on the turn signal.

"Peter, what are you doing?" his mum asked.

"I'm turning off. We'll be on this road all day if we stay behind this timber truck. And have you seen the way those logs are strapped up? It's an accident waiting to happen."

"But we don't know the roads."

"We've got a map. In the dashboard."

Uh-oh.

Samuel and Martha knew what the map meant. It meant their mum and dad having a massive row for an hour, arguing about where they should have turned left.

"Okay," said their mum. "We need the B642. Kids, look out for the B642."

"B642," sang Martha.

The car went round a roundabout three times, until Samuel spotted the B642, hiding in brackets on a small green road sign.

"There it is," he said.

The car turned off the roundabout, and within five minutes, the map had managed to create the usual left-turn row. Samuel kept staring out of the window and the birthday girl kept singing as their mum and dad's argument took root and began to grow.

"Left."

"What?"

"Too late. We should have turned left back there."

"You could have told me. You're the one with the map."

"I did tell you."

"Well, you could have told me before we reached the flaming turnoff."

"It's this stupid old map. It's too hard to read."

Samuel thought about what his mum had just said and he wondered how a map could be stupid. And then he thought about the tree that was turned into paper to make the map. Maybe the map was hard to read as a kind of revenge.

Whatever the reason, they missed the left turn and were now stuck on the B642.

"If we keep going, we'll be able to get back on the dual carriageway," Samuel's mum said as she analyzed the map.

"Fan-flaming-tastic," said Samuel's dad. "Back where we started!"

"It was your idea to turn off."

"Well, we'd have been fine if you could just read a flaming map!"

"Oh no," said Samuel's mum.

"What's the matter?" Samuel's dad shook the question out of his head.

"It doesn't join the dual carriageway . . . It goes *under* it."

And, to prove her point, the view around the next bend revealed a large concrete bridge, directly above the B642.

Samuel saw, to his far left, the timber truck rising at a steady angle toward the bridge. What he couldn't see was that the loose gray straps that helped fasten the logs had come completely undone.

As the car headed toward the bridge, Samuel tried to keep his eyes on the lorry. He had worked out that if they kept going at the same speed, the car would go under the bridge at the exact moment the truck would go over it.

So when he saw the first tree trunk bounce off the truck, he knew the danger.

"Dad! Stop the car!"

"Samuel, what on earth's the matter?"

"Stop the car! The logs! Falling off the truck! Stop the car!"

"Samuel, what are you talking about?" His dad was showing no sign whatsoever of stopping the car.

The first log broke through the roadside barrier one hundred meters before the bridge and started rolling down a slope toward the field at the side of the B642.

"Stop the car! Stop the car!"

"Samuel?" His mum always added a question mark to his name when she was cross.

"Stop! Stop! Just stop!"

But the car kept going, the logs kept falling, and his sister kept singing.

And when Samuel's dad finally decided to brake, it was too late. The last of the logs rolled off the truck and fell off the bridge.

*Smash!*

Within less than a second from it hitting the thin metal, Samuel and Martha lost both of their parents, while they themselves, along with the entire back half of the car, remained physically unharmed.

Samuel and Martha stayed sitting on the backseat. They were too shocked to move. Or to speak. Or to make any sound at all.

Neither of them knew where their parents had planned to take them for Martha's birthday. All they did know was that whatever else happened, nothing would ever be the same again.

# Aunt Eda

The crushing of their parents by a giant log wasn't Samuel and Martha Blink's first encounter with death.

Indeed, most of their direct relatives had been wiped out within the two children's lifetimes, although they hadn't been present at most of these other deaths.

They weren't there, for instance, when Granddad had a heart attack carrying a box of ornamental gnomes into his back garden. Or when Nan, two months later, tripped over one of the gnomes and fell headfirst into the greenhouse.

Nor were they there when Uncle Derek electrocuted himself trying to rescue a tiny piece of toast from the bottom of the toaster with his fork. Or when Aunt Sheila collapsed and banged her head against the doorstop after getting five numbers in the lottery.

And they weren't there when their Norwegian uncle Henrik had . . . Well, the case of Uncle Henrik was something of a mystery.

Unlike all the other deaths, Samuel and Martha were

never told how Uncle Henrik had died. In fact, they weren't told much of how he lived either.

You see, Uncle Henrik was from Norway. That is the country where Samuel and Martha's mum, Liv, was from and a country the two children had never visited. Their mum had a twin sister called Eda. Liv and Eda grew up in a town called Fredrikstad, near Norway's capital city, Oslo. When they were twenty, their long-widowed mother died. The next year Liv moved to England, to study at university, where she met her future husband, Peter. That same year, Eda fell in love with a ski jumper called Henrik in Norway.

Samuel and Martha knew very little about Aunt Eda and Uncle Henrik. But one thing they did know was that Aunt Eda had been a very good javelin thrower, the best in the whole of Norway, and she made it to the Olympics in Moscow. Samuel had always thought this was an amazing fact—that a blood relative had made it to the Olympics—and it always had made him try harder at Sports Day. But when a javelin he had thrown nearly skewered his gym teacher, he realized he probably wasn't going to be following in his aunt's footsteps.

Whenever Samuel and Martha had asked about Aunt Eda, their mother had always given the same reply. "She is a kind and wonderful woman."

So why had they never seen this very kind and wonderful woman?

You may well ask. Samuel and Martha certainly had done, about one hundred times each, but they never got a satisfactory answer.

Here are three of the not-very-satisfactory answers they received:

1. *"Your aunt Eda is scared of boats and airplanes, so she never leaves Norway. Now, no more questions, I have got a headache."*
2. *"We cannot afford to go to Norway, as it is a very expensive country and we are not made of money. Now, no more questions, I have got a headache."*
3. *"It is very cold in Norway. I am sure you would like to go somewhere warm with nice beaches. Now, no more questions, I really have got a very bad headache."*

And that was it.

Well, it had been it until six days after their mum and dad died. That was the day the letter came, placed in Samuel's hand by Mrs. Finch, the kindly old neighbor who had been looking after them.

Samuel looked at the handwriting, but didn't recognize it. The letters were tall and leaned back slightly, like people that don't like the smell of something.

He opened the envelope and found two airplane tickets along with a letter, which he started to read.

Eda Krohg
1846 Flåm
Norway

Dear Samuel and Martha,

I am the sister of your mother and, as I am to understand it, your only surviving relative. It is a terrible shame that the first time I write to you is under these most horrid circumstances, but it is important for you to know that you are not on your own. You will not have to go to a children's home, or be passed around like a parcel no one wants to open.

As your next of kin, I invite you both to come and live with me here in Norway, and have included two airplane tickets for that purpose.

I don't know what your mother has told you about me. You are probably aware that we never saw each other, and little more than a Christmas card has passed between us since before you were born. It is a shame we did not speak to each other more often, as your mother was a kind and wonderful woman.

I live near the pretty village of Flåm, which I am sure is not as big or exciting as Nottingham, but we have a fjord and snowcapped mountains nearby. I also have a dog called Ibsen, who is an elkhound, which is a Norwegian breed. He would very much enjoy the chance to sniff new people for a change!

There is a school in the nearby village. It is a

small school, with only twelve children in total, and I am sure it will suit you very much. I have already spoken to the principal and you will be able to enrol (is that the word?) in two weeks.

As for me, well, I have certain rules that you must follow. These rules must not be broken, as they are there for good reasons.

There is an old expression in Norway—

"A life without rules is a drink without the cup!"

Without the cup, what good is the drink?

Anyway, I am sure we will get along just fine, and I look forward very much to the meeting of both of you.

Oh, we will have such happy times, you will see!

Your loving aunt,
Eda

# The Yes-No Girl

Aunt Eda was waiting for them at the airport, with a piece of cardboard that said SAMUEL + MARTHA. HELLO, I AM AUNT EDA.

Samuel saw the sign. "There she is."

Martha looked and saw a tall and thin woman with graying hair tied into a bun. The woman, wearing a long stripy scarf and a big orange coat, was smiling straight at her.

Martha followed her brother through the crowds of people and tried to smile back at the woman, but she couldn't. She had lost the ability to smile seven days ago. The day she stopped speaking.

In the case of Samuel, he didn't smile because he didn't like the look of Aunt Eda. She certainly didn't look like someone who had ever been in the Olympics. She looked tall and strict, and wore weird clothes. He didn't like her stupid long scarf or her silly round-toed ankle boots or her big orange coat. He didn't like her red cheeks or her long neck or her weird sloping shoulders that gave her the look of a wine bottle.

When they reached their aunt she held out her arms.

"Samuel," she said, still smiling broadly. "Martha."

She hugged them both, squashing their faces together as she brought the children into her arms. Samuel couldn't help but notice that these arms—although thin—were very strong. The wiry hairs on her chin and upper lip prickled his cheek.

"You poor children," she said, holding the hug for as long as possible. And then she whispered something in Norwegian, which neither Samuel nor Martha could understand. It was something that seemed to mean a lot, because when she stood back there was a tear in one of her eyes.

She looked into both their faces, searching for something that wasn't there.

"Oh dear, oh dear," she said. "We'd better go to lost luggage and ask if they haff seen the smiles of two children."

"I'm twelve," Samuel said crossly. "Martha's ten. You don't have to speak like we're babies."

Aunt Eda looked like she was ready to tell Samuel off but she thought twice about it.

"Right," she said, nodding toward the luggage trolley Samuel was pushing, "I'll take your bag, shall I, Mr. Twelf Years Old?"

"I can manage it," Samuel said, tightening his grip on the metal handle of the trolley. In fact, he had chosen the one trolley with a wobbly wheel and couldn't manage it very well at all, but he tried to hide the strain on his face.

"Werry well. Then let us go to the car, shall we?"

Aunt Eda had a slight accent that sounded slightly surprised, as if the words had never expected to be used. It also turned all *vs* into *ws* or *fs*, which Samuel would have found quite funny if he wasn't so cross about being in Norway.

"She looks stupid," whispered Samuel as he and Martha followed their aunt through the airport.

Martha gave her brother a look. *No, she doesn't,* she thought (but she was too sad to say it). *She looks nice. She's got Mum's eyes and Mum's smile and she's being very friendly.*

"Look at her clothes," Samuel went on. "Look at her stupid scarf. And those boots. And what's she wearing that weird big coat for? She must spend an hour buttoning it up to the top."

Aunt Eda turned around. "Sorry? Did you say something?"

"Er, I was just saying how much I like your clothes," he said.

"Oh," said Aunt Eda. "Thank you werry much."

The children followed their aunt through the door that had a sign saying UTANG—EXIT and outside into the cold air. Suddenly Samuel realized Aunt Eda's scarf and coat weren't so stupid.

"I hate this country," Samuel told his sister. "I've been here five seconds and I know I hate it."

His words were lost on the wind as they walked across the tarmac to a scruffy-looking white car on its own in a far corner of the parking lot.

"Look at her car," he mumbled to Martha as they helped put their luggage in the battered old trunk. "It's ancient!"

Samuel climbed in the back, and was surprised when he saw Martha sit in the front.

"Now, it is old," said Aunt Eda, acting like she'd heard Samuel talking about the car. "But cars are loyal, I think. If you stand by them, they won't let you down."

The car coughed its disagreement as she tried the ignition.

"Come on, you old thing," said Aunt Eda. "Come on . . . Ah, there it is . . . purring like a Skogkatt."

Samuel felt a sense of unease in his stomach as the car pulled away, as if he expected another log to fall out of the sky.

"It was terrible, what happened," Aunt Eda said. "I couldn't beleef it. Your mother was a brilliant person. And your father—"

The softly spoken words ran through Samuel like nails down a blackboard.

"You didn't know my dad," Samuel said. "You hardly knew Mum either. You never saw her, so I don't know why you want us to live with you. You never wanted to see us before."

"This is not true," said Aunt Eda quietly.

"Why did you never see our mum, if you liked her so much?" Samuel asked, surprised at how angry his own voice sounded. "Mum said you were scared of flying in planes. And going on boats."

"She did?" Aunt Eda looked confused for a moment, as

if she was learning new things about herself. "Oh yes . . . yes . . ."

Her words trailed off.

Samuel looked at his sister. She was tracing circles on her palm with her fingertips. A week ago, Samuel had prayed for her to stop singing and now he wondered if he was ever going to hear her sing again. He wondered if there was a song sad enough.

*Probably not,* he thought.

Probably not.

Samuel had only been in Norway for thirty-six minutes but he was already sure that it was the worst country he had ever visited. What was the point of all the mountains and trees and water? Why live somewhere so cold you have to wear big coats and woolly hats? And what was with the words on the road signs?

**ENVEISKJØRING**

**REKVERK MANGLER**

**ALL STANS FORBUDT**

The names of the towns they were driving through were just as weird—

**LØKKEN VERK**

**SKOGN**

**KYRKSÆTERØRA**

The small town they were in now was called "Hell." It even had a sign, written in English, that said WELCOME TO HELL.

And what did Hell look like? The same as all the other villages they had been through.

Bright-colored three-story houses and a fat gray church that clung to the gentle slope of a hill, with a short steeple that seemed scared to reach too high to the sky.

"In Norway, Hell is the word for prosperity," explained Aunt Eda. "Do you know what *prosperity* means?"

She looked at Martha and then in the rearview mirror at Samuel. Neither was about to tell her if they knew what *prosperity* meant or not.

"If you prosper at something, it means you are successful, like if you earn a lot of money people say you are prosperous," Aunt Eda said. "And Norway is always called a very prosperous country. Everybody earns a nice amount of money. The postman earns nearly as much as the doctors and lawyers. It is a very equal society. In Norway, people don't get too jealous of each other. We are a peaceful people. There is enough money and enough land to go around so efferyone is happy . . . That is what they say."

Samuel could see his aunt's face in the mirror and noticed that her eyes were not showing the happiness she described. *She doesn't want us here,* Samuel thought. *That is why she has unhappy eyes. She probably hated Mum, really. And she probably hates us.*

He didn't care about peace or rich postmen. He just wanted it to be the week before, when everything was normal.

"How far is it?" Samuel asked his aunt.

They had gone past Hell now and they were somewhere else, without houses or a name.

"Oh, not too far now," she told him. "But on the way we must stop and get some food at the grocer's shop in Flåm. Flåm is the village nearest to my house. It is a lovely place."

The words were no comfort. Samuel had never felt farther away from home in his whole life. And it wasn't just the two plane journeys or the long car ride or the weird scenery that was making him feel like this. It was the thought that even if he made the long car ride and two plane journeys back in the opposite direction, he would be no closer to home. He knew, ever since his parents died, that he would never feel at home again—even if he lived to be a hundred years old.

"I have a dog," Aunt Eda said. "A Norwegian elkhound. He is a werry good dog, if a little bit greedy. He is called Ibsen. I told you about him in the letter. He barks a lot but he is a big soft thing really. Do you like dogs?"

"No," said Samuel.

Martha said nothing.

"Oh well, I am sure you will like Ibsen."

The scenery suddenly disappeared, replaced by darkness on both sides of the road.

"This is a werry long tunnel," explained Aunt Eda. "It is elefen kilometers, and goes right under the mountain."

Samuel looked at his sister. She used to be scared of tunnels, but her blank face showed no sign of fear.

"You are werry quiet," Aunt Eda said, turning to Martha.

"Why don't you tell me about your hobbies? What games do you like to play?"

The questions made Samuel cross. "She can't answer you. She doesn't . . . speak."

Aunt Eda made a questioning face, so Samuel explained.

"She hasn't said anything since Mum and Dad died. She only nods and shakes her head. Only ask her things that need a yes or no for an answer."

Samuel thought the idea of his silent sister might shock Aunt Eda, as she seemed the shockable type, but she took this piece of news as if it was perfectly normal. He watched his aunt's face under the flickering lights of the tunnel and detected nothing except a warm smile below the same sad eyes.

# The Tale of Old Tor

"Now," said Aunt Eda, turning a corner. "This is Flåm, the nearest willage to my house. This is where we must stop here and get some food from the grocers."

Flåm was a very quiet and clean village with hardly any traffic. It reminded Samuel of a model village he used to own when he was little, but this was a model village blown up so big it was full-sized. Like Hell and all the other places they'd driven through, the streets were lined with gabled timber houses—some painted white or blue, others left dark and natural. Aunt Eda drove them slowly past a church, which was also made of wood, and shaped like all the other buildings, except for the short, pointed steeple sticking out of it.

"Your uncle Henrik used to joke that it wasn't a church at all," said Aunt Eda as she waited at a crossroads. "He said it was just an ordinary house that had ideas above its station."

Aunt Eda parked the car in the middle of the high street.

"Come on, children. Let us get some food, shall we?"

Samuel huffed, but he and Martha did as their aunt said, following her past a bookshop, then an art shop, toward a shop which had a sign outside, painted in bold yellow letters, that said:

**DAGLIGVAREBUTIKK**

"This is Oskar's shop," explained Aunt Eda. "Oskar is the grocer. This is where I get my shopping. It is a werry friendly place."

She pushed open the door and a bell rang.

Samuel nearly choked on the smell. It was like walking into a giant block of smelly cheese.

The shop was busy with villagers talking and laughing, but when they heard the bell, and turned to see Aunt Eda and the two children, their conversation stopped.

"*Goddag!*" Aunt Eda said, cheerily, but the greeting bounced off their stony faces.

Aunt Eda did her best to ignore the villagers staring at her, and picked up a shopping basket. She began to pick groceries from the shelves—a packet of flatbread, a carton of cloudberry juice, a jar of pickled herrings—while Samuel and Martha shuffled along behind her.

When she reached the cheese counter, another customer—a chubby woman in three cardigans—tutted at Aunt Eda and shook her head at Samuel and Martha.

"What's her problem?" Samuel muttered.

But it wasn't just the cardigan woman. All the other customers were giving Samuel and Martha equally funny looks.

"Now, Samuel and Martha, is there anything you would

like to add to the basket?" Aunt Eda asked, doing her best to ignore the villagers.

Martha shook her head.

"No," said Samuel, because he wanted to leave the shop as soon as he possibly could.

"If you're sure," said Aunt Eda, with a smile, as she waited at the cheese counter for Oskar to appear.

"*Goddag,* Oskar," she said to the shopkeeper, once he'd walked over.

Oskar was a rather odd-looking man. He was short, with a bald head and an impressive yellow mustache. He also wore a yellow bow tie and yellow shirt, tucked tight over his round belly. He didn't return Aunt Eda's greeting. He just stood there, silent in his yellow clothes, as if he was just another cheese waiting to be picked.

"Oskar?" Aunt Eda enquired. She then began talking in Norwegian and pointing at different cheeses.

Oskar began slicing cheese, but didn't talk.

It was then that a boy appeared from the doorway at the far end of the shop. The boy was about Samuel's age, with white-blond hair and green eyes magnified by thick, gold-rimmed glasses.

He came and sat on a stool behind his father, Oskar, and began playing with a calculator.

*It must be the closest thing to fun round here,* thought Samuel. *Playing with a calculator.*

"*Goddag,*" the boy said to Samuel. His smile revealed a silver brace.

"Hello," said Samuel.

"Fredrick!" Oskar clicked his fingers, and sent his son away, as if Samuel was infected with something dangerous.

To Samuel's surprise, the poor boy did exactly as he was told, disappearing from where he had come without question.

The other villagers in the shop were leaving, each one tutting or grumbling or throwing scornful looks as they passed Aunt Eda and the children. When the last villager had left, Oskar's face softened, like a chunk of cheese that had been left too near a fire. And, in a voice that sounded both friendly and cross all at once, he began to talk.

But what it was he said to her Samuel and Martha couldn't imagine, although the bulging eyes made it clear it was something quite serious.

Samuel wished he could speak Norwegian so he could understand properly. But if he *had* understood the conversation, he might have wished it the other way round, as the words coming out of Oskar's mouth would have made him think everyone round here was totally mad. Including Aunt Eda.

# The Conversation between Aunt Eda and Oskar (That Samuel and Martha Couldn't Understand)

**AUNT EDA:** What is the matter with everyone today, they seem so unfriendly?

**OSKAR:** Eda, it seems strange that you have to ask.

**AUNT EDA:** Well, I am asking.

**OSKAR:** The children! Who are they? What are you doing with them?

**AUNT EDA:** They are my sister's children. They have come from England. My sister and her husband died in a terrible accident and they have no one else. No one. They must come and live with me.

**OSKAR:** Near the forest?

**AUNT EDA:** Yes, near the forest.

**OSKAR:** Then you might as well kill them now. It would be kinder. Because you know if they go into the forest they won't ever come back.

**AUNT EDA:** They won't go into the forest. I will make it clear that they must never go in.

**OSKAR:** (shaking his head) As soon as they hear about all the creatures that live there—the huldres and the pixies and the trolls and all the others—they will want to see them. You know what children are like.

**AUNT EDA**: No, I will make it very clear to them that they must not go near the trees. So long as they never go into the forest, they will be safe.

**OSKAR**: (leaning over the counter) No, Eda, forgive me, but I fear you are wrong. You might be able to keep the children away from the forest, but can you keep the forest away from the children? Did you hear about Old Tor, the painter?

**AUNT EDA**: Old Tor? Who has the art shop down the street? Whose wife was just so rude to me? I have bought pictures from him before. What about him?

**OSKAR**: Well, he says he was out near the fjord on Friday, painting a moonlit scene, when he saw a great monster. A monster that had run out of the forest. A troll with two heads!

**AUNT EDA**: (gulping) A troll with two heads?

**OSKAR**: Yes, and it was being chased by even uglier creatures. Huldres!

**AUNT EDA**: Huldres! Just like the Professor said.

**OSKAR**: Yes. They were on horseback. Old Tor saw them throw a net over the two-headed troll and then beat him to the ground. They dragged the troll back to the forest.

**AUNT EDA**: So what did Tor do?

**OSKAR**: He hid behind his canvas and prayed to God that no one would notice him. He sat there shaking for two hours before he dared make a move.

**AUNT EDA**: And it was dark. How could he see? He only has one good eye, hasn't he?

**OSKAR**: Yes. I know. But it is a *very* good eye. You have seen his paintings. Old Tor is the most respected man in the village . . . And if the creatures are stepping out of the forest, you can see why people worry. About the children. Your house is too close, Eda.

**AUNT EDA**: Yes, it is close. Don't you think I know that? But what do these worried people think I am going to do? Do they think I am going to send the children into the forest? Do they think I won't tell them not to go there? Do they think I won't tell them not to be outside after dark? Of course I will. What else can I do?

**OSKAR**: You could . . . move. Maybe.

**AUNT EDA**: Oh, and what would my dear Henrik say then?

**OSKAR**: Henrik? Eda, Henrik has . . . gone. You must realize that.

**AUNT EDA**: Yes. Of course. I know that. I know that just as well as I know that he is coming back.

**OSKAR**: But it has been ten years, Eda. Ten years since he walked into that forest. You must know he isn't coming back.

**AUNT EDA**: If I knew that, I would have gone into the forest years ago, and finished myself off too.

**OSKAR**: Eda, you don't mean that. There are plenty of men out there, you know. Maybe some who need a little company too, from time to time.

**AUNT EDA:** Well, yes, maybe. But now I've got Samuel and Martha to look after. And anyway, I know Henrik is still alive. Somewhere. Inside that forest. And I know he is going to come back.

**OSKAR:** Yes. But now? After ten years? Wouldn't it be easier if you—

**AUNT EDA:** No. He is alive. And he is coming back. I can feel it in my heart. If you believed in love as much as you believed Old Tor, you would understand me.

**OSKAR:** Oh, Eda, if only you realized how much I believed in true love.

**AUNT EDA:** And what does that mean?

**OSKAR:** (blushing) Nothing. It means nothing.

**AUNT EDA:** Now, here is twenty krone for my groceries. You can keep the change. *Morna,* Oskar.

**OSKAR:** *Morna.*


And then, in a strange kind of English, Oskar said to the children: "Remember, do as your aunt does tell you so—stay away from the cheese."

*The cheese?* thought Samuel. *What's so dangerous about the cheese?*

(He didn't realize that the shopkeeper had been talking about the forest, and meant to say "trees," not "cheese.")

Aunt Eda, Samuel and Martha left the shop and walked back to the car. On the way, Samuel looked inside the window of the art shop run by Old Tor.

He saw the chubby woman with the three cardigans who had been so rude. She was talking to a man with a very long beard and clothes specked with paint. Catching the old man's stare, Samuel saw that one of his eyes was as white as milk. Samuel pretended to be interested in the canvases by the window. Most were of mountains and fjords, but then he saw another picture. It wasn't in the window, but hanging on the wall behind the old man. It was a picture of a wild-looking creature, with two heads. It was so lifelike it made him jump, as if the creature could have leaped out of the painting.

Samuel shook the picture out of his mind, like a dog shaking off water, and followed his aunt and sister to the car.

"Why is everybody so creepy around here?" he asked his aunt as they loaded the shopping into the trunk.

"They're not creepy, really. Not when you get to know them. They are just a bit frightened, that's all. And fear can make you act a bit strange."

"Why are they frightened?" Samuel asked. "What is there to be scared of?"

"Nothing," Aunt Eda said, too quickly to be believed. "That is, nothing if we all follow certain rules. Now, Samuel, I can see from your face that you don't like the sound of that werry much. But they are not just for you, they are for me as well. If all three of us follow the rules, we will be fine. And we will not become strange like those scared old willagers."

Samuel curled his lip as he climbed into the backseat. All his life he'd had to listen to other people's rules. *Do your homework on time. Make your bed. Change out of your uniform after school.* And where had following these rules got him? All the way to Norway and his hairy-faced aunt.

No. That was it. Samuel Blink wasn't going to listen to rules anymore.

After all, what else had he got to lose?

# The Unmentionable Place

Aunt Eda lived in a white wooden house with a steep sloping gray roof, a few miles outside of Flåm.

Most visitors to the house would have been mightily impressed with its setting, as it perched on a lush green hillside overlooking one of the most beautiful Norwegian fjords. The fjord was called the Aurlandsfjorden—a giant inlet of water so still and so pure that it looked like a massive mirror reflecting the tree-covered hills and snowcapped mountains all around.

Samuel, however, was not like most visitors. He hated the house and he hated the view from the first time he saw it. He felt exactly the same about the grassy slopes of the hills that led up to the thick, dark forest behind the house.

"This is the worst place ever," he mumbled to his sister, who neither nodded yes nor shook her head no.

Where were the people? Where were the *things to do*?

"Come on, children, let me show you inside," said Aunt Eda as she walked them from the car to the narrow front door. Samuel couldn't help but notice the easy way Aunt Eda's skinny arms managed to carry both the suitcase and the shopping bags, as if they contained nothing but feathers.

"This is the hallway, where we leave our coats and our hats and where we take off our shoes," she said, placing the bags and suitcase down. "And there is the kitchen and the wash-room, on the left . . . and on the right, if we go on through, is the liffing room."

She walked them into a large room with wooden walls, rugs on the floor and a fireplace. A shiver went through Samuel as his eyes scanned the room. He had a very strange feeling he had been here before. He recognized everything, but couldn't think where from. The rocking chair, the sofa covered with a multicolored woolen blanket, the dark wooden table, the shelves full of glass vases and ancient-smelling books, an empty dog basket, the framed paintings of the mountains and fjords on the wall, and more mountains and fjords out-side the front window.

"Ah yes," said Eda, noticing Samuel was looking at the paintings. "They were painted by an old man in the willage. Old Tor they call him. He sits out sometimes, late at night, painting the water and the mountains under the stars."

Outside the back window was a different view entirely—the grass slope stretching toward the strange army of dark pine trees on the horizon.

Samuel shook off the feeling that he had been here be-fore, and noticed something even more unsettling. "Where's the TV?"

"There's no telewision here," Aunt Eda told him. She almost seemed proud of the fact. Proud of not having a television!

"But I've brought my video games," he said. "And I need a TV to play them."

Aunt Eda did not seem to appreciate the seriousness of this situation, as she said: "Well, for now you will haff to find someone else to play with."

"Like who?" sulked Samuel.

"Like . . . like . . ." Aunt Eda nearly said "like your sister" but decided against it after looking at Martha's somber, speechless face. " . . . like dear old Ibsen."

At the sound of his name, a large, gray and black dog padded his way into the living room and introduced himself by wagging his tail. The tail was white, and curled around so that the tip touched his back, as if it was the handle of a dog-shaped jug.

"Get off me," Samuel said, pushing the dog's snout away.

He expected the dog to growl at him, but he just wagged his curly tail and looked up at Samuel with complete love in his eyes. Then Ibsen padded his way over to Martha, and just for a second she seemed to forget herself. Happiness tugged the corners of her mouth—not into a smile exactly, but into something that might grow into one.

"Martha!" Samuel said, pointing at her face. "You're smiling!"

But as soon as the half smile was pointed out, it disappeared, like a frightened deer, and Martha remembered her sadness once again. A sadness that was mildly comforted by Ibsen's rough tongue licking her hand.

"Looks like you haff got a friend," Aunt Eda said, but it was unclear whether she was talking to Martha or Ibsen.

The dog followed everyone upstairs, where the children were shown their bedroom. There were two beds with sheets and blankets tucked in tight in a way that reminded Samuel of a hospital. A tall antique wardrobe stood like an awkward stranger in the corner of the room, from where it seemed to look down on the children.

*"I know that wardrobe,"* Samuel said. *"I've seen it before."*

Aunt Eda looked frightened for a moment, as if Samuel's words were dangerous creatures let out into the room.

"It is a werry popular type of wardrobe," she said.

"But I've seen the wallpaper too."

"The wallpaper is especially popular, all over the world I am sure . . . Now, here are your beds . . ."

The beds faced two windows, out of which Samuel could see the green sloping field and the dark forest behind.

Ibsen, who was now at Samuel's side, looked up at the boy and began to whimper. And he kept whimpering until Samuel stopped staring out at the forest.

Aunt Eda was busy showing Martha where to put her clothes in the wardrobe when Samuel asked: "What's in the trees?"

Aunt Eda's head spun around as if Samuel had just said the worst swearword he knew.

"In the forest," Samuel went on. "Are there bears? Or wolves? Or something else? Is that what those stupid villagers were scared of?"

Aunt Eda walked from the wardrobe to Samuel, and bent down until her face was level with his.

As Samuel looked in her eyes he felt his heartbeat start to quicken. His question about the forest had a transforming effect on his aunt, making her face look so stern it could have been carved from stone.

*"Don't mention that place,"* she said in the most serious voice Samuel had ever heard. *"Don't let your mind think about what is inside there. When you go outside you must stay on the grass, where I can see you. Both of you. This is the most important rule I will tell you. Neffer go in the forest. Neffer. And don't talk about it effer again. Do you understand?"*

Of course, Samuel didn't understand. He had more questions in his head than ever before. What was so dangerous about the forest? And if it was so dangerous, why live so close that you can see it from your windows?

But Samuel was so shocked by the sudden change in Aunt Eda that he found himself unable to say anything except: "Yes, I understand."

Aunt Eda breathed in through her nose, as if testing the truth of his words by smelling them.

"Good," she said.

And then she straightened herself back upright and forced the smile to return to her face.

"Right," she said. "Now, let's go and feed those empty stomachs."

# Rudolph Soup

"What is it?" Samuel asked, looking at the bowl of murky brown liquid.

"Reindeer soup," Aunt Eda replied, as if it was the most normal thing in the world to eat a reindeer.

Samuel looked at the hairs on her chin and upper lip.

*She's as disgusting as the soup,* he thought to himself, finding it hard to believe she and his mum had been twin sisters.

His mum was pretty, and always wore nice clothes and makeup. She used to put stinky cream on her upper lip that got rid of her mustache, and she used to do workouts twice a week to keep her figure. She wore jeans and bright-colored T-shirts, and went to the hairdressers every Saturday morning to get it styled or to put highlights in.

Samuel looked at the gray-and-black hair his aunt scraped back in a bun. He looked at her red cheeks. He looked at her blouse and her cardigan that looked two hundred years old. It was hard to believe she and his mum belonged to the same species, let alone were twins.

"Reindeer? That's disgusting."

*Ugh,* he thought. *Rudolph soup.*

"It is really werry nice," said Aunt Eda. "I think you'll find it tastes like beef." Samuel watched his sister take a sip from her spoon, with no visible pleasure or disgust. He did the same, and nearly retched.

"That *is* disgusting," he confirmed.

"It was Henrik's favorite," said Aunt Eda.

"Well, Henrik must have had very bad taste," said Samuel.

Aunt Eda leaned across the table. *"Don't talk that way about Uncle Henrik. Do you hear me?"*

Her voice wasn't much louder than a whisper, but it had the sudden quiet anger of a cat's hiss. It wasn't her voice that worried him, though; it was the expression on her face. Her eyes looked so hurt that, for the first time since he had arrived, Samuel felt guilty for being so rude.

He wanted to say "I'm sorry" but somehow couldn't get the words out. However, the apology was there on his face as Aunt Eda nodded, and sipped her soup.

There was an awkward silence, which was only interrupted by the sound of Ibsen's whimpering. "Oh, Ibsen, what is it?" Aunt Eda asked.

Ibsen was looking at the window, pointing his nose toward the forest. Samuel looked at the dog and thought there was something strange about it, but couldn't decide what.

Aunt Eda ignored Ibsen and carried on sipping her soup.

"Now," she said. "After we haff eaten, I will explain the

rules to you both. After all, you can't follow rules unless you know what they are in the first place. Okay?"

Martha nodded. Samuel did nothing. He didn't want to hear the rules. Why should he do as his aunt said? After all, no one ever did what *he* said. Not even when doing what he said was a matter of life or death—like stopping his parents' car before a log crushes it.

"Rules keep things in place," Aunt Eda said. "And me and you must be kept in certain places too. And for our own good."

Samuel looked at her cardigan buttoned right up to the top, and realized exactly what Aunt Eda was. She was a person buttoned right to the top. He wondered what it was that kept all her invisible buttons in place.

"Okay," said Aunt Eda. "Now you haff finished your soup, it is time to hear the rules."

Samuel was going to argue, but he looked at his sister and saw she was listening to his aunt. *Maybe Martha's interested,* he thought. *Maybe she wants to know the rules.* So Samuel decided to be quiet, and sit perfectly still, as his aunt ran through her list from one to ten.

# The Rules

The Rules

1. Never go up to the attic.
2. Don't say anything bad about Uncle Henrik, as he is not here to defend himself.
3. Take your shoes off at the front door.
4. Never feed Ibsen between mealtimes, even when he begs.
5. Eat all of your meals. One day, you might need all the strength you can get.
6. Always ask my permission before you go outside.
7. Don't ever go outside after dark.
8. If it starts to get dark when you are already outside, come in straightaway as fast as you can.
9. **NEVER—UNDER ANY CIRCUMSTANCES—GO INTO THE FOREST.**
10. Never question any of the rules. Especially number nine.

# The Huldre-folk

It was dark outside the windows.

Samuel and Martha had never known darkness like this. In England, the nights were always softened by some distant streetlight. But here, next to a dense forest and miles from the nearest village, the darkness was so intense it almost had a weight. You could feel it pressing in, outside the windows, like the whole house was in the grip of a giant.

Samuel saw something reflected in the glass and turned around. "What's that?" he asked. He was pointing to the weird light that shone up at Aunt Eda's face.

"It's a special lamp," she said softly. "A happiness lamp. It stops me getting too sad when it is so dark."

Samuel looked at his sister and wondered if the lamp might help her.

"Could Martha have a go?" he asked.

"If she wants a go. Martha, do you want to use my happiness lamp?"

Martha looked at the ultraviolet tubes of light and shook her head.

Aunt Eda turned from the lamp and smiled at Martha. "You might be part huldre," she joked.

"What's a huldre?" Samuel asked, on Martha's behalf.

Aunt Eda paused for a long time, and looked through the gap in the curtains at the darkness. *Maybe it would be a good idea to tell them about the huldres,* she thought. *Just in case anything happens.*

"The huldre-folk are creatures who are said to be scared of light," she said eventually, changing the angle of her lamp. She was trying to make the huldres sound less serious than she knew they were, as if they were just something out of a storybook, rather than creatures living in the forest behind her house. "They effaporate if they are exposed to the sun. They liff in a separate world under the ground, and only come out at night. They get jealous of the humans who don't have to spend their days in the dark. *Huldre* in Norwegian means 'underneath.' The huldre-folk are supposedly as tall as you and me, but they are werry ugly. They haff a tail and gray skin and strange eyes and bony bodies. They are said to trap humans and other creatures in prisons underground . . ."

She went quiet suddenly, remembering what Old Tor was said to have seen.

Samuel thought of the nightmares he sometimes had, about gray-skinned monsters with tails and wide-apart eyes. But these were only nightmares. He knew they weren't *real*.

"Do you believe in the huldre-folk?" Samuel asked.

Aunt Eda moved her mouth as if the question was something to chew on. Then she said: "I believe there are more things out there than we understand."

*She's mad,* thought Samuel. *Absolutely raving mad.*

Okay, so Mum might have believed in star signs but she didn't believe in creatures with tails who lived in underground worlds. Maybe the happiness lamp made her mad. A madness lamp, sending mad ideas into her brain.

Later on, lying in bed, Samuel told Martha: "I hate this place."

Martha said nothing.

"And I hate her. I hate her hairy chin and her Rudolph soup and her no TV and her buttons and her rules."

Martha still said nothing.

"Martha . . . Martha, say something . . . Please . . . Just sing a song . . . make a sound . . . Please . . . I can't take it just listening to her all the time. Please, sis. Please . . ."

But still Martha said nothing. Somewhere, deep inside, she wanted to talk to her brother, but the words weren't there.

"Do you know what you are, Martha?" he asked, getting out of bed. "You're a selfish cow. You might as well have a cow's tail because that's what you are. You're selfish and I know it's because you're sad about Mum and Dad, but I'm sad too and I'd be less sad if you spoke to me. Martha? Speak! Say something!"

He was shaking her now, but she still didn't say a word.

She just scrunched her eyes shut and—when his hands left her—burrowed deep down into the darkness under the blankets.

*Like a rabbit,* thought Samuel. *Or a huldre.*

When she heard Samuel climb back into bed, Martha came out from under the duvet and stared at him, at the dark, crumpled silhouette lying in the next bed. She felt as if there was a whole universe between them. In fact, she felt as if there was a universe on every side now.

She didn't mind feeling like this. She knew, actually, that it was the best way to be. If you weren't really a part of the world—the world that spoke and smiled and sang—then you could never feel truly upset.

After all, she had felt close to her parents and look what happened.

No. This was how it was going to be. Martha Blink, with a universe on every side, to defend herself against all the pain and tears and happiness of the world.

# The Cat with Two Collars

The next afternoon, having asked his aunt for permission, Samuel was out playing on the grass that ran from the back of the house to the border of the forest. He knew Aunt Eda was watching him, from the kitchen window, making sure he didn't head too far toward the trees.

*What can I do?* Samuel thought.

He had only wanted to go outside because there was nothing to do inside. No TV. No video games. A sister whose voice had died with their parents.

Bored of reading old books, he'd headed out onto the grass slope that ran between the house and the trees. But now that he was outside he realized there was nothing to do out here either. Just a forest he couldn't enter, and grass. Lots and lots of grass.

He was about to head back inside when he saw a black cat with the brightest green eyes, staring straight at him.

*Strange,* thought Samuel. *Aunt Eda doesn't have a cat.*

As Samuel got closer, he saw that the cat was wearing two collars. One black. One white. Both made from a kind of cloth, with a small metal disc attached to each.

"Here, kitty kitty."

Samuel crouched down, and beckoned it closer with his fingers, but the cat didn't make a move. It just stayed there, as proud as a queen, watching the boy with its dark and weary eyes.

"Here, kitty kitty. Here, kitty kitty."

Samuel moved his hand closer, stroked the cat's head, and tucked his finger inside one of the collars. He tried to lead the cat forward with the collar, but met resistance. The cat tried to reverse away, and did so, but lost its collar in the process.

Samuel examined the metal disc that was fastened to the white fabric, and read the engraving.

HEK

"Hek," said Samuel. "It suits you. Weird name for a weird cat."

The cat stayed sitting in the same spot, and hissed up at the boy who had just stolen one of its collars.

"Nope, I'm sorry," Samuel said. "It's mine now. And what do you need two collars for any—"

Samuel's question sank into a shocked silence. He was sure—as sure as you can be about such things—that the cat's eyes had just changed. He could have sworn that they switched from green to black, or a very dark gray, just for one second.

He felt a coldness run through him, a coldness that was more than a product of the chill wind as he realized there was something unnatural about the feline creature in front of him.

"Creepy cat," mumbled Samuel. "Freaky, creepy cat."

Samuel turned and looked toward the house. Through the living-room window he could see Aunt Eda as she walked toward the kitchen to begin preparing Ibsen's supper.

Although he was scared, he was reluctant to go back inside. After all, finding this strange cat was probably going to be the most exciting thing that could happen to him in this boring place.

"What are you looking at?" Samuel said.

The cat's eyes, which were now back to normal, were staring directly at the white collar Samuel had just stolen.

"You really like this collar, don't you?"

The cat hissed again, but this wasn't a normal hiss. It was a hiss that drew from its mouth a small cloud of black smoke that rose out into the air.

It was then that Samuel began to feel a slight dizziness. A kind of confusion that made him forget himself.

*Who am I? Where am I?*

*I am Spamuel Link.*

*I am in Boreway.*

*I am Lambuel Sink.*

*I am in Snoreway.*

During this strange state of mind, Samuel's whole body felt itself loosen, including the hand that had been clutching on to the white collar.

His fingers fell open and the collar dropped down to the

ground. He blinked his eyes, and blinked again, and gradually the feeling of dizziness went away.

*I am Samuel Blink. I am in Norway.*

He looked down onto the grass and saw a black cat with a black collar staring up at him.

"Here, kitty kitty. Here, kitty kitty."

Samuel looked at the cat's green eyes, and had no idea that only a few moments before he had seen them switch to black. Nor did he remember the small cloud of black vapor that had been hissed toward him, or the white collar that now rested on the ground underneath his feet.

The cat hissed, and kept hissing, frustratedly trying to produce another vapor cloud, but none came. Of course, Samuel didn't realize this was what the cat was trying to do, as the events of the last minute were no longer inside his mind.

"What's your problem?" Samuel asked as the cat kept hissing out nothing but air. He crouched back down and reached again toward it. "Come on," he said. "You could be my pet."

Just as he was about to touch his finger inside the black collar, the cat turned and ran as fast as it could toward the forest. Samuel began running up the slope after it, but only made a few steps before hearing his aunt behind him.

"Samuel! Stop! Stop! Come here this minute!"

He turned to see Aunt Eda standing outside the house, holding the knife that was being used to chop up Ibsen's dinner.

Under normal circumstances, he would have carried on running. After all, the things parents and aunts don't want you to do are normally the best type of things to do, and worth double effort.

But when Samuel saw the black cat dart over pinecones and disappear into the soupy darkness between the trees, he stopped. Not because Aunt Eda told him to. Not because he was getting out of breath as he pushed against the wind. No, he stopped because of a sudden fear as he got closer to the forest, a fear that felt as real and solid as a brick wall.

He stood still for a moment, looking at the rough trunks of the pine trees that were only a few meters in front of him. They stood like awesome gateposts to the shadowy and unknown land beyond. He thought he heard something, a strange and distant calling, that didn't seem to belong to the world he knew.

Then he saw a shifting shape. Darkness moving amid darkness, where the cat had just been. A bird? He didn't know. He didn't want to. He turned around, and walked the way of the wind back to his rather frightened-looking aunt. And as he headed down the slope, he did not see the white collar lift up on that same wind and roll off down the grass, over the drive, tumbling closer toward the distant fjord.

# The Flight of the Shadow Witch

With a simple arch of her neck, the Shadow Witch turned from a black cat into a raven, and the remaining collar shrunk around her to become the most perfect fit.

She flew low through the trees, past the old huldre village, where skeletons lay inside the houses, on and on she kept flying, past the stone cottages of trolls, weaving her way through pine trees until she reached the clearing in the North of the forest.

There was a tree there. A broad and dark-trunked tree, larger than any found in the outside world, with a wooden palace cradled in its branches. The vast tree stood alone, away from the pines that bordered the clearing, and was known—by those who called it anything at all—as the Still Tree.

The Shadow Witch flew inside a window of the large tree palace, and turned into her true form. A gray and wizened old woman, with black eyes, and shadows leaking from her mouth as she breathed.

"Master, I have news."

The man she was addressing was hunched over his desk, with a quill in his hand and a blank piece of parchment in front of him, both of which had been conjured with the help of his servant the Shadow Witch. This was the room in which he now spent most of his time. It was his study, and his desk was by a bookcase containing nothing but the best-selling book he had written many years ago, *The Creatures of Shadow Forest*. There were other shelves in the room, but instead of books they contained heads. Pickled heads. In jars. The heads of what he called the Enemies of the Forest. All those creatures who had tried—and failed—to escape to the outside world.

The man, whose name was Professor Horatio Tanglewood, had been working on his latest book for ten years. He was trying to write his life story, but he was still struggling to find the right first sentence.

" 'I was born on a clear and star-filled night,' " he mumbled aloud. "No! Rubbish! Useless!"

The Shadow Witch cleared her throat. "Master."

"Yes! What is it?" he barked, but didn't turn around.

"Master, I bring you some news." The Shadow Witch could hear the weakness of her own words. After all these years, she was still terrified by the man who controlled her.

"Go on," he commanded. "Go. On."

So the Shadow Witch carried on talking to the back of the man's head.

"Master, I was outside of the forest, keeping an eye on the white wooden house as you told me to do. I was just sitting on the grass when I saw . . . a boy. A human boy, master."

"A boy?" Professor Tanglewood turned around in his chair. He had a long and thin face, aged but not as ancient as the witch. Underneath his left eye there was a thin and horizontal scar. His hair was still dark, and in a more evil version of the world, he could have almost passed for handsome.

"Yes. A boy, master. He came to me. And I stayed still so I could observe him better, but then he tried to take hold of me and—"

Her master's sharp eyes were staring at her wrists. "You are only wearing one bracelet, Shadow Witch. The black one. Where is the other?" He stood up from his chair and came toward her.

"Master, he tried to grab me, so I pulled away but he still had hold of the white collar—the bracelet I stole from my sister. I tried to use my powers to retrieve it, but you know how weak they are outside the forest. The most I could manage was a memory spell, so the boy had no knowledge of the bracelet. Master, I am sorry."

Professor Tanglewood closed his eyes and sighed, and said in a voice as calm and eerie as a graveyard wind, "You lost the bracelet."

"Master, I am sorry."

"Sorry? A rather useless word, isn't it? What can it do, this 'sorry'? Can it retrieve a bracelet? Can it stop a curious child from entering the forest? Can it write my memoirs?"

"No, master, it cannot."

Professor Tanglewood stared at the Shadow Witch for a

long time, wondering when it would be, the day he was going to kill her and steal her powers.

"I had a dream last night."

"A dream, master?"

The Professor nodded. "A dream that two children entered the forest." The memory tugged his mouth into a smile. "And they were killed by creatures. A flock of Flying Skullpeckers, I think it was. Oh, you should have heard that delicious sound. I watched them die. I watched and I heard their screams, and I was comforted. And after the children died, the whole forest applauded. All the huldres and the trolls and the pixies and all the others. They applauded me, as if they realized why I made the changes. They knew, in that moment, that I was their savior from all the other humans. Which I am, of course. You see, even your foolishness cannot endanger the forest, Shadow Witch. For what is the worst that could happen? That the boy found the white bracelet and came to pay us a visit. We know that light magic is no match for the dark. And, as is more likely, what if he entered the forest completely unprotected? If that were the case, his death would be as certain as the sunrise."

"Yes, master," the Shadow Witch said, coughing shadows.

"Leave me," he said. "I must get on with my writing, for when the creatures know about how much I have done to protect them, they will love me. And there shall be no resistance, and no attempts at escape, and everywhere I walk in the forest there will be the same cry: 'Hail, Professor Tanglewood, for he is the Changemaker!' Now go, Shadow Witch. Go. But stay inside the forest. You cannot be trusted beyond the trees. Do you understand me?"

"Yes, master."

The Shadow Witch bowed her head, and became a raven once more. She flew out of the window she had entered, and soared aimlessly over the trees, feeling deep sorrow for the bracelet she had lost. But the Shadow Witch's sadness was also for the boy she had seen. A boy she felt was one day going to cross into the forest never to return, or return so different he would never be recognized.

She flew so high she could see the distant white wooden house, and thought of the humans inside.

*Stay there,* she thought.

*Stay safe.*

# In the Kitchen

The wind beat against the kitchen window with an anger that was only matched by Aunt Eda's face.

"You broke my rule," she said, chopping up the last slab of red meat for Ibsen's supper. "The most important rule."

"I didn't break it," Samuel said. "I didn't go *into* the forest."

"Well, what were you doing? You were right on the top of the . . ."—she searched for the word—"of the *slope* . . . you were about to go in, weren't you?"

Samuel paused. "There was a cat."

"A cat?"

"A black cat. I was following it. And it went into the forest. Keep your knickers on."

Aunt Eda looked confused. "I don't see what my undergarments have to do with anything."

"That's just a *saying*."

"Well, it's not a saying in Norway. Anyway, you have to understand that I do not make rules just for fun. It is not a hobby of mine. I do not sit and think, 'Let's make up a rule today just for the sake of it. Let's only wear green clothes because it is Tuesday.' I tell you not to go into the forest for a reason."

"Well, I'm going to go into the forest." Samuel was only testing his aunt. He didn't really want to go into the forest, but he wanted to know why it was so important.

And it was then, as he looked at his aunt's cross face with her tight mouth, that he realized something. *She has no control over me.*

All his life Samuel's parents had controlled him by stopping him from doing things.

If he got a letter from school, he was stopped from playing his video games.

If he stayed out too late, he was stopped from going out the next evening.

If he fought with his sister, he stopped getting his pocket money.

So most of the time he kept himself in check by thinking of what he might lose if he misbehaved.

But what could he lose now?

He had lost his mum and dad. He had lost half of his sister (the half that spoke and smiled and sang). He had lost all his friends. He couldn't watch TV or attack alien planets on his video games.

What punishment could Aunt Eda dish out?

He hated the food anyway, so the thought of missing dinner was less than terrifying. She could send him to his room, but so what? It was no more boring than all the other boring rooms.

She could inflict nothing so terrible as the memories he held in his head of what happened on the B642, so he had absolutely nothing to lose.

"I am going to go to the forest," he told her. "One day, when you aren't looking, I'll go and see what is so special that you can't even talk about it. You won't be able to watch me all the time."

Aunt Eda threw him a severe look. "And why would you do that, when I have explained that it breaks the most important rule?"

"Because I'm bored," said Samuel. "What am I supposed to do? There's no TV. There's nothing. Just loads of books written in Norwegian with stupid words and stupid letters like æ and ø and å."

"Oh," said Aunt Eda. "You think this is some game? You think it is fun to break the rules of your boring old aunt and her boring old house? If I told you not to run off the edge of a cliff, would you run off the edge?"

"It's not a cliff," said Samuel. "It's only trees."

Aunt Eda laughed. It wasn't a happy laugh. It was a wild, high-pitched noise that shot out into the living room: "Ha!"

In the living room, Martha looked toward her brother standing in the kitchen. The loud sound of her aunt's laugh had brought her back into the world, if only for a moment.

"Ha! Only trees!" said Aunt Eda. "If it was only trees, do you think I would not show you the forest myself?"

Samuel shrugged.

"Please, Samuel." As Aunt Eda struggled to saw the knife through a particularly tough part of the meat, Samuel noticed she was nearly crying.

And then he managed to say what he had found so hard yesterday.

"I'm . . . sorry," he said. He realized it felt good saying it, rather like taking off a heavy backpack.

"Oh, Samuel," said Aunt Eda, buttoning up her tears. "You are right. Rules aren't enough. I can't just tell you not to go into the forest. You are a boy, after all. And boys see a rule as a kind of toy—something to pick up and play about with and see how it breaks."

Aunt Eda closed her eyes and blew air slowly out of her nose, to show she was making a very big decision.

"I must tell you about the forest," Aunt Eda whispered so only Samuel could hear. "I must tell you what happened to Uncle Henrik."

"What about Martha? Are you going to tell her?" Samuel asked, looking behind to see through to the living room, where Martha was sitting on the rug with Ibsen.

Aunt Eda frowned. "Do you think she needs more dark terrors inside her brain?"

Samuel shook his head.

"No. We will tell her, but not yet. It will be our secret, do you understand? Our secret. A werry serious secret. Now, I will go and give Ibsen his food in the hall and then I will tell you. Okay?"

"Okay."

"Ibsen! Ib-sen! *Mørbrad!* Steak!"

The dog looked up from his position on the rug, and glanced at Martha, as if to tell Eda: "I'll have my steak in a minute. But right now I'm keeping Martha company."

Samuel watched as Aunt Eda lay the bowl of meat down in the hall.

When she returned she had a look of determination, because the story she was about to tell required a lot of strength and courage. She closed her eyes again and took a deep breath, as if she was about to go underwater.

"Are you listening?" she asked.

"Yes," said Samuel.

"Then I will begin . . ."

# The Story of
# What Happened to Uncle Henrik

"Uncle Henrik was a wonderful man. He was the greatest I ever met. And it is only down to amazing luck that I met him in the first place. He was a ski jumper, and I was a jaffelin thrower.

"This was twenty-fife years ago. We were both sports people and it is not too much of a boast to say that we were rather good sports people, as we both made the Olympic Games . . . Yes, Samuel, that's right . . . Your boring old aunt once made it to the Olympics. I threw the jaffelin! I never won a medal, but I came close. Werry close. I sometimes think that if I'd had one more hour of sleep, or had one more egg for breakfast that morning . . . But anyway, I am not one for regrets.

"Two years later I was inwited to the Closing Ceremony of the Winter Olympics in Lillehammer, which is a town on the other side of those mountains you can see out of the window. This was the Winter Olympics where Henrik won his silfer medal for ski jumping . . . Oh, your uncle was an amazing ski jumper . . . He had no fear. None at all. He used to jump so far through the air it was like watching a man who had stolen the secret of flying from a bird. He would spend what seemed like whole minutes in the air, leaning so far forward his nose was nearly touching his skis. Oh, it was an incredible sight!

"Anyway, I met him and we fell in luff and we got married and it was luffly. We wanted to spend effery moment together.

" 'I haff the perfect idea,' Henrik told me. 'We will moof to a house further north and buy goats. We can make our own cheese.'

"I thought this was a ridiculous thing to do, and I worried Henrik would regret the decision later. He had always luffed cheese, but he had a good chance of winning a gold medal at the next Winter Olympics. And a gold medallist sounded a lot better than being a goat farmer!

"But Henrik was insistent. 'You are the only prize that matters to me now,' he told me. So we did it. We drofe through the tunnels in the mountains and arrifed at this house where we are right now. It was perfect. Too perfect, I thought, because it only cost one hundred krone. And I was right. You see, we soon discovered that the last person who had lived in the house had gone missing . . . in the forest.

"The people of Flåm talked of creatures. Huldre-folk, witches, trolls, pixies, and a hundred others. They talked of a terrible being who ruled all the forest, called the Change-maker. Of course, I thought the willagers were talking ignorant rubbish. Surely, the only places such creatures existed were in fairy tales and storybooks.

"But still, I was curious how a man could simply disappear. So I did a bit of research on the prefious owner. He was an Englishman called Professor Horatio Tanglewood. The willagers told us all about him.

"They said he was a werry arrogant man, who had asked Old Tor to paint his portrait ten times.

"He was a professor of Norse folklore, which means he studied the kind of strange creatures that people in Norway used to believe in, before science and the Bible had shown them that trolls and huldre-folk and pixies couldn't really exist.

"It turned out that Professor Tanglewood had gone missing on his second wisit to the forest. He escaped the first time and it was then that he gave the forest its name. Shadow Forest, or Mørke Skog, as we Norwegians call it. He told everyone about his experiences in a book called *The Creatures of Shadow Forest,* which said that the stories of trolls and huldre-folk were all true. He wrote about lots of other creatures too. Over a hundred in all. And all were equally deadly. He wrote that the creatures were all governed by an evil being called the Changemaker, who stopped at nothing to prevent humans from ever entering or leaving the forest.

"This book made the Professor a laughingstock at the University of Bergen, where he worked. They said he'd been studying myths for so long he had lost touch with reality. But no one was brafe enough to go into the forest and see if he was telling the truth. And people became efen more scared later.

"Why? Because when the Professor made his second trip to the forest, he was never seen again.

"I told Uncle Henrik we must neffer go in the forest and Uncle Henrik agreed.

"Effery morning we would get up and milk the goats we had bought and then Henrik would make the cheese in that room just ofer there—past the kitchen. The one with the yellow door. It is a washroom now.

"Our Gjetost cheese soon became the most popular in the area. The people in Flåm were no fools when it came to cheese.

"It had the most perfect taste and texture and it was lighter than normal Gjetost. It was a golden color, not too brown. This is why Henrik named it 'Gold Medal Cheese.' He said to me: 'You see, I have my gold medal at last!'

"He was so proud of his cheese. So so proud. He was starting to luff cheese more than he had ever luffed ski jumping. Oskar the grocer also luffed Henrik's cheese and ordered a year's supply . . . Me and Henrik were both so happy, and we were making a lot of money. We were *prosperous*—do you remember the Norwegian word for prosperous? . . . That's right, Samuel. *Hell.*

"Anywhere, where was I? Oh yes, the cheese. We were making lots of money and everything was perfect and it was a golden time of laughter and log-fires and cuddles and tasty cheese, but then something happened. Something bad. And it changed our lifes for effer."

# The Creatures of Shadow Forest

Samuel was now gripped by Aunt Eda's story. He wondered if she had been the same, then. If she'd been so strict and buttoned up. He doubted it. And what had happened to Uncle Henrik?

As she approached the crucial part of the story, Aunt Eda was clearly finding it difficult to go on talking. Her words had stopped as suddenly as people who have just realized they are running toward a cliff. She made herself a cup of egg coffee, and poured Samuel a cloudberry juice.

Outside the door, Ibsen was dragging his metal bowl across the hallway as he licked the last remains of his steak.

"Right," Aunt Eda said, blowing ripples across the surface of her coffee. "I will tell you the rest of the story now."

She took a deep breath, as if she was about to go underwater. And when she started talking the wind that had been rapping against the window suddenly went quiet, as if it too had stopped to listen.

"We realized something was wrong.

"Our goats were going missing. Effery night one would

simply disappear. Uncle Henrik was in such despair that he went to Flåm and he told the willagers . . . well, you can guess what they said. They blamed it on creatures in the forest. Trolls, in particular. Trolls were famous for stealing goats, they told him.

"I told Henrik not to listen to these ignorant people, who lived by their superstitions. But Henrik said there was no other way to explain it. There were no other goat farmers in the area to steal our goats, and Henrik said that it was impossible to lose a goat effery night *by accident*.

"So on the day we had lost our eleffenth goat, he went into the bookshop in Flåm and purchased a copy of Professor Tanglewood's book. And it said that trolls were known to steal goats, as well as to kill humans.

"The more he read, the more he beleefed in *The Creatures of Shadow Forest*. He sat there and his eyes would feed on the words for hours at a time.

"After he'd read the book, Henrik said that there was only one way to find our goats and that was to go into the forest. I reminded him of the promise he had made to me—about never being tempted to head into the trees where a man had gone missing. But I knew it was no good. He had the same eyes he had before a ski jump. He just kept on saying 'No one can get away with stealing—not even trolls.'

"I told him, 'I'll come with you,' but he said I had to stay and look after the nine goats we had left. I told him, 'People don't come out of that forest.' He said that 'The only people who don't come out of forests are people who don't *want* to come out of forests. Don't worry, Eda, my sweetheart, whateffer happens, I will find my way back to you. No troll will stop me. I promise.'

"So he headed out to the forest and I waited for him. I waited and waited. After three days I went to Flåm. I told the police he had gone missing, but they made excuses. They said Shadow Forest wasn't part of their area. I told efferyone he had gone missing, but no one dared to go into the forest to look for him. Not even Oskar, who had made so much money from Henrik's cheese.

"I would watch guard of the goats effery night like Henrik had told me, but I couldn't stay awake for effer and when I eventually fell asleep another goat went missing. And this happened, until there were no goats. No goats, and no Henrik.

"On the morning the last goat disappeared, it had been snowing heavily. I went out early into the field and I saw footprints in the snow, heading away from the forest. My heart lifted for a moment. Henrik had returned! But then I realized the footprints curfed back round into the forest. I took a closer look at the footprints and realized it wasn't the pattern of a shoe, but the mark of a bare foot. And not just any foot—a big foot with three toes. *A troll's footprint.* Henrik had been right all along. Trolls had been stealing our goats and taking them back into the forest! And heffen knows what they had done to Henrik.

"I was in despair. I didn't know what to do. I would lie

awake thinking about what might haff happened to him in the forest. But I got hold of such thoughts and kept them in check—I wasn't ready to lose my mind just yet.

"I know what you're thinking. You're wondering if I was tempted to go and follow him into the forest. Well, I can tell you, there were many occasions when I packed my rucksack, put on my boots and grabbed hold of my jaffelin, ready to go and find him.

"But effery time I headed up through that goatless field, I always felt something hold me back. I remembered him telling me to wait in the house and I kept on hearing his last words: 'Whatever happens, I will find my way back to you.' Maybe it was my own weakness. Maybe I was too frightened. But I never was able to step into the forest.

"I just stayed in the house and occupied myself as much as I could with books or knitting or other things that might distract me. I kept praying for some company, for something to keep me busy, and someone decided to take note of my prayers because one morning I found a stray dog asleep on the grass. That's right. It was Ibsen. He might not have been as good company as your uncle, but he was certainly a lot better than a goat. And he made me feel safe. He was my protector from the trolls.

"Over time, I am pleased to tell you that the horrible thoughts about what might have happened to Henrik in the forest were replaced with better things. Like memories of him flying through the air on his skis, or smiling at the smell of his 'Gold Medal.'

"Of course, it would be easier if I didn't have to look at those horrible dark trees every day. But I can't moof house, any more than I can head out into the forest. And anyway, I've got you and Martha now . . . What a team, eh? Ibsen, Samuel, Martha and old Aunt Eda."

Samuel looked at his aunt and saw the tears she was trying to hold back glaze her eyes. He sipped his cloudberry juice, as if trying to get rid of a bad taste.

Trolls and huldres and a hundred other creatures, all living in the forest behind the house. It was too much to believe in, and he didn't. Not fully, anyway. After all, what does a footprint in the snow prove? And why should anyone believe a mad professor?

But he remembered his own fear when he had stared into the darkness of the forest, and gulped back the rest of the juice.

"So," said Aunt Eda. "Now you know."

"Yes," said Samuel, although he didn't really.

He went and joined his sister in the sitting room. She was staring out of the back window, toward the forest.

"Martha," he said.

His sister turned to him.

"Martha—"

But he didn't know what to say.

# Night Songs

Samuel woke up in the middle of the night to the sound of singing.

It was only a faint sound, but as he couldn't sleep deeply, it was loud enough to make him open his eyes and wonder at what he'd heard.

He lay in the dark, and waited for the voice to return, but there was nothing. Just the gentle patter of rain against the window. He rolled over, and saw the dark shape of his sister, sleeping her deep and dreamless sleep.

Then he heard it again. The singing.

*"I once knew a tree,*
*That could talk like you and me,*
*And I taught it how to smile.*

*"I said, 'Excuse me, tree,*
*If you wear a face like me*
*You'll never go out of style.' "*

It sounded familiar, like a nursery rhyme his mum used to sing, and he recognized the voice. And the language. Samuel pulled back the covers and went to the window. Peeping through the curtains, he looked out into the dark and rainy night and couldn't see anything at first. Everything was the same purple black as the sky.

But then slowly, as his eyes adjusted to the pale moonlight, he could see varying degrees of darkness. The thick black of the distant forest and the lesser dark of the grass slope in front. He scanned the grass slope, letting his ears lead his eyes until he saw a small round shape, like a walking barrel, heading down the hill toward the fjord. *A creature. From the forest.* He opened the window, to hear the creature's voice a bit clearer.

*"It's raining, it's raining,*
*But I'm not complaining.*
*For what's the worst it can get?*

*"It might soak your clothes*
*Or drip on your nose,*
*And make you a little bit wet.*

*"But why try and be dry,*
*When the sky wants to cry,*
*And send tears that rain down on your head?"*

Samuel stayed there at the window, listening to the creature's funny songs as he watched its small, fat silhouette walk down the hill.

> *"I'd better be right,*
> *To escape in the night,*
> *When the darkness wears its cloak.*
>
> *"But if I am wrong,*
> *I'll be singing my song*
> *Till the huldres make me choke."*

The rain stopped and the singing died with it, after which there was nothing to be heard but the eerie silence of the moon.

Samuel lost sight of the creature, and the pitter patter of the rain began again. Or at least, that is what it sounded like. Yet when Samuel put his hand out of the window, he felt no drops on his skin.

*That's not rain.*

He was right. And within moments he saw something in the distance. A dull throb of light from inside the forest, like a dying and fallen sun. As this golden glow grew closer, Samuel felt his heart begin to race, almost in time with the sound that was moving forward, out of the forest.

And then he realized what the noise was. It was horses.

Three white stallions, and the figures riding them were each holding a flaming torch. They were out of the forest, now, although the faces of the riders were still too dark and far away to be seen.

Samuel, believing he'd get a better view downstairs, left the bedroom. He tiptoed past Aunt Eda's door, and headed softly down to the living room. Once there, he went to the window and pushed his head between the curtains. He could see the flaming torches move closer, illuminating the three riders. At first he'd thought they were humans, but now, by the light of the flickering torches, he could see that they were strange and bony gray-skinned creatures, with wide-apart eyes and flattened, screwed-up noses. It was them. The monsters of his nightmares. *I'm dreaming,* he told himself. *I must be dreaming.*

They were shouting orders, and whipping their horses, as they galloped after the barrel-shaped singing silhouette.

"Samuel? Samuel? What is the matter?"

Aunt Eda was standing behind him, in her nightgown, looking very worried indeed.

"I don't know," Samuel said as his aunt joined him at the window. He now realized this wasn't a dream.

"*Huldres,*" his aunt whispered urgently.

The huldres rode out of view, heading toward the fjord. It went quiet for a while, and Samuel and Aunt Eda stood as still and silent as the glass vases on the shelves. When the huldres galloped back into sight, they were dragging the singing creature inside a net.

"Come away," Aunt Eda said. "Away from the window. Away! Now!"

"Ow," said Samuel as she yanked his arm. "Get off me."

Samuel resisted his aunt's grip and stayed looking out of the window.

"Samuel. Come away or they'll see you. Come away. Now . . . If they see you, they will come for you. And me. And your sister."

"You're boring," he told her, but he couldn't hide the fear in his voice.

"Boring people stay alife," she said.

Samuel could hear the genuine terror in his aunt's voice, so he stepped back and listened as the huldres and their horses dragged the poor singing creature back to the thick darkness of the trees.

Aunt Eda held Samuel, and this time he didn't resist. He felt the fading gallop of her heart and the tight grip of her strong arms.

"Who was that creature? The one who sang?" Samuel asked.

"A Tomtegubb," said Aunt Eda.

"Have you seen one before?"

"Yes," she said, her voice trembling like a loose log. "Yes, I have. And . . . and so have you."

Samuel didn't understand. "I don't understand."

"Was that singing not familiar to you? Like the wardrobe and the wallpaper you recognized."

"I . . ." said Samuel, pulling away, "I . . . don't . . . I . . ."

And that is when Aunt Eda told Samuel something she hadn't told him before. About the time her sister—Samuel's mother—came to visit, bringing her husband and children along too.

"That's right, Samuel. You . . . you . . . came here when you were two and Martha was just a baby. Your mother heard about Uncle Henrik going missing and came to comfort me. She didn't beleef my stories about the creatures of the forest, of course. Well, not until she heard you scream in the night."

Samuel was more than confused as he stood there, straining to see his aunt's face in the dark.

"No. My mum said she'd never gone back to Norway. You're lying. She said—"

"She said that to protect you, Samuel," interrupted Aunt Eda. "She wanted you to forget you'd ever been here and forget that you saw something similar to what you've just seen now. Your parents never came back after she knew the creatures were real because they thought you and Martha would be unsafe here. And I was never able to see you in England, because I wanted to stay here for when Henrik returned."

Samuel wanted to think this was all a lie, but he remembered the strange dreams he had always had, about creatures he now knew were huldres.

"I've been here before," he whispered as the thought became solid in his mind. "I knew it. I've been here before. The monsters were real."

"Yes," said Aunt Eda. "And now do you realize why my rules are so important? Why you can't go out after dark or go near the forest?"

"But I don't get it," Samuel said. "Why don't you just move?"

He could hear his aunt gulp back her sadness. "I told Henrik I would stay," she said. "If I left the house, I'd be giffing up on him. Do you understand?"

"Henrik's not coming back," Samuel said.

"No," said Aunt Eda. "He will. I know it. He made a promise, and he never broke a promise in all his life."

# Five Slices of Brown Cheese

The next morning, Samuel was surprised to see Aunt Eda acting like nothing had happened. He wanted to talk about huldres, but knew he shouldn't in front of his sister, so he tried to act normal too.

Unbeknownst to Samuel, Aunt Eda had made a decision. They were going to move. They could not stay another night here. Oskar had been right. It was one thing stopping them from going into the forest and quite another stopping the forest from coming to them. It was what Henrik would want, she'd told herself. But she wasn't going to tell the children until later, until she'd done all the washing and the packing, because it would only worry Martha and put her off her breakfast.

"Take this to the table," Aunt Eda said, handing Samuel a breakfast tray full of plates of flatbread and cheese.

Samuel didn't like cheese at the best of times, but he had never seen one that looked like the one on the tray. The cheeses he had tried at home had been yellow or white, but this one was a strange brown color.

"What is the matter with your face, young man?" Aunt

Eda asked him as she handed both children glasses of cloud-berry juice. "Haven't you seen cheese before?"

"Not cheese that is brown," came Samuel's reply.

"That is because you haff neffer seen Gjetost cheese," said Aunt Eda. "Like the cheese Uncle Henrik used to make. It is very popular with skiers. They take chunks of it on the slopes to keep themselves going. This particular one is not as nice as Henrik's 'Gold Medal' cheese, but it is still a Norwegian speciality. It's a sweet goat's cheese. The taste is a little bit like caramel. Or even chocolate. Children haff it for breakfast, and grown-ups haff it as well." She was speaking faster than usual, as if scared of the silence between words.

As she spoke Aunt Eda was peeling paper-thin slices of the strange cheese with a funny looking slicer. Samuel noticed her hand was trembling. Ibsen was also watching very closely, as he loved cheese more than anything. Even steak. Not that he was ever given any. He just had to make do with the smell, which teased his nostrils and made him drool saliva into his basket.

"You see this handle?" Aunt Eda asked Martha, but didn't wait for a reply. "It is made with the horn of a reindeer."

Samuel sighed, remembering the sight of the huldres. "Who cares?"

Aunt Eda decided to ignore the sulky face that accompanied the question. "Well," she said. "I should imagine the reindeer cared werry much indeed."

She smiled, like she had made a joke, but her eyes looked scared.

"I don't like goat's cheese," said Samuel. "I like cow's cheese."

Aunt Eda's shaking hands placed five thin slices of Gjetost on his plate, along with some flatbread. "Well, young man, in this part of Norway we haff goats, not cows."

She gave Martha the same amount of cheese and flatbread, and Samuel watched as his sister started to eat it without any sign of complaint or enthusiasm. Then he looked out of the dining-room window at the empty grass fields that lay in front of the forest, and thought of the charging huldres and the creature they had captured. A shudder went through him.

Again, Samuel shook the feeling away and picked up his brown cheese and flatbread.

If a stranger had arrived in the room during those five minutes it took Samuel to finish his breakfast, he could have been perfectly mistaken for thinking that the suddenly quiet young man was the most well-behaved twelve-year-old on the face of the earth.

However, if the stranger had a sharp eye—a sharper eye than those belonging to Aunt Eda—he would have noticed that Samuel was only eating the flatbread.

He flicked his wrist before taking his first mouthful. This meant the cheese fell onto his lap. He could then place the fallen slices in his pocket with the hand he kept out of view under the table. He smiled, knowing he was breaking his aunt's fifth rule.

And then, right after breakfast, Samuel decided to break another of Aunt Eda's rules.

"I'm going to go up to the attic," he told his sister, when they were sitting upstairs on their beds.

Martha shook her head.

"Yes," said Samuel. "When she goes out to the washing line, I'm going to see what's so special up there that she doesn't want us to see." Samuel was determined to find out more about the forest, especially after last night, and he was convinced there would be clues in the attic.

Again Martha shook her head, for a moment looking like she was genuinely concerned.

"Yes," said Samuel. "I'm going."

And so, when Samuel heard his aunt head out to the washing line, he left his sister on her bed and walked down the landing toward the ladder. The ladder led up to a small, square wooden door in the ceiling.

Halfway up, Samuel faced a problem. The problem had four legs and a wagging tail and was starting to bark.

"No, Ibsen! Sssssh!" pleaded Samuel.

But Ibsen was not a dog to be shushed, and kept on barking the news of Samuel's rule breaking out to Aunt Eda.

And then Samuel remembered. The cheese! He pulled out

the thin slices of Gjetost from his pocket and let them fall onto the landing.

It worked. The barking stopped. Ibsen's silence was bought for five slices of brown cheese.

He undid the latch and pushed open the door, before clambering up into a room full of dust and cobwebs.

# The Tea Chest

It was dark in the attic, and Samuel had to wait for his eyes to adjust. There was a tiny window, but it was so caked with cobwebs that the weak Norwegian sunlight hardly made it past the glass.

The ceiling was low, and anyone taller than Samuel would have had to hunch their back as they walked over the creaking floorboards. Being considerably smaller than his aunt, Samuel could walk around the dark room with relative ease, although he did manage to bang his knee on a tea chest that had been sneakily hiding in the semidark.

"Ow!" Samuel said, then covered his mouth.

He felt inside the box, expecting to find something interesting, but found nothing but old clothes. They were men's clothes, so Samuel guessed they had belonged to his uncle Henrik.

There were pictures on the wall. Photographs in frames. Samuel squinted and saw a man standing on a snowy mountainside, clutching a pair of skis. The man was smiling—or laughing maybe—and he was wearing a purple bodysuit that clung so tight to his body that if his skin had been purple, you wouldn't have been able to tell where the bodysuit ended and his skin began.

There was another photograph, next to it. A man jumping through the air on his skis. And another, of the same man standing in front of a large block of brown cheese.

Samuel looked back at the photo of him standing in the snow, and as he looked Samuel got a strange feeling that he had seen this man only yesterday. The laughing eyes seemed as familiar to him as those of Aunt Eda. He realized it was Uncle Henrik, but the sense of recognition was still strange.

"Weird," he said to himself.

He looked around and saw something lying behind the tea chest along the side of the room. It was the skis that he had seen in the photo. Then he noticed something else on another wall. A framed glass case, containing his uncle's silver medal.

Samuel went over, to get a closer look, but became distracted by another tea chest. The chest was covered with an old tablecloth, as if it was hiding something. He looked around at all the other tea chests, but it was the only one hidden in this manner.

Intrigued, Samuel started to peel back the checkered cloth. Before he had seen what was inside, he jumped, startled by a sudden gust of wind slapping against the attic's small window.

He didn't know why he was so scared. Maybe it was because of what he had seen last night. Or maybe it was just because of the strange feeling he had gotten when looking at the photograph of his uncle.

Anyway, Samuel knew he didn't have long before Aunt Eda would catch him nosing about up here, so he closed his eyes and whipped the tablecloth off the chest as fast as a magician wanting to keep a tea set in place.

He opened his eyes and became instantly disappointed. The chest was full of books, and not even interesting-looking books. These were old books, in boring hard covers with dull colors and no pictures on them. And they were written in Norwegian.

Samuel hadn't read a book since his parents died. He had tried. Mrs. Finch, the neighbor who had looked after Samuel and Martha before they flew out to Norway, had suggested that Samuel should read to take his mind off things. But he hadn't been able to concentrate enough to finish reading a single sentence. His mind was still so full of the car accident that his eyes had slid off words like feet on an icy pavement.

Picking through the books in the tea chest, Samuel looked at the titles on the spine.

*Niflheim og Muspellshein*
*Ultima Thule*
*Ask og Embla*
*Æsir*
*Per Gynt*

And then he saw another book, underneath all the others. It was right at the bottom and Samuel had to stretch his arm as far as it would go in order to reach it.

It was heavy—heavier than its average size suggested—as if the words weighed more than in the other books. The cover was the dullest of greens, like grass in a March fog, but it somehow looked better than the rest.

Samuel looked at the spine, and felt a chill as the wind kept blowing against the side of the house.

The book had a title he could understand. It was called *The Creatures of Shadow Forest,* by Professor Horatio Tanglewood.

# The Fascinating Darkness

While her brother was nosing around in the attic, Martha stared out of the bedroom window and watched her aunt collect the washing from the line. The wind was strong, and kept blowing the vests and long johns and jumpers into Aunt Eda's face as she unpegged them.

What was Martha thinking about as she stared out from that upstairs window? Whether you were ten thousand miles away or right in the same room, you wouldn't have been able to understand what was going on behind those dark brown eyes as they observed her aunt battling the wind.

The truth is, she wasn't paying much attention to anything her eyes were witnessing. Since her parents' death, everything she saw in the outside world struck her as being pointless. What was the purpose of doing anything? Where did it get you? Everybody dies in the end, whether that end comes sooner or later it didn't really matter. She knew that some people—like Aunt Eda—could try to spend time talking and smiling to cover up the sadness inside them, but words and smiles belonged to another world now. A world to which Martha knew she would never be able to return.

So when she watched a bedsheet that her aunt had placed in the basket fill like a cotton balloon and fly up into the air, she didn't open the window and tell Aunt Eda that the washing was escaping in the wind.

It was only when her aunt turned around from unpegging her last pair of long johns that she caught sight of the rebellious bedsheet.

Aunt Eda shoved the long johns into the basket and started running after the white sheet as it swooped up in the air, and back down, cartwheeling over the grass toward the forest.

Martha saw other items were now leaving the basket as well, due to the increasing strength of the wind. And pretty soon all of the washing was traveling through the air toward the trees, flying over Aunt Eda's head or whizzing past her on the grass.

Undershirts, long johns, woolly socks, underpants—all tumbling and soaring like birds with injured wings . . .

Aunt Eda managed to catch hold of some socks and a shirt, then she saw the bedsheet come to rest only a few steps away from the forest. She ran toward it, pinning the rescued items of washing to her chest with her left arm. Then, once she had gotten to the bedsheet she stretched out her other arm—her javelin arm—but just as she was about to clutch hold of the white cotton, it escaped her, as it responded again to the call of the wind.

Aunt Eda ran a few more steps forward, awkwardly holding the bundle of dry washing, but then stopped suddenly as the sheet disappeared into the darkness of the forest.

Martha watched as her aunt stood facing the trees.

Aunt Eda was either unable or unwilling to step forward and retrieve any item of washing that made it beyond the giant trunks in front of her. And it was right then, at the moment Martha was reminded of the dreaded fear that the forest seemed to inspire in her aunt, that the ten-year-old girl at the window started to become interested in what she was watching. As her aunt began to walk back, toward the empty basket and the washing line, Martha's eyes stayed rooted on the darkness between the trees.

It seemed beautiful.

Beautiful, and strangely inviting. She became fascinated by it, as she stood there, at the window. It seemed so different from the pointless smiles and pointless words she had been surrounded by since her parents died.

Something about the black spaces between the trees seemed to speak directly to her, drawing her in—the darkness as irresistible in a world of false smiles as a cool pool of water on a hot summer's day.

. . .

As Martha stared out of the window, Samuel was a floor above her, opening *The Creatures of Shadow Forest*. He turned to the first page and began to read:

*There is a place you must never enter. It is a place where evil has many faces, and where creatures of myth and legend live and breathe. And kill. It is a place beyond dreams or nightmares—a place that has so far been too feared to be called anything at all. Now, in this book, I will explain the unexplained, and give fear a name that suits it well. That name shall be* Shadow Forest, *and it will plant terror in your hearts.*

Samuel gulped, and sweat moistened his palms. Then he flicked to the next page and began to read about the creatures of his nightmares.

### The Huldre-folk

*The huldre-folk are human-sized creatures who spend most of their lives underground. They have very bony bodies and long tails and claws instead of fingernails. They have scrunched-up noses and their eyes are set wide apart, and never blink or cry. They only come above ground in the dark—to hunt for caloosh, to catch creatures trying to escape and to es-*

cort doomed prisoners to the clearing in the forest where the Changemaker lives. The Changemaker is the fearsome overlord of Shadow Forest and he is loved and worshipped by the huldre-folk.

Years of living underground have had a very negative effect on the huldres, leading to a profound jealousy and hatred of creatures who live freely in the forest.

Their natural cruelty was one of the reasons the Changemaker chose them to be his prison guards, stopping all humans from entering and leaving the forest.

Most creatures in the forest speak Hekron, a universal language that everyone—even humans—can understand. The huldre-folk are the exception. They hate being understood almost as much as they hate the sunshine and so they invented their own language called Okokkkbjdkzokk, a language which sounds almost as cruel and sinister as the huldres actually are.

Weakness: Their flesh evaporates if exposed to daylight.

Samuel turned over the page, and he read as fast as he could about another kind of creature—*trolls*:

## Trolls

Trolls are the most terrible creatures in the whole of Shadow Forest. These are the creatures a human should be most scared of meeting, as they are horrible right down to their bones.

*Not only do they steal people's goats, but they also kill any humans they can get their hands on. They come out when it is dark and can smell human blood from a great distance away, and are drawn to it like bees to pollen.*

*They are generally very strong, and use their strength to drag people back to their homes, where they cook them alive in a giant pot. All trolls have three-toed feet and they are universally ugly, but the type of ugliness varies greatly. There are two-headed trolls. No-headed trolls. One-eyed trolls. Four-armed trolls. Despite their differences of appearance, trolls are all equally dangerous and should be avoided at all costs.*

*Weakness: Trolls have no weakness at all. They are pure evil.*

Samuel shivered with terror after he had finished reading, and flicked through the pages, catching glimpses of other creatures' names—Slemps, Truth Pixies, Tomtegubbs and many others. He decided to keep hold of the book, tucking it in his trousers and hiding it under his sweater. He then put the checkered cloth back over the tea chest. He stepped across the creaking floorboards, toward the ladder that leaned against the opening in the floor.

*I'd better go.* He realized his aunt would have probably finished taking the dry washing off the line.

As he placed his foot on the ladder he noticed an object like a spear leaning against the corner of the room.

*Aunt Eda's old javelin.*

But there was no time to inspect.

He heard Aunt Eda downstairs, so he quickly climbed down the ladder and tiptoed back to the bedroom where he had left Martha.

"Martha, there's a jav—"

Samuel's sentence was left unfinished, hanging in the air as he scanned the room for his sister. But it was no good.

Martha was nowhere to be seen.

# Martha Goes Missing

"Martha? . . . Martha?"

Where was she?

Samuel ran downstairs and looked in the living room but the only presence was that of Ibsen, his four legs jerking as he lay in his basket, lost in cheese-fueled dreams.

Martha wasn't in the hallway or the kitchen either. Maybe she was in the washroom, helping Aunt Eda sort out the dry clothes. This possibility led him through the length of the kitchen to the yellow door with the wobbly handle. He opened it and walked inside the small room, which had once been used as a tiny cheese factory. Aunt Eda was grumbling to herself in Norwegian while trying to match socks together on top of the washing machine. After she finished with the washing, she was going to phone Oskar and ask if it would be all right to stay with him until she had found somewhere else for them all to live. These thoughts preoccupied her so much that she was completely unaware that Samuel had stepped onto the stone floor beside her.

"Where's Martha?"

His question made Aunt Eda jump. She turned from her half-rescued pile of washing.

"Good heffens, Samuel. You shocked the life out of me." Then she remembered his question, and frowned. "Martha's upstairs. In the bedroom. With you. By the way, I haff made a decision. Today we are going to moof—"

"No," Samuel said. "She's not there. Martha. She's not in the bedroom."

Aunt Eda turned toward Samuel, and as she looked him in the eye a sudden terror seemed to grip her.

"When did you last see her?" she asked him.

"Ten minutes ago," Samuel said. "I went to—" He managed to stop himself from telling her "the attic."

Aunt Eda looked around the small, windowless washroom. After all those years, it still smelled of cheese. "I haff been in here fife minutes," she said, as much to herself as Samuel. Then, with a sudden urgency: "Look out of the window."

Samuel went back out of the yellow door and looked out of the kitchen window, with *The Creatures of Shadow Forest* still under his sweater. He saw nothing except empty fields with the fjord and the mountains in the distance.

"No!" barked Aunt Eda, behind him. "The window at the back of the living room!"

They ran toward the living room, but Aunt Eda paused by the doorway.

"Her shoes," she said. "Her shoes are missing."

Samuel looked out of the window that was positioned above Ibsen's basket. (Ibsen, owing to the sudden commotion, was now yawning himself awake.)

Samuel strained his eyes but saw nothing except the empty washing line and the grass field sloping up toward the—

He saw something. A figure in the distance. A figure heading straight to the forest.

"No!" Samuel screamed, when he recognized the dark blue of his sister's dress, blowing forward in the wind.

Samuel ran out of the room, down the wooden hallway, shot past his aunt and opened the door. Once outside, he started sprinting up the slope toward Martha and the forest. As he ran he pulled the book from under his jumper and held it tight with his right hand. He thought about dropping it, but if Martha reached the forest, he would need to keep it with him.

"Martha! Martha! Stop!"

As he got closer, he was hardly conscious of the wind that blasted him or the soft muddy grass that pressed into his socks.

"Martha!" Aunt Eda called. Then: "Samuel! Samuel!"

Even his aunt's voice was only half in his mind. It was as if the Samuel she was calling was someone else, running alongside him.

"Marth-aaaaa!" he called.

The only thing he focused on now was his sister, so he wasn't aware of all the muddy hoofprints left by the huldres' stallions the night before.

"DON'T GO IN THE FOREST!" Samuel screamed, pushing the air out of his lungs. He could see her long hair blowing forward like the branches of the tall trees in front of her.

"MARTHA! STOP! CREATURES! HULDRES! TROLLS! IN THE FOREST!"

Martha was only walking, but she was so far ahead that Samuel knew he couldn't reach her.

"MARTHA! NO! COME BACK!"

Martha didn't turn or show any outward sign of having heard her brother. She just kept on walking—neither quickening her step nor slowing down—until she had reached the trees.

And even then she kept on going, farther and farther, until she disappeared into the darkness of the forest.

# Running Up the Hill

She had gone.

Samuel kept running toward the space between the trees, where his sister had been visible only a moment before, and tried to see farther into the darkness.

"MARTHA! COME BACK! MARTHA!"

He was running fast. Faster than when he had run to the forest before, in pursuit of the cat. And Aunt Eda was finding it difficult to catch up with him.

True, he'd had a head start. He had shot, shoeless, out of the front door while Aunt Eda was still looking out of the window. But Samuel was running at such speed, and with such single-mindedness, that his aunt's old legs couldn't narrow the distance.

"Don't follow her!" she cried, breathless, as she ran. "Don't go into the forest!"

Of course, her words were useless. The fear of the forest was never going to be as great in Samuel's mind as that of losing his sister.

Even though she had explained to Samuel the story of what happened to Uncle Henrik, Aunt Eda knew that he would imagine he could enter the forest and bring his sister back. After all, Martha had only walked between the trees a few seconds ago. She wouldn't have gotten very far, so Samuel would have every reason to believe he could find her.

But Aunt Eda knew better. She knew that in this instance the usual rules of space and time couldn't be trusted. She knew that whoever or whatever entered the forest never returned. It didn't matter whether it was a white cotton bedsheet or a flesh-and-blood husband—the forest never let go of whatever came its way.

And so when she saw Martha disappear between the trees, Aunt Eda knew she was already lost. The only hope she had now, as she ran up the grassy slope, was in reaching Samuel before he too disappeared forever.

*Damn these old legs,* she thought as she struggled against the angle of the ground to gain speed.

"SAMUEL! STAY THERE! SAMUEL!"

But the boy still wasn't listening. He was sprinting ahead with unlimited energy, desperate to catch a glimpse of his sister's long hair or navy dress.

He was nearly there.

"SAMUEL! SAMUEL! STOP!" The words stole Aunt Eda's breath, and seemed to make the ground even steeper.

But then, just when she thought it was too late, she heard something. A noise. Behind. In an instant she recognized it as the jangle of Ibsen's collar.

And sure enough, the dog was there, galloping fast across

the grass toward Samuel. It was an incredible sight. The dog who had always been too scared even to point his nose in the direction of the forest was now charging headlong toward it at ferocious speed. It was as if something had been woken up inside him. Ibsen, who of late had shown little interest in anything other than begging for cheese and snoozing in his basket, was tearing across the grass as fast as a cheetah chasing a gazelle.

Not that Samuel was aware of his canine pursuer. For Samuel, everything that was now behind him might as well have stopped existing. He was nearly there now. He could see other trunks of pine trees, farther into the dark.

But just as he was ready to dive headlong into the shadows, he felt something tug his arm.

At first he thought it was Aunt Eda's hand.

"Get off me!" But then he saw the hand had teeth—teeth that weren't letting go of his sleeve.

Ibsen, having jumped into the air to catch hold of Samuel, was now digging his four paws into the ground to stop the boy from running into the forest.

Although the dog was lighter than the twelve-year-old he held on to, he had gravity and the force of two extra legs on his side.

"Get off me, you stupid dog!"

But Ibsen held firm. Samuel raised his arm, causing the dog to stand on only his hind legs. Despite such rough treatment, the steadfast elkhound didn't once let go, or seek a better grip by sinking his teeth into the arm itself.

"Get off! Get off! Get off!" Samuel cried, staring into the dark abyss of the forest.

Samuel kept shaking his arm, and threatened to hit Ibsen with the book. Then he turned to see Aunt Eda running up the hill toward him.

"NO!" screamed Samuel, the word rising with his foggy breath into the cold Norwegian air.

At that moment—the moment just before his aunt's hand would have been able to reach him—Samuel's jumper ripped, leaving Ibsen with a ragged patch in his mouth.

Realizing he was free of the dog's grip, Samuel darted straight into the forest. As he ran into the darkness, he ignored Ibsen's barked warning and the screams of his aunt. A scream so agonizing it sounded like a woman giving birth.

Or mourning the dead.

# Part II

# The Feather Pit

Martha walked in as straight a line as she could manage, which wasn't very straight at all given the number of pine trees in her way.

She didn't know where she was going.

There was no plan involved with her walking other than to head as deep into the darkness of the forest as possible. So she just kept on walking, through the green plants that brushed against her knees, toward a thin dirt path lined on both sides by little shrubs filled with berries.

And then she heard something.

A kind of squawking.

It was a horrible noise, and it was getting closer.

*Squawk! Squawk! Squawk!*

That was when she saw them.

Three giant birds, taller than her, running fast on thin legs. The birds had gray feathers and tall, swanlike necks. Their heads were darker gray than the rest of their bodies, with a white stripe on their foreheads and with very long (and very loud) squawking beaks.

As they kept running straight toward her she saw the front

bird's fat body and tiny, flightless wings. She kept looking for the other birds' bodies but couldn't see them.

And then she realized.

It wasn't three birds at all.

It was one bird with three heads on three separate necks. A "caloosh" was one of the many creatures described in Professor Horatio Tanglewood's book *The Creatures of Shadow Forest*, but Martha didn't even know anything about this book, as neither her brother nor Aunt Eda had told her about it. (Calooshes, by the way, are as scared of leaving Shadow Forest as humans are of entering it, and never head out into the open, which is why you've probably never bumped into one.)

Martha stared at the caloosh running toward her. Then the bird suddenly stopped. All of its three beaks squawked at the same time as the ground opened up and the bird fell down a hole. Then the ground closed back up again, and looked exactly as it had before. Martha looked around, wondering if there were any other hidden holes in the ground.

"Martha! Martha!" It was the faint call of her brother.

*He must be getting close to finding me,* she thought. And she suddenly realized that wasn't such a bad thing. Maybe she had been hasty coming into the forest. Maybe she should have listened to Aunt Eda.

She decided to go to her brother, but she couldn't work out where he was. His voice bounced off the trees, making it seem like he was everywhere. She walked a bit in one direction, then another, watching the ground for holes, but Samuel still sounded just as far away.

She kept walking, then started to run, and she sensed she was now getting closer to Samuel.

"Martha! Martha!"

Yes, he was definitely near now.

She ran faster.

One step after another after—

Her foot fell into nothing, and her body followed. The ground had opened up and now she was falling down a hole into darkness. There was a low branch of a tree hanging over the hole but she couldn't reach it in time.

She screamed.

It was the first sound her mouth had made for over a week, and she only made the sound because she had no choice. That is simply what mouths do when they find they are falling down a black hole into apparent nothingness. They scream.

"Aaaaaaaaagh!"

Martha landed on something soft and feathery. In fact, it was so feathery that she had to conclude it was indeed feathers. She looked up at the small circle of light. A hidden trapdoor. It shut as quick as it had opened.

She rolled over and tried to stand up but she only managed to get onto all fours. She clambered over the feathers as her eyes slowly adjusted to the darkness. Her hand reached out and touched the dug-out earth on the side of the giant hole.

There was a soft yellow lightness, getting slowly brighter. Soon she could see the feathers—they were gray, like those of the three-headed bird that had fallen into the other hole.

She looked around her and saw the source of the light. An underground window, with metal bars. Moving closer to the window, she heard voices, and glimpsed the fire of a torch. The torch and the voices were coming closer toward her, down some kind of corridor.

*Maybe they are coming to rescue me,* she thought.

But even as she had the thought, she realized it wasn't true. People don't set traps in order to let you go again.

Martha knew that whoever or whatever was coming toward her was not wanting to make friends. So she lay down and covered feathers over herself, hoping she wouldn't be seen.

# The Scream

"MARTHA! MARTHA! MAAARTHAAAAAAA!"

Samuel kept calling his sister's name, but only received an echo in response. He looked around, trying to locate Martha amid the trees, but he could see no sign of her.

This was odd, to say the least. After all, she couldn't have gone that far. She only ran into the forest two minutes ago.

He kept running through the green vegetation, book in hand, and tried to ignore the pain of his shoeless feet as they cracked twigs and landed on stones.

"MAAARTHAAAAAAA!"

He stopped again. It was like she had vanished into the air. He stared up at the tall trees, as if they were strangers who might be able to help, but he was greeted with nothing but silence. He tucked his book back under his sweater, and scanned three hundred and sixty degrees.

The trunks were so close together that it was hard to see for a long way in any direction. The closeness of the trees seemed to steal the sky, or at least smash it into so many little pieces that it was only visible through the leaves like stars on a clear night.

Samuel strained his eyes around the dark and green land-scape, but he still couldn't see Martha. Nor could he see back where he came from. None of the gaps in the trees revealed a view of the distant fjord and mountains. There was no sign of Aunt Eda.

The compass of his brain no longer worked properly. He couldn't tell which way would lead him back to the soft grass and the white wooden house, any more than he knew how to get to Martha.

It was as though the trees had somehow moved around behind him, the way clouds change position when you aren't looking at them.

"Martha. Please. Martha."

Samuel's voice was quieter now. Not scared exactly, but not confident either.

"Who's there?" he said as he stood still. He thought he had heard the cracking of a twig behind him. "Martha? Is that you?"

But she wasn't anywhere to be seen.

He heard another twig-snap, and another. Definite foot-steps, coming closer toward him.

Samuel waited to see who it was. "Hello?" he said.

There was no answer, which made him think it could still be his sister. Samuel felt sick with panic as he waited to see who it was.

"Martha?"

Samuel tried to move, but fear rooted him to the ground.

In the distance he heard a sound. A faint scream and then what sounded like someone falling. Could it be Martha?

"Martha!" Samuel called as he carried on walking. But then he heard something else.

A bark.

He turned around and saw Ibsen.

The dog barked again.

"Go back!" Samuel told him. "Go to Aunt Eda!"

Ibsen seemed to be barking exactly the same thing, but neither of them listened to the other.

"Go home!" Samuel tried again.

More barking.

"Go home, you stupid dog! Go back home!"

Ibsen stopped barking but stayed precisely where he was.

Samuel began walking deeper into the forest. Ibsen followed.

"Do what you want," Samuel muttered, and kept on going. "But I'm not going back, so you can rip my sweater all you want."

The dog lowered his head, as if he had understood, and Samuel kept calling his sister's name.

"Marth-aaa! Marth-aaa!"

He headed in the direction of the scream, with a terrified Ibsen close at heel.

# The Sneeze

While Samuel and Ibsen kept trying their hardest to find her, Martha herself was trying her hardest to hide. She had managed to cover herself entirely with feathers and now she lay at the bottom of the hole as still and as quiet as she could manage.

This is what she heard:

Footsteps, getting closer.

A clinking sound—keys.

Muffled voices.

A key sliding in a lock.

A door creaking open.

The voices got louder, but they spoke a language Martha had never heard before. A bit like Norwegian, but completely different at the same time.

First voice: *"Enna fregg oda blenf?"*

Second voice: *"Ven! Froga oda klumpk!"*

First voice: *"Kyder fregg lossvemper."*

Second voice: *"Froga oda blenf. Froga oda caloosh!"*

The whispery voices hardly sounded like voices at all.

They were more like a sinister wind blowing through leaves, only a wind that had shaped itself into words.

Unbeknownst to Martha, the voices belonged to huldres, and she had just fallen into one of the many traps designed to capture calooshes and stray forest wanderers. Yet, even though Martha couldn't understand their language, she sensed correctly that she was in grave danger. She didn't want to stay trapped in the feathers, but she thought that whatever fate awaited her beyond the door would be even worse.

So she decided to stay quiet, and wait for the two creatures to leave.

But deciding to be quiet and actually being quiet are two very separate things. Although Martha had hardly made a sound since her parents were crushed to death, she was on the verge of blowing her cover.

You see, the thing with feathers is that they tickle. And the thing with noses is that when they are tickled they have a tendency to sneeze.

Martha knew the sneeze was coming. She just hoped it would be after the two creatures shut the door and walked away.

"*Froga oda blenf,*" the first voice was saying, which roughly meant "I heard something," but it has no exact translation.

He thought he had heard a caloosh, the squawking three-headed bird that huldre-folk depend on for meat and eggs and feathers, as well as for entertaining them with caloosh fights.

"*Nip. Keider fregg lossvemper,*" said the other huldre in a slightly less sinister voice than his fellow guard. He was convinced that there was no caloosh or anything else amid the feathers.

They were just about to shut the door when they heard:

"A-a-a-a-atchoo!"

And when Martha sneezed, the feathers that had been lying over her face shot high into the air, making it easy for the two huldre guards to spot her straightaway.

Martha saw them for the first time. Their too-far-apart eyes, their claws, their gray skin and their cow's tails that flicked at the sight of the human girl lost in the caloosh feathers. They were two of the huldres Samuel and Aunt Eda had seen the night before, who had chased the singing creature and taken him back to the forest. They were wearing clothes made from caloosh skin, with weapons strapped to their belts. A sword, a small throwing ax, daggers, and something Martha didn't recognize.

"*Ig kippenk,*" said the slightly less sinister huldre, whose far-apart eyes had a deep sadness to them.

He was called Grentul, but it wasn't the name his mother had given him. It was a name he had given himself, a long time ago. A time when everything changed and the huldres had been forced underground.

"*Ig kippook,*" said the other, who was so skinny it seemed his ribs were about to burst out of his skin.

He leaned over the feather pit at Martha, tilting his head the way a cat does before pouncing on a mouse. He was called Vjpp, which is an impossible name for human tongues to pronounce.

Martha didn't know what they were saying, but judging from their gestures, they seemed to be debating how they should get her out. At first Vjpp smiled an evil smile and beckoned her with one of his clawed fingers.

Needless to say, Martha did not do as the finger asked her and stayed exactly where she was.

The two creatures debated a little while longer, and Martha saw Vjpp point to the flaming torch Grentul was holding. This prompted the other huldre to nod reluctantly, and hand it over.

"*Fugappuk ky brekk!*" Vjpp shouted.

The next thing Martha knew, the flaming torch was flying through the air above her head. She turned and saw it land with a crackle, as rising sparks danced upward in the dark.

Feathers quickly turned to flames as the fire roared and spat its way toward her.

"*Fugappuk!*"

Vjpp was rattling his keys in excitement. This was the cruellest and most enjoyable thing he had done all day.

"*Fugappuk! Fugappuk!*"

Martha could feel the heat blast her cheek as the fire inched closer and knew she had no choice.

She had to get out of the feathers, or else share their fate.

So she sat up, choking on the smoke, and raced on all fours against the fire.

The huldres' clawed hands pulled her out just in time, then shut the thick heavy door, leaving the fire to burn itself out. She was led down a dark corridor, but was too busy coughing to worry about the caged creatures on either side, their faces grotesque in the flickering light.

# Prison Songs

Martha was thrown into a cell at the end of the corridor, which had metal bars instead of walls and nothing much else.

No bed. No toilet. No window.

No hope of escape.

*"Ob kenk,"* said Vjpp, his ribs shaking under his tight skin as he laughed.

Grentul looked at Martha with his sad wide-apart eyes as if he wanted to tell her something. An apology? An explanation? Whatever it was wouldn't have been understood, so he walked away. Vjpp waited a moment longer and spat blue spit through the bars at Martha. Then he too turned and walked down the corridor.

When Vjpp's cruel laughter had faded, and his flickering tail had vanished into darkness, Martha looked around at the inhabitants of the other cells.

An old woman, with long white hair down to her ankles and wearing a white tunic and shawl, stood watching her from the cell opposite.

Farther down the corridor she saw a fearsome-looking creature, with two heads and four eyeballs peering at her from behind the wooden bars. Both heads had shaggy black hair and beards, but the head on the right looked a lot grumpier than the head on the left. Martha guessed, rightly, that the creature was a troll. A two-headed troll. She had never read about trolls in *The Creatures of Shadow Forest*, but the sight of the creature was enough to terrify her.

Then she heard a noise, coming from the cell next to hers. The noise was singing, and not particularly good singing either:

*"There's nothing wrong*
*With a little song*
*When things aren't going your way.*

*"For there's no crime*
*In a silly rhyme*
*On the most unhappy day . . ."*

She looked to see who would be capable of singing so happily while trapped in an underground prison. The creature she saw was a Tomtegubb (although she didn't know that yet), the exact same Tomtegubb that Samuel and Aunt Eda had seen get caught by the huldres (although Martha didn't know that either). He was shaped rather like a barrel, with a short roundish body and no neck, or none that she could see, anyway. He had golden skin, very hairy eyebrows, and a flat nose with long blond whiskers that shone from his face like rays from the sun.

His clothes were most unusual too. A tunic made of multicolored patches—bright green and bright yellow and shiny red. The tunic was short, and only covered half his body. The other half was covered by purple trousers. Indeed, his trousers—as the other prisoners would have been able to tell her—were the subject of one of the Tomtegubb's self-written songs, called "The Purple Trouser Song." It was a very long song, with twenty-two verses and three different choruses, and the Tomtegubb regarded it as his masterpiece.

His clothes looked quite ridiculous in the dark and dingy underground prison, but even more ridiculous was his broad smile when his circumstances should have made him very sad.

It went quiet for a moment, a moment during which the troll with two heads seemed very relieved, then the Tomtegubb launched into another song.

"There may be no window,
There may be no bed,
But at least there are no prison bars,
Inside my happy head."

The song prompted the two-headed troll to rub both his foreheads.

"Tomtegubb, please stop, I'm begging you," he said, out of his grumpier head, which was on his right side.

*"If our shared tomorrow*
*Is filled with death and sorrow,*
*There's only one thing to say.*

*"And that's get up and dance,*
*Let's sing and let's prance,*
*For we've still got today!"*

The Tomtegubb's singing, accompanied by the troll's moans about his double headache, kept going for quite a while.

During this time, Martha sat herself down in one of the back corners of the cell, with her legs out straight in front of her. She looked around at the other prisoners, and wondered what they would do to her if there were no bars between them. Would they kill her? She looked at the old, white-haired woman in the opposite cage, who was staring at her with kind eyes. Could that kindness be trusted?

She didn't know.

All she knew was that she was dirtying her dress on the ground—a dress her parents had bought for her birthday—but no one was there to tell her off about that.

# Rising Smoke

Still walking in the direction of the scream, Samuel now noticed something else.

Smoke.

It was rising from the ground in the distance ahead of him and Ibsen. They walked through the ferns toward it, but kept looking around for a human form amid the trees.

"Martha? Martha? Are you there?"

If she was near, she certainly wasn't making any sign of the fact.

Then something weird happened.

The smoke, which had until that point been thick and heavy, stopped completely. Samuel sped up, to see how the fire had gone out so quickly, but Ibsen stayed behind and growled.

"What's up, you hairy idiot?" Samuel asked him.

Seeing that Samuel wasn't going to listen to his growled warning about the imminent threat lying ahead, Ibsen followed a few paces behind. He kept growling and even barked as Samuel got closer to where the smoke had been.

"Ibsen, shut up! I'm trying to li—"

Samuel stepped onto the same trap as Martha and fell into empty nothingness. The smoke hadn't stopped at all. It had just been hidden when the trapdoor had closed. Now it was all around him, and he could feel the terrible heat of the fire below.

As he'd been turning to talk to Ibsen, his hands were able to reach the side of the hole just in time. His fingers clawed desperately into the earth, trying to get a better grip.

Looking up, Samuel could see the low branch of a tree hanging over the hole, too far out of reach.

"Help!"

He looked down. Clouds of black smoke hit his face, and he flinched away from the intense heat of the fire. The blazing flames below almost reached his shoeless feet. Sparks rose and singed his socks.

"Ibsen!" he choked. "Ibsen! Help!"

Samuel managed to pull himself up enough to see Ibsen backing away from the hole.

"Ibsen!" he shouted as he started to lose his grip. "Come back!"

Of course, he didn't know what Ibsen would have been able to do. He was only a dog, after all. But when you find yourself clinging on to the edge of a hole, hanging above a blazing fire that is already starting to cook your feet, you hold on to even the slightest of hopes.

"Ibsen . . . Ibsen, come here. Help! Come back, you coward!"

But Ibsen, although terrified, wasn't a coward. He was only walking away from Samuel to take a run-up. Having paced back a few steps, he now ran directly toward the hole and jumped through the smoke to land on the other side. This was a truly remarkable thing to happen, especially as the size of the hole was considerably more than the size of the dog.

Once Ibsen was safely landed, he got his footing and jumped again, pushing off from his front paws first, then lifting up with his back legs. A second later, he had the low branch in his mouth and was dipping it down into the choking smoke.

"Help! Help!"

Earth crumbled under Samuel's fingers. He was about to lose his grip and fall into the hellish flames below.

But then he felt something, prodding his shoulder. Turning his head, he saw it was the low branch that had been such a cruel tease moments earlier.

He didn't know how the branch came to be there, but he was very pleased to see it. He had to be quick, though. The crumbling earth under his left hand meant that his right hand couldn't take too long to grab hold of the branch.

It was an awkward move, especially in the smoke. But he did it. Once both hands were around the wood, the branch snapped and swung Samuel to the other side of the hole. The branch hung on just long enough to let him climb out and clamber away from the smoke.

He coughed, bending double, for about five minutes. Then

he looked at Ibsen and realized he must have jumped over to save him.

"Thank you," Samuel said, checking he still had the book tucked under his jumper. "And, I'm . . . er, sorry. For calling you stupid. And I don't think you're a hairy idiot."

Ibsen gave a brief wag of his tail. "Apology accepted," the wag seemed to say.

Then a terrible thought hit Samuel. What if Martha had fallen down the hole? What if she had been burned alive? There was no way of answering those questions, as the hole was now concealed again.

"Martha, where are you?" Samuel mumbled, looking around at all the trees for anything that might give him a clue.

Then he saw something. A flash of gray amid the landscape of tall brown trunks.

A house.

He felt cold with fear, yet there was a chance that whoever lived there might be able to help him find his sister. It was a small chance, but no smaller than that of escaping from the fire. So Samuel started walking toward the house, with Ibsen treading carefully by his side, checking the ground for hidden holes.

# The Village

As they got closer, Samuel's heart began to race. He realized the small house wasn't on its own. There was another, farther back. And another, and another . . .

"It's a village," Samuel told Ibsen, although what Ibsen was to do with that information wasn't exactly clear.

The village consisted of twelve small houses, with stone walls and wooden doors and roofs. The windows of each house were round, as was the layout of the village itself. Together, the houses formed the circumference of a perfect circle.

In the middle of that circle, there were tree stumps with pictures carved onto the part of the wood that faced the sky. Each picture was of the sun, with its rays flowing like a kind of mane. The exact same image was also carved into each of the houses' doors.

Samuel went over to one of those doors and knocked, his hand beating against the middle of the wooden sun.

"Hello? Is anyone there?"

No answer.

"Hello? Excuse me, is anyone home?"

He went over to the glassless window and asked the same question. Poking his head inside the window, he got his answer. No one was there.

In fact, it looked like no one had been there for quite some time, as the whole place was shrouded in a veil of dust and cobwebs.

He found the same situation at the next house along. And the next. By the time he and Ibsen reached the fourth house in the circle, Samuel decided to try the door.

It creaked open, tearing the mesh of cobwebs along its top edge.

Ibsen growled his nervous warning.

"Stay there if you're a scaredy-cat," said Samuel, "I mean, scaredy-dog."

But Samuel was the one who was really feeling scared. If it hadn't been for his desperate need to find his sister, and find any clues that might lead to her, he would have been running as fast as he could in the opposite direction.

But what was he hoping to find?

A map of the forest? Some kind of creature, still living among the dust and cobwebs, who might be able to help him?

He looked right and saw a small kitchen with a wood-burning stove. There were logs inside, still waiting to be set on fire.

*That's strange*, thought Samuel. *Why put fresh logs in the stove if you were never going to use them?*

There was a pot on the stove, which stank of rotten food. A meal no one ever got to eat.

Samuel inched his way into the dining room, which had a round wooden table with the same image of the sun carved upon its surface. Around that image were four wooden bowls and four wooden spoons.

As well as rotten food, there was another smell in the house. A foul, even more putrid smell that Samuel couldn't quite identify.

"Ow!"

His toe hit something.

Something hard but light, that skidded a short distance across the floor.

He looked down and what he saw caused him to lose his breath.

It was a skull.

A skull that Samuel's foot had just detached from the rest of its skeleton.

For the second time today he was wishing he'd listened to Ibsen.

He was torn between the two different Samuels that lived inside his head. There was the Samuel who wanted to run away and the Samuel who wanted to stay and look. It was that second Samuel who won a short victory as he stared at the remains of the dead body on the floor.

The skull wasn't human.

The eye sockets were too wide apart, as close to the sides

as the front of the head. Samuel remembered the creatures of his nightmares—the huldre-folk he had seen with Aunt Eda—and thought of their strange eyes.

*No*, thought Samuel. *It can't be a huldre. Their homes are under the ground.*

Samuel dared his own eyes to scan the rest of the skeleton, and tried to compare it with the pictures of human bones he had seen in science books. There were clear differences. Too many rib bones. Longer feet and hands. A tailbone. It *was* a huldre.

*Whatever has killed this creature could be still around to kill me.*

The door creaked shut behind him, in the breeze.

It was then that shock turned into total fear.

Samuel was so scared he felt sick.

His heart was a mad drum beating three times too fast.

Ibsen barked.

This time Samuel listened, and headed back outside.

"Come on," he told the dog. "Let's go."

And they both ran as fast as they could away from the empty village. But even as they ran Samuel couldn't shake the image of the skull, and the secrets that seemed to be lost somewhere in the hollow darkness of those wide-apart eyes.

# A Rude Interruption
# from the Author

Now, you may be wondering what exactly Aunt Eda was doing at this time.

Of course, you may not be wondering this at all. You may just be wondering about what had happened to the huldre-folk to make them go underground, or you might be thinking about Martha in her prison cell, or you might just be wondering what you are going to have to eat for breakfast tomorrow. I don't know. I'm only the author, I'm not a mind reader. But if you *are* wondering about what Aunt Eda was doing, then you'd better read this next chapter. If not, then you can skip this one and go straight to the one after, which is called "Troll-the-Left and Troll-the-Right." But if you do that, it might make the ending a bit confusing. Not that I'm trying to tell you how to read the book or anything. You can read it back to front if you really want. It's your book. Anyway, I just thought I'd better let you know that the next chapter is about Aunt Eda just in case she's your least favorite character. She's one of my favorites, but everyone's different. And also, if you've just eaten your evening meal, you might want to let it digest before reading "The White Bracelet," as it contains a rather disgusting kiss involving cheesy breath and a furry mustache.

Don't say I didn't warn you.

# The White Bracelet

Aunt Eda had never driven fast in her life. She had always been scared of the roads, and the wheeled boxes of metal they were made for. Since she had heard what had happened to her sister, Liv, fear had turned into mild terror.

But as she drove toward Flåm, she traveled so fast her battered old car had no idea what speed it was traveling. The numbers on the speedometer only went up to ninety, and she had passed that as soon as she'd hit the main road.

"Come on, old car," she begged. "You can go faster than this."

The car moaned its disagreement, but kept racing toward the village.

Outside the window, the grass became a blur. Only the distant mountains and fjords stayed still, as calm and beautiful as one of Old Tor's paintings.

The car screeched into the village, past the houses, past the church, left at the crossroads and down the main street. Aunt Eda slammed on the brakes just outside Oskar's store and ran inside.

Some of the villagers were there. Eda looked around to try

to see Oskar, but he was nowhere to be seen. Instead, she saw his blond son, Fredrick, sitting on a stool and playing with his calculator.

"Fredrick, where is your father?" Aunt Eda asked in Norwegian.

The boy looked confused, as if Aunt Eda was a sum he couldn't solve.

"Er . . . He's upstairs."

"I need to see him. It's an emergency."

Aunt Eda pushed past the tutting villagers and went through the doorway at the back of the shop.

"Wait!" said Fredrick. "My dad will kill me! I've broken his rule."

But Aunt Eda knew there was no time left for following rules. She climbed a dark narrow staircase and followed the sound of Oskar's voice to a large white room with wooden floors and a reindeer's head looking down from one of the walls.

Oskar was on the phone to his new cheese supplier, and had his back to Aunt Eda.

"No, no, we don't want any more of your Gjetost cheese. Your Jarlsberg cheese is fine. Very white and very creamy. But I am afraid your Gjetost cheese is no good. It is too brown. It needs to be more of a golden color, and it has to taste more like caramel . . . At the moment, I am afraid to say that it tastes like it came out of a reindeer's—"

Aunt Eda cleared her throat.

Oskar jumped out of his skin, but looked relieved when he saw who it was. Maybe he thought it was going to be a two-headed troll.

"Eda. What are you doing here? Who let you up? Didn't Fredrick try and stop you?"

"He tried," said Aunt Eda. "But there is no stopping me today. I am sorry but I have come to ask you a very big favor."

"A favor? Eda . . . I don't know . . ."

"Well, think of it more as Henrik asking you a favor. After all, a favor for me is a favor for him. And you do remember how he helped you out, when your shop had no customers. He gave you free 'Gold Medal' cheese. A month's supply."

Oskar looked sorrowfully at the phone. "Oh, if only he was still here! If only I didn't have to rely on these dimwits from Oslo with their stinky brown cheese. It's like eating socks. They wouldn't know proper Gjetost if it threw them down a mountain. If I still had Henrik's 'Gold Medal,' I would have queues from my cheese counter all the way to Lillehammer."

"So you will help me?"

Oskar nodded. "All right. What is it?"

Aunt Eda took a deep breath and then came straight out with it. "I need a man."

Oskar straightened his yellow bow tie and raised his eyebrows.

"Aha," he said. "Well, I must tell you, it is not a big surprise."

Aunt Eda looked confused. "It isn't?"

"I have a nose for these things, you see." He wiggled his gigantic nostrils, to prove his point. Suddenly he was feeling quite happy that Henrik *wasn't* there.

"You do?"

"Love is much like a cheese. It gets stronger with time. And people like us, Eda, we are not good at being alone. Sleeping in an empty bed is too much like eating flatbread with nothing on it. Don't you think?"

He walked over to Aunt Eda and held her head in his hands, and before she had time to object, she was being kissed. Aunt Eda pushed Oskar and his cheese breath and furry mustache away.

"No," she said, wiping her mouth. "No! Oskar. *No!*"

She was going to be cross but then she remembered why she was here. "Listen, Oskar, I think you might have gotten the wrong idea. You are a lovely man, but I don't need you to warm my bed."

Oskar paused, and looked up at the reindeer head as if he was worried it might tell someone what a fool he'd just made of himself.

"Oh, I see. So what do you need me for?"

Aunt Eda closed her eyes and blurted it out: "To go with me into the forest."

"The forest? As in Shadow Forest? As in the most dangerous place in the whole world? The place where people disappear and never come back?"

"It's Samuel and Martha," Aunt Eda explained. "The two children I am looking after. They have gone into the forest. With Ibsen. And I have to find them."

"Oh no. The children. Those poor children."

"I have to bring them back, but I can't do it alone. I know you've said no before, when I wanted you to help find Henrik. But you've got to help me this time. Please. I beg you."

But Oskar was already shaking his head and talking over her words. "Eda, Eda, listen. I so want to help you, and I would do anything else . . . Anything . . . It's just . . . terrible things are in that forest. Even the creatures are trying to escape. Old Tor saw another last night. I told you he had seen the two-headed troll. Well, he went back to the fjord last night and saw something else. A Tomtegubb, and more huldres."

Aunt Eda gulped, knowing she and Samuel had seen the same thing.

"But this time they saw him," said Oskar. "The huldres. They saw him and chased after him. And he ran away."

Aunt Eda remembered how the huldres had galloped toward the fjord. "But Old Tor can't run. He can hardly walk."

Oskar nodded. "I know, it is something of a mystery . . . but he swears it is true."

Aunt Eda didn't see what this had to do with going into the forest, so she asked again.

"Please . . . Please, Oskar . . ."

But there was no persuading Oskar.

"I can't go with you into the forest," he said. "I'm sorry. I can't do it. I have responsibilities. I have the shop. I have Fredrick. I'm sorry, I can't help you. I am too old to be a hero."

"Then what can I do?"

He shrugged his shoulders. "You must ask the other men in the village. Maybe they will help."

"I might as well ask your reindeer for help. You know what the villagers think of me. They will think it was my fault for letting the children be so close to the forest."

The rising of Oskar's eyebrows told her that maybe he shared the same view. She thought about pleading some more, but she didn't have the time. She left the room, and ran to Old Tor's art shop.

Old Tor was perched on an antique chair painting a hideous-looking huldre on horseback, riding by the light of the moon.

"Old Tor, you must help me, the children I am looking after have gone missing in Shadow Forest,"

The old man's eyes widened in terror, and he fell into a kind of trance.

"Old Tor? Old Tor? Can you hear me?"

At that point his wife walked in, the chubby woman with three cardigans who had been so rude to Eda at the cheese counter.

"Leave us alone," she said. "We can't help you!"

"My children have gone missing in the forest. I can't find

them alone. And your husband has seen the forest creatures before . . ."

"You don't have to tell me," said the old woman, nodding at the canvas. "He hasn't seen anything else since. People want paintings of mountains and fjords. Nice scenic things. They don't want to be hanging pictures of monsters on the wall. We haven't sold anything in days."

The cardigan woman was making Aunt Eda quite cross.

"You don't seem to understand. The children are missing in the—"

"Well, that is your business. If you are foolish enough to keep them so near to such a dangerous place."

Aunt Eda decided to ignore that last comment, and plead again with Old Tor. "Listen, I know you will not come to the forest with me, but I am going. I have no choice. I have no more to lose. Please, is there anything you can tell me about the creatures you have seen?"

Old Tor turned away from his painting for the first time, and looked up at Aunt Eda. One of his eyes had a milky-white surface, and Aunt Eda remembered what Oskar had told her. *He's lost all his sight in one eye.* She wondered how old he was. Eighty? Ninety? *How could a man like that outrun a galloping horse?* she wondered as she looked at the time-withered hand that held the paintbrush.

The hand, and the paintbrush, stayed motionless in the air as Old Tor made some sort of decision. Then he stood up and walked in a slow painful way over to his jacket, which was hanging on a hook in the corner of the room. His hand reached inside and pulled something out. Something white. Like a bracelet. Or a cat's collar.

He hobbled back over, ignoring the grumbles of his wife, and handed it to Aunt Eda.

"Take it," he said, placing it in her hand. What was it? Some kind of charm?

Old Tor's wife made a grumbling sound, as if a miniature explosion was going off inside her head, and she walked in disgust out of the room.

"What is it?" asked Aunt Eda.

"I found it by a rock near the water's edge, last night when I went to paint the fjord . . . Do you see that pewter disc, hanging from it? Well, read what it says."

Aunt Eda looked at the white cloth bracelet, and the silvery disc attached to it. She saw there were three letters engraved in capital letters:

# HEK

"*Hek,*" whispered Aunt Eda. *Witch.*

Old Tor nodded. "I had it in my pocket when the huldres chased after me."

Aunt Eda still didn't understand. "I'm sorry," she said. "I don—"

Old Tor pointed to his blind eye. "It came back. The sight

in this eye. Just for those few seconds I needed it, when I was running away. I could see better than ever, even though it was dark. It was the most amazing thing. And my legs too. It was almost as though my feet had sprouted wings, like I was a boy again, but the fastest boy who ever lived."

Aunt Eda clutched the bracelet in her hand. "Maybe it was fear," she said. "Fear can have powerful effects."

The old man shook his head. "It can't make you see the brightness of colors in the dark. It can't make an old man outrun a horse."

Aunt Eda looked at the painting he was halfway through. The scary wide-eyed creature with pointed ears and a cow's tail, on top of a galloping white stallion. "And now? Can you run?"

He smiled. "No. You've seen me. It takes me a minute to cross the room. The bracelet gave me certain . . . abilities . . . but only when I was in danger. Take it, please. If there are more of those creatures in the forest, you will need it."

Aunt Eda slipped the white bracelet onto her wrist. "Thank you, Old Tor," she said. "But what about the children? They have no bracelet to protect them."

"No, but they have you," he said. "Now go. And may God bring you luck."


A quarter of an hour later Aunt Eda was upstairs in her attic, searching for *The Creatures of Shadow Forest*.

"Where is it? Where is it? Where is it?" she asked as she

dug through the contents of the tea chest. "Oh no," she said. "Someone's taken it."

But who?

It could only have been Martha or Samuel. She looked around, to see if there was anything else to help her.

Old clothes. No.

Photographs of Henrik. No.

And then she saw it, leaning against the wall. The javelin. She hadn't used it for years, as her arms weren't what they used to be. It felt strange, looking at it, as if she was looking at her younger self.

"You are coming with me," she said as she picked it up.

She went downstairs, left the house, and climbed the hill as fast as she could. When she reached the pine trees she stopped, and called into the forest once more.

"SAMUEL! MARTHA! IBSEN!"

But the only response was the echo.

"Well, Eda," she said to herself. "This is it."

She tightened her grip on the javelin and made sure the white bracelet was still on her wrist, with the pewter disc attached. Finding everything where it should be, she inhaled a deep breath of cold air, as if sucking in courage, and stepped forward into the shade of the trees.

# Troll-the-Left
# and Troll-the-Right

Martha was still sitting down on the hard floor of the prison cell.

"You do not speak, human child," said the white-haired woman in the cell opposite. "Where are your words? Where did you lose them?"

Martha said nothing, but the old woman nodded as if there was an answer inside her silence.

"Do you know why they have locked you up?"

Martha shook her head.

"You are a human. Humans are forbidden from the forest . . . All except one. It's not fair, but nothing in this forest is fair. Not anymore. Not since the forest was transformed. No one in here deserves their fate, none of us are criminals."

"None of us except the Tomtegubb," said the troll's right head. "His singing should definitely be illegal. The Changemaker should see to that."

The troll looked at Martha with both its heads, and decided to introduce his selves.

"I'm Troll-the-Left," said the left head.

"And I'm Troll-the-Right," said the right head.

"Some folk think of us as one troll because we've got just the one body, but we're not."

"We'll be no troll in no body tomorrow," moaned Troll-the-Right. "We'll be nothing but a couple of stones. And it's all your fault."

"Oh, stop your moaning," said Troll-the-Left.

"If you'd have listened to my moaning, we wouldn't be here now," said Troll-the-Right.

"I've been listening to your moaning all my flenking life. I could never bathe in the lake because you said the water was too dangerous."

"The water *was* too dangerous."

"No wonder we stink."

"Better to stink than to be dead."

"You're a big flenking coward," said Troll-the-Left.

"And you're a flenking maniac," said Troll-the-Right. "I told you what would happen if we went out of the forest. I told you, but would you listen? No."

Then Troll-the-Left remembered they were in the middle of introducing themselves to Martha.

"You must excuse our manners," he said. "We're only trolls. We're not evil, like a lot of folks think. We be good creatures, really. But we're not clean and polite like you humans. And me and Troll-the-Right don't get on too well, you see. Living in the same body doesn't give you much space. And he's a flenking coward, if you pardon my Hekron."

"I'll give you coward," said Troll-the-Right as the right hand pulled Troll-the-Left's hair.

"Scared of having a wash. That's a flenking coward in any language," said Troll-the-Left as the left hand yanked Troll-the-Right's beard.

The fight between the two troll sides had no clear winner as both halves of the body had an equal amount of strength.

"Take that," said Troll-the-Left, twisting the other's nose.

"Take that," said Troll-the-Right, yanking the other's bottom lip.

After the trolls eventually fought themselves into exhaustion, the old woman with the long white hair spoke again to Martha. And when she began to speak the whole prison fell quiet, as if they knew the old woman was about to reveal the deepest secrets of the forest.

## Golden Circles
## and Heavy Shadows

"I am the Snow Witch," the old woman said to Martha. "Have you ever met a witch before?"

Martha shook her head.

"Don't be scared, human child. Magic is not an evil thing. It is only the reasons for using magic that can be evil. And the magic I have is fading. I hardly have a spell left. Even to make the tiniest bit of frost, it sends such pains through every part of me. It is my sister. The Shadow Witch. She stole something from me. A bracelet. A Hek bracelet. It offers protection from harm in the forest. And then, once she had stolen my bracelet, she stole my magic."

"Do you hate her?" asked Troll-the-Left, with a grudgeful side glance at Troll-the-Right.

"No, I don't hate her," said the Snow Witch. "She is my sister. And besides, it's not her fault . . ."

Troll-the-Left frowned. "She stole your magic but it's not her fault? That doesn't make sense."

"She was forced to change," explained the Snow Witch. "The Changemaker who rules the forest forced her to steal the shadows of good creatures and make them evil. The forest was once a paradise, but now it is a terrible place."

Martha looked into the other cells, at the two-headed troll and the Tomtegubb, and wondered if they were dangerous. Troll-the-Left had said trolls were harmless, but maybe he was lying.

"I know what you're thinking, human child," said the Snow Witch. And she did, because the next thing she said was: "You don't have to worry about trolls and Tomtegubbs. They're the Unchanged. Their shadows have never been stolen. Tomtegubbs never even had shadows to steal."

Martha looked to the Tomtegubb, who was smiling at her like a best friend, and saw that the Snow Witch was right. Instead of a shadow, there was a faint circle of golden light around his feet, as if he were a kind of lamp. She then looked toward the two-headed troll, but saw he *did* have a shadow. Even in the dim light of the prison, it was clearly there. The blackest shadow she had ever seen.

Again, the Snow Witch knew what she was thinking.

"Yes, human child, trolls do have shadows, but a troll shadow can't be lifted off the ground. They're too heavy, even for magic to lift."

Troll-the-Left and Troll-the-Right looked at each other in surprise, and then shrugged a shoulder each. "Well," said Troll-the-Left. "That explains a few things."

The Shadow Witch sighed. It was a sigh that seemed to

contain the sadness of a whole forest. "This is what this prison is for. If the Changemaker can't change you, he can't control you. So he has to use fear. If you break his rules, if Unchanged creatures stray out of their villages, or out of the forest, they end up here."

"Waiting to go to our deaths," added Troll-the-Right miserably.

The Snow Witch nodded. "Yes. I have been here many, many years. All the other creatures have been sent to the Changemaker and sent to their deaths. Fear is his weapon. Those he can't change, he fills with terror. And terror is everywhere. Many creatures are evil and dangerous now. And the most evil of all are huldres. The ones who locked you in here. Yet you must know, human child, if you hadn't fallen down the trap, you would have been caught soon enough by someone else. Even the most honest and pure of all the creatures—the Truth Pixie—has been turned into something most violent. Most violent indeed. Oh, it chills my fragile heart just to think of it. That dark and most terrible day."

# Icicle Tears

After the Snow Witch had finished talking, everyone fell into a glum silence. Even the Tomtegubb stopped his humming for a short while and thought of all the other Tomtegubbs who had been killed by the Changemaker. It was only Martha who felt no fear at what the Snow Witch had to say.

She knew how cruel life liked to be, and she expected nothing better.

If she didn't feel anything, cruelty wouldn't work.

*I'll give up feelings as well as speaking,* Martha thought to herself. But giving up feelings is not as easy as all that. And the feeling that wouldn't let go was the one called guilt. She felt guilt for her brother, for leading him into the forest. She thought of the scary creatures, like the Truth Pixie. They were out there now, ready to harm any human who crossed their path. She closed her eyes and prayed for her brother and spoke silent words in her brain.

*Samuel.*

*I'm sorry.*

*I'm very, very sorry.*

It was then that she began to cry.

She hadn't wept since the day of the falling log. Her tears had been kept prisoners the way she was kept prisoner now, but the thought of her brother lost in this terrible forest released all those locked-up tears all at once.

It wasn't her normal type of crying.

It wasn't the type of crying she had used when Samuel had hidden all her hair bands. Or when her mum had been late to pick her up from horse riding. Or when her parents hadn't stopped shouting at each other.

Those tears were always used to get something.

The tears she cried now were a different variety. They were quieter, for a start. And much less blubbery. And there was no practical use for them whatsoever. They were like the wrong money in a foreign country and couldn't get her anything at all.

"Don't cry, human child," said the Snow Witch.

But the quiet tears kept on coming, enough to fill a glass of water.

The Snow Witch began to mumble something under her breath, and seemed to be in some kind of pain.

"What's up with the Snow Witch?" Troll-the-Left asked.

"You ask too many questions," said Troll-the-Right.

"You're just scared of answers," said Troll-the-Left.

"A world with no questions is the safest world," said Troll-the-Right.

"You mean the dullest world," said Troll-the-Left.

"I mean the safest."

"That's what I said."

Martha felt a coldness in her eye and on her cheeks. She looked at the Snow Witch, who still seemed like she was in great pain.

Then Martha realized something.

She wasn't crying anymore.

Her hand raised to her cheek. She felt her tear. It was hard. Frozen. It was exactly the same on the other cheek. Another thin icicle.

The tears broke off in her hand, and turned to little puddles on the floor.

"I have gotten rid of your tears, human child," said the Snow Witch. "But my powers are too weak to take away your sadness."

Or Martha's sadness was too strong.

"Come on," said the Tomtegubb, in the kind of light sing-song voice Martha herself would once have used. "Cheer up. It's not all bad, you know."

But Martha knew the Tomtegubb was wrong.

It was all bad.

And what was more, it was only going to get worse.

# The Magical Smell

Samuel and Ibsen had been walking for hours, and had no idea where they were going. They had run so fast and so far away from the deserted village and the huldre skeleton that they had no idea where they were.

"My feet are killing me," the boy told his canine companion. "It's all right for you. You've got paws." Samuel tried to keep his shoeless feet on the grass at the side of the path, rather than the hard earth in the middle.

Samuel's cries for his sister were less frequent now, and increasingly hopeless. His sister's name bounced off the trees like a ball no one wanted to catch.

"Martha! Martha! Martha!"

He felt weak with hunger. His feet had cuts and blisters. The wind chilled his bones. He wondered if he should try to find his way back to Aunt Eda, but decided against this idea. Martha was all that mattered, and he wouldn't leave this forest without her.

On and on he walked, with a weary Ibsen beside him, not knowing if they were heading closer or farther away from the girl they hoped to find. Samuel held Professor Tanglewood's book, *The Creatures of Shadow Forest,* close to his chest, and looked at his watch with his free hand. It said half past ten, but it had said half past ten ever since he had entered the forest. It was as though time had halted the moment he had stepped foot between the trees.

He stopped.

There was a rumble, like distant thunder.

When it happened again, Samuel realized what it was.

*That's not thunder. That's my stomach.*

He thought longingly of those five slices of cheese he had given Ibsen earlier. He could eat a whole block of brown cheese now.

His hunger was weakening him. He saw food everywhere and nowhere. Tree trunks became giant slabs of well-cooked meat. The muddy path took on the sight of gravy.

As he staggered on, memories came back to him as smells and tastes.

He remembered his dad coming in on a wet Friday evening with warm parcels of fish and chips for the family. The magical smells of malt vinegar and his dad's rain-soaked coat had filled the house.

He remembered the day before the accident. His mum had made a birthday cake for Martha, and he'd been allowed to lick the icing out of the bowl.

He shut his eyes, as if closing them could take him back to that kitchen two weeks ago. Back to the sugary mixture on his tongue, and the safe warmth of his mum's smile.

But it wasn't enough. Memories can only tease you, they can't fill your stomach any more than they can bring the dead back to life.

Then, in the darkness of his closed eyes, a scent tickled his nostrils. It was a real smell this time, and not a remembered one.

In fact, Samuel's nose had never sniffed anything quite so delicious.

He opened his eyes and found himself faced with a decision. The path made a *Y* in front of him, breaking off in two directions. One way led up a steep hill, the other slightly down.

His nose made the decision. Although his legs were tired, Samuel's nostrils directed him up the thin winding path on his right and this time Ibsen didn't growl any obvious objection.

Samuel had no idea what the smell was. He had never smelled anything like it before. It was sweet and savory all at once. Strong yet subtle. It was a smell that made every other smell in the world completely pointless.

"Mmmm," he said, because his nose was now commanding his mouth as well as his feet.

The path flattened, and the canopy of leaves became less dense, letting in more of the soft evening light. A small log cabin appeared in a gap between two trees.

The cabin had an arch-shaped green door and two windows, one of which was open. *This is it,* thought Samuel. *This is where the smell is coming from.*

He stopped, worried. He thought of the last house he had seen, with the skeleton inside. He remembered what his aunt and the book had told him about all the different deadly creatures who inhabit the forest. But then, maybe whoever lived in this house knew where Martha was.

He staggered forward, along the light-dappled path, still entranced by the smell that had seduced his nostrils and teased his stomach. Ibsen whimpered, but even he seemed to be captivated by the dreamlike aromas wafting over the air.

"Food," mumbled Samuel.

Then the door opened, and out of the log cabin stepped a small creature—a man about three feet tall. No. Not a man. It was a small, childlike being, with pointed ears and an angelic little face that looked as pure and delicate as a snowflake.

It would have been very hard to imagine that such a face could belong to a murderer, but murderers come in very many shapes and sizes. As Samuel was about to find out.

# The Truth Pixie

Samuel's heart began to race, and fear traveled through his every nerve. The skull had been scary, but at least it had been dead. Sure, he had seen huldres and a Tomtegubb before, but only from a distance, and in the dark. Now in broad daylight he was faced with this living creature, who wasn't a human or an animal; it seemed very different. He felt like he couldn't trust his own eyes.

"Hello there, friend," the pixie said, as if he had been expecting Samuel to arrive.

*Friend.*

Samuel was worried. Why was the creature calling him his friend? And how could he understand what he was saying? He remembered what he had read in the book he held in his arms.

*Most creatures in the forest speak Hekron, a universal language that everyone—even humans—can understand . . .*

He held the book close to his chest. In a world he no longer trusted, Professor Tanglewood's book was going to be a lifeline. It gave him faith.

"Are you all right, friend?"

There it was again. *Friend.*

Samuel was suspicious of the word.

But the innocent little creature had the kindest eyes and the kindest smile Samuel had ever seen. Everything about him seemed so welcoming—even his strange, upturned nose and pointy ears had a softness to them. Samuel felt the terror leave his body, and the hunger return.

"Hello," Samuel said as the smell surrounded him like an invisible cloud.

"You look tired, friend. And hungry. Why don't you come inside and have some soup?" The creature stepped out onto the grass, but Samuel didn't notice that he had no shadow. And even if he had noticed this, he wouldn't have known to run away.

"I'm looking for my sister," Samuel said. "She went into the forest but I can't find her. She's ten years old and is wearing a dark blue dress. Have you seen her?"

"No, friend. I have seen no sister."

"I have to find her. Do you know—"

Before Samuel had time to finish his question, the creature interrupted him and said: "Well, an empty stomach won't help, will it? Come on, what do you say?"

Samuel didn't say anything, but his stomach answered with the most enormous rumble.

The pixie clapped his hands. "Exactly!"

One minute later, Samuel and Ibsen found themselves sitting inside the log cabin, watching the creature stir a pot of soup on top of an iron stove. It was sort of like being in a doll's house, as everything seemed out of proportion. Samuel looked around and noticed the strange way the cabin had been decorated. The log walls were painted white, with splodges of purple and gray.

"I really need to find my sister. Are you sure you haven't seen her?"

"No, friend. I am sure."

While the pixie had his back turned, Samuel opened the book under the table.

Why weren't there any pictures? It would have been much easier if Professor Tanglewood had taken photographs of the creatures, or even drawn illustrations.

Instead, he had just written the name of each creature in capital letters at the top of every page, with a written description underneath. This meant it would take Samuel longer to work out which of the many forest creatures his host was.

A huldre? No.

A troll? No.

A Tomtegubb? No.

A Slemp? No.

A Flying Skullpecker? No.

He turned over the next page but didn't have time to look at it as the creature came over with a bowl of bright yellow soup. The bowl looked very big in the pixie's hands, but was a normal size for a human.

The flavor rose up with the steam and delighted Samuel's nostrils. He trembled with hunger. Even if it had reindeer in it, he knew he would gobble up the soup in five seconds flat.

"Mmmm," he found himself saying. "That smells delicious."

The creature rubbed his hands together in excitement, as if he was going to enjoy watching his guest taste the soup almost as much as Samuel was going to enjoy eating it.

"It is my special recipe. Special, *special*."

"Oh," Samuel said.

Ibsen barked and Samuel took the bark to mean "I'd like some soup too, if you don't mind."

"It's all right. I'll save you some."

Samuel picked up his spoon and was about to start tucking in when Ibsen jumped up at him, causing the soup to shake off the spoon and land on the page he hadn't yet seen.

Samuel looked down at the book and saw the words *TRUTH PIX*. It was meant to say *TRUTH PIXIE* but there was a splodge of soup over the *IE*.

Samuel read on:

*This creature lives in a small log cabin high on one of the Eastern hills. He is three feet tall, and has the most innocent looking face imaginable. Distinguishing features include pointed ears, an upturned nose and feet that look too big for the pixie's body. Don't be fooled by his appearance, as this creature is VERY DANGEROUS.*

Samuel stopped reading because the Truth Pixie was talking.

"What is that matter? Do you not want to eat the lovely soup?"

"No," said Samuel, staring at the Pixie's large feet. "I mean yes . . . I mean I wasn't not eating it. I just dropped a bit. On my knee."

He pushed the book farther under the table so the Truth Pixie couldn't see. The creature gave his guest a suspicious look.

Samuel didn't want to explain what he was reading, for obvious reasons.

He spotted a brown loaf on top of the small oven in a silver tray. "Can I have some bread, please? It's just . . . I like to dip it into my soup."

The Truth Pixie stood as still as a picture, with a face halfway between a smile and a frown.

"You want bread with my soup?"

"Er . . . yes . . . please."

"Bread with soup! What a funny request!"

"It's . . . um . . . quite normal where I come from. And I can share it with my dog."

The Truth Pixie looked like he was about to get very cross, but he kept the crossness inside and said: "Very well. Bread with soup."

So the creature turned and walked over to the silver tray and started slicing the bread with a knife. While Samuel wasn't being watched, he quickly pulled the book from under the table and carried on reading.

*Truth Pixies are very dangerous because they lure other creatures (including humans) with kind smiles and promises of rest and food, before serving them a poisonous soup. The soup smells delicious but contains a deadly herb called Hewlip that grows naturally on the hillside.*

*One minute after tasting the soup, the Hewlip expands your brain until your head explodes. This inevitably is a bloody and painful death, which the Truth Pixie enjoys—occasionally applauding this most terrible sight.*

But then, in smaller print at the bottom of the page, there was something else.

**WEAKNESS:** *An inability to lie.*

# A Few Factualities

"Five slices."

Samuel jumped. He hadn't heard the Truth Pixie walk back over to the table with the bread.

The book slammed shut between Samuel's legs. "Thank you," he said.

"What is that?" The Truth Pixie's finger was pointed toward Samuel's lap.

"Oh, it's just . . . er . . . a book. A book of stories. It's nothing important. It's all made up."

"Stories." The Truth Pixie made a face and stuck out his tongue as if a story was a type of disgusting food. "I hate stories very much. I like factualities, not fictionalities."

The Truth Pixie slumped his shoulders, and Samuel wondered for a moment if such a sweet-looking creature could really be very dangerous.

"It is getting cold."

"What?"

The Truth Pixie pointed now at Samuel's bowl. "The special soup. It is nicer when it is warm. You should eat it— mmmm. Good soup. *Special* soup."

Samuel picked up one of the pieces of bread and tore it in half. The Truth Pixie's eyes were wide with excitement as the bread was dunked into the soup.

Of course, Samuel had no intention of eating the soup but he still hadn't thought of how he was going to escape. He knew he had to do something, but what?

Then he remembered—

WEAKNESS: *An inability to lie.*

"Are you a Truth Pixie?" Samuel asked as the bread hung between the bowl and his mouth.

The Truth Pixie screwed his face up, as if the question had just punched him on his upturned nose. "Yes," he said, then covered his mouth with his hand.

Samuel nodded. "And is this soup poisonous?"

The Truth Pixie scrunched his face even more. "Yes," he said as his hand left his mouth.

"What will it do to me?"

The Truth Pixie winced. "It is very poisonous and it will make your brain burst out of your head and splatter on the walls and give you a death of the most horrible pain you can imagine."

Samuel kept asking questions and the Truth Pixie kept blurting out answers in between slapping his own face and biting his hand.

"So you are trying to kill me?"

"Nnnnnnn—yes!"

"Why?"

"Because I enjoy it! It makes me feel not so small!"

"What will happen if I don't eat the soup?"

"Nothing!"

"Won't you try and hurt me?"

"No!" By this point the Truth Pixie was biting his hand so much he was bleeding.

"Why not?"

"Because I am scared you will hurt me back!"

"Why?"

"Because I am a small weak pixie who feels pain more than any other creature."

"What would you do if I stood up and walked out of your house? Would you follow me?"

"No!"

"What if I took your sandals?" Samuel asked, staring at the sandals on the pixie's big feet. "Would you do anything?"

"I might call you names."

"What names?"

"Stinkymudfungle. Elf-breath. Bottom-squelch."

"Those names wouldn't hurt a five-year-old."

The Truth Pixie sighed. "They're the worst I know."

"And would you do anything else?"

The Truth Pixie desperately tried to lie. "*Yo.* I mean *nes.* I mean—"

"You mean no, don't you?"

"Nnnnnnnn—yes!"

The Truth Pixie was exhausted with all his hopeless efforts at lying. "Don't hurt me. Please. Please. I can't help it. I didn't used to be like this . . . I didn't used to try and poison anyone. I used to be good. I didn't used to put Hewlip in my soup, I just used to enjoy being a good . . . a good . . ."

Samuel couldn't believe it. A minute ago the pixie had been trying to kill him and now he was on the edge of tears.

"Why did you change?" Samuel asked. "Why can't you make normal soup? Why can't you just . . . be good?"

"It's my shadow," he said. He looked surprised at his words, as if three little mice had just ran out of his mouth. "I don't . . . understand. When I had my shadow I used to like gentle things. I used to like spickle dancing and singing flower songs, but no pixies do those things anymore. They aren't enough. We take darker pleasures now . . . violent things. Exploding heads. Trolls, mainly. Stupid creatures not worth their height. Think with their stomachs. Make a great mess when they blow, though, that's the problem. Their blood and brains stain the walls."

Samuel gulped as the gray and purple on the walls gained new meaning. But the thought of splattered brains wasn't enough to ruin his appetite.

He picked up the slices of bread. "Are these poisonous?"

"No."

Samuel shared the bread with Ibsen and didn't stop munching until there wasn't a crumb left. Then Ibsen fell asleep on the floor and Samuel decided to find out as much as he could from the murderous little creature with no shadow.

# The Questions Samuel Asked the Truth Pixie and the Answers He Received

**SAMUEL**: What happened? Who stole your shadow?

**TRUTH PIXIE**: It was the Shadow Witch. She is one of the two Forest Witches. I didn't understand it. She had been here before and I had cooked her soup. Soup without Hewlip in it. Her and her sister. The Snow Witch. They had been nice to me. And I had been nice to them. And I had shown them my spickle dancing. But then one day, two ravens landed on the grass outside my cabin. One of them transformed into the Shadow Witch; while the other just stayed there, outside on the grass. The Shadow Witch knocked on my door, and I let her in. She had a much sadder and older face, even though it had only been six moons since I had last seen her.

**SAMUEL**: What happened? What did she do?

**TRUTH PIXIE**: She kept mumbling things under her breath. Things that were less than words but more than silence. After she finished mumbling, she left and I saw her out, but when I looked on the ground I realized something was missing. I looked down on the grass and realized I had no shadow. And it was a sunny day. Without a cloud in the sky. Look now, even as I stand by the window, I have no shadow whatsoever.

**SAMUEL**: Are you a ghost?

**TRUTH PIXIE**: No. But sometimes I . . . I feel like I am. I have changed so much I might as well have died. All that was good has been lost . . . Oh, it is terrible. I am terrible. How I would love to see your head explode. That sounds so bad, doesn't it?

**SAMUEL**: A bit. Yes. Do you know where my sister might be?

**TRUTH PIXIE**: No. No. I don't know that.

**SAMUEL**: I heard a scream. Near the edge of the forest. And then I found a hole. With smoke coming out of it. I think she might have fallen down it.

**TRUTH PIXIE**: The huldres. They have holes all along the border. They work for the Changemaker.

**SAMUEL**: (remembering what he had read earlier) The Changemaker? The huldres work for him.

**TRUTH PIXIE**: Yes. The Changemaker is the overlord of the forest. I have never seen him, but his name chills the hearts of every creature in the forest, especially those creatures who still have their shadows. They are the Unchanged. Like you. Criminals. And if your sister is caught by the huldres, she will be sent to the Changemaker, like all the other prisoners.

**SAMUEL**: And what will happen to her?

**TRUTH PIXIE**: I don't know. All I know is that those who are sent to the Changemaker don't come back.

**SAMUEL**: I wish you were a Lie Pixie.

**TRUTH PIXIE**: So do I.

**SAMUEL**: (who did not know the Changemaker was really Professor Horatio Tanglewood) But who is the Changemaker? And why did the Changemaker want to do all these things?

**TRUTH PIXIE**: I do not know.

**SAMUEL**: Is he evil?

**TRUTH PIXIE**: Evil is not what you are. It is what you do. He does evil. And so do I.

**SAMUEL**: I must find my sister. What is the best chance of finding her?

**TRUTH PIXIE**: The best chance is to go to the Changemaker. That is where the huldres will take her if she's in prison.

**SAMUEL**: Where is the Changemaker?

**TRUTH PIXIE**: The Changemaker lives in a clearing in the North of the forest. He lives with the Shadow Witch in the middle of a clearing in a tree called the Still Tree.

**SAMUEL**: How do I get there?

**TRUTH PIXIE**: You must follow the crooked path down the hill. Then turn right and keep going. Keep walking in a very straight line. Not too far left. Not too far right. After a while you will see the Hewlip bush. You will recognize the Hewlip bush from its bright yellow leaves with a jagged edge like this one I have here. Once you have passed this bush, you will be entering THE MOST DANGEROUS PART OF THE FOREST. The closer you get to the Changemaker, the more deadly the forest becomes. And remember, the creatures with no shadows are the deadly ones. You must keep on walking in a straight line for a long while until you reach a road. It is a wide road with wagon tracks pressed into the earth. You turn right when you reach that road and it will lead you past the lake and toward the Changemaker's clearing.

**SAMUEL**: What else must I look out for?

**TRUTH PIXIE**: Flat circles of earth with no plants growing on them. They are caloosh traps. If you step on them, you will fall down into the huldre territory below the ground. You must also be careful to keep hold of your shadow. So long as you have your shadow, you are always going to be you. If your shadow is stolen, you are whatever the Changemaker wants you to be. If you try and challenge him, he will kill you.

**SAMUEL**: What are the chances of escaping the Changemaker once I find my sister?

**TRUTH PIXIE**: One in trinkinion.

**SAMUEL**: Trinkinion?

**TRUTH PIXIE**: It's a pixie number. It is higher than infinity.

**SAMUEL**: There's nothing higher than infinity.

**TRUTH PIXIE**: Yes, there is. Trinkinion. It is so high it makes infinity look small. It is the number that is used to count sadness and happiness and memories.

**SAMUEL**: So there is not much chance of escaping the forest with my sister?

**TRUTH PIXIE**: No. Not much. It is about the same chance as the sun turning to butter.

**SAMUEL**: Can I have your sandals now?

**TRUTH PIXIE**: They are my only pair.

**SAMUEL**: You tried to poison me. The least you can do is give me your sandals.

**TRUTH PIXIE**: Oh, all right.

**SAMUEL**: Thanks. They're a good fit . . . Ibsen, Ibsen, wake up. We've got to go and find the Changemaker.

**IBSEN**: (jolting awake) Woof.

**TRUTH PIXIE**: Are you going?

**SAMUEL**: Yes. We are.

**TRUTH PIXIE**: Very well.

**SAMUEL**: Try to be good.

**TRUTH PIXIE**: (waving from the door) I always try . . . good-bye.

**SAMUEL**: Good-bye.

**TRUTH PIXIE**: (under his breath) Stinkymudfungle.

# The Tightrope Walker

Samuel and Ibsen walked down the steep crooked path as the Truth Pixie had instructed, and kept a lookout for shadowless creatures.

Like his sister, Samuel was feeling rather sad. But unlike his sister, Samuel's sadness was mixed with crossness and so Samuel didn't really know what he was feeling. It wasn't pure sadness or pure crossness but more of a *cradness*. He knew that wasn't a word but he thought it should be.

As he saw it, the two main things that had gone wrong with his life were to do with people not listening to him.

If his dad had listened when he'd said "Stop!," then both his parents would have still been alive.

If Martha had listened when he'd told her not to go into the forest, then he wouldn't be facing a one-in-trinkinion chance of successfully rescuing her from the Changemaker.

"Why don't people listen to me?" he asked Ibsen. "Why can't they just do as I say?"

Ibsen wasn't listening. Or if he was, he couldn't provide a satisfactory answer.

"If they did as I say, everything would still be all right. Mum and Dad would still be here and Martha would still be singing stupid songs and I wouldn't be in a dangerous forest, checking that everything has got a shadow."

As he kept treading farther down the twisting path, he thought briefly of this other world. The world where he was listened to. What would he be doing there, right at the moment? He would be at school. His old school, in Nottingham. It was a Tuesday afternoon, so he would probably be having a math lesson. Square roots or something. He would be bored, flicking bits of rubber with his ruler, but underneath the boredom would be a happiness. The happiness he used to take for granted. The happiness that came from having a mum and a dad—even if they never listened to you. Because mums and dads weren't just people, they were a kind of safety net. You always knew that however boring math lessons would be, or how much trouble you got into at school, they would always look after you. They might tell you off, but they would always be there to help you bounce back up.

And now that they were gone, it was like he was high on a tightrope all on his own. If he fell, if he made one tiny mistake, then that would be it. There would be no net to catch his fall.

"Walk in a straight line," said Samuel the tightrope walker, staying close to the tree trunks in his path. "Not too far left. Not too far right."

He passed rabbits and a caloosh and an elk and Samuel breathed relieved sighs at the sight of their shadows, and kept on his way toward the Changemaker.

But as he walked, Samuel felt tears roll down his face. Not cold icicle tears. These were hot and angry tears that leaked from his nose as much as his eyes. They were as unstoppable as a waterfall no matter how many times he wiped them away.

Ibsen looked up, offering as much comfort as he could with his floppy tongue and dopey eyes, but the boy kept on crying.

"Get a grip," Samuel told himself. "You big baby!"

And then he saw it. The bush with yellow, jagged leaves.

"The Hewlip bush," mumbled Samuel as he recalled what the Truth Pixie had said.

Ibsen whimpered, as if understanding the bush's significance.

*Once you have passed this bush, you will be entering THE MOST DANGEROUS PART OF THE FOREST . . .*

Samuel touched one of the poisonous leaves, and gently ran his finger along its jagged edge.

He looked beyond the bush at the slope of the land in front of him, studded with the same type of tall pines he had just passed. He could see no creatures, shadowless or otherwise. No signs of danger. But as he stood and stared in front of him, he sensed something. A brooding kind of menace that seemed to charge the air, warning those who were about to head closer toward the Changemaker.

The feeling made him tingle with fear, as though he was about to jump off his imaginary tightrope and land on hard ground miles below.

Samuel wiped away the tears. That was the last time he was going to feel sorry for himself.

"Right," he told Ibsen. "This is it."

He carefully picked some of the jagged yellow leaves off the poisonous bush, placed them inside his wet pocket, and then headed into the danger zone.

## Another Rude Interruption
## from the Author

Hello. It's me again. The author.

Yes, I know, no one likes to be interrupted, especially when they're reading a book. But I should just warn you that the next two chapters are about how Professor Horatio Tanglewood became so evil. Some people like to think people are born evil, and if you want to stay thinking that, then why don't you skip the next few pages and head to "The Wagon."

Go on.

Off you go.

Now, is there anyone left?

Oh yes. Just you.

Well, never mind.

I suppose I had still better tell you a bit more about Professor Tanglewood and his very peculiar type of evil.

# The Tragedy and Triumph
# of Professor Horatio Tanglewood

While Samuel continued his journey, Professor Horatio Tanglewood sat alone in his tree palace trying to work out exactly what to call his new book. He was feeling very happy with himself, as he had just given the order to the huldres to deliver the Snow Witch to him tonight, along with the other prisoners. Recently he had been sensing a weakness in the Shadow Witch, especially when the Snow Witch was mentioned. So he had decided it was best to finish off her sister once and for all.

Excited by this prospect, he felt a new energy and decided to get working on a title. He hadn't written any of his autobiography yet, but was sure that if he found the right title, all the other words would fall like rain into his head, just like they had for *The Creatures of Shadow Forest*. Up and down he paced, past the jars of pickled heads, thinking of different titles.

And then, when he'd thought of something, he stopped pacing and stared into the face of a Tomtegubb, a cousin of the Tomtegubb who was in prison with Martha. Like all Tomtegubbs, this one had died with a smile, a smile that was now preserved for eternity.

"What do you think of *Professor Horatio Tanglewood: The Reluctant Hero,* or how about *Making Change: The True Story behind the Changemaker?*"

The pickled head said nothing, but kept smiling.

"Yes, I agree," said the Professor. "They're good, but they're missing something. Ah! I have it! A name that wraps it all up and puts a bow around it. Are you ready? What about *The Tragedy and Triumph of Professor Horatio Tanglewood?* Yes, it's perfect, isn't it? Absolutely perfect. Oh, it will come to me now, don't worry, my old golden friend. I can already feel my life bleeding into the words as I stand here. It will be written in a month. No! A week. Not even that! A day! And then the Shadow Witch will conjure a thousand copies and do a translation spell so every single creature can understand exactly who the Changemaker is and what he—or rather *I*—have been through. It will be exactly the same as *The Creatures of Shadow Forest.* That is to say, it will be the exact opposite. Instead of telling humans about the dangers of the forest creatures, it will tell the forest creatures about the dangers of the humans in the outside world. Not me, of course. I shall be the hero. The tragic, triumphant hero. The creatures shall worship me. They shall know then that the Changemaker is really just me, just Professor Tanglewood. And they shall love me, as much as they have feared the Changemaker. This book shall become their sacred text. Oh, there might be the odd creature to overcome—the trolls, for example. We'll have to get them to overcome their book phobia, of course. But no.

These obstacles are nothing. This book is going to capture their hearts, I know it. I have ruled them by terror for too long. After this book has been written, love will make them obey. They shall love me, you heads. Love me, Professor Horatio Tanglewood—the Changemaker. Do you hear?"

The pickled heads in the jars said nothing as Horatio walked back over to his desk and began to write his life story. He sat there, with his quill and pages of parchment, and wrote one hundred thousand words without once getting up, not even for the toilet. He just sat there, with tears running down his face, as he relived his horrendous life.

Professor Tanglewood was an evil and cruel man who could imagine no music more pleasant than the scream of a dying child. But you must know that he did not start off this way.

On the contrary, Horatio Tanglewood began his life as the most adorable baby any parent could imagine. Indeed, his mother and father would spend whole hours gazing over his crib, in wonder at their calm and happy only child.

When he grew a little older, it was clear that Horatio was turning into a model of politeness. His first spoken word was "please," his second was "thank you." He loved all vegetables, especially carrots, and never left any food on his plate. Unlike other boys his age, he had no interest in pirate swords or cowboy pistols. He preferred to learn how to spell words like *d-i-s-s-i-m-u-l-a-t-i-o-n* and *a-n-t-h-r-o-p-o-m-o-r-p-h-i-z-a-t-i-o-n* and *f-r-a-c-t-o-c-u-m-u-l-u-s*.

He particularly enjoyed reading folktales, and could read them on his own when he was still only two years old.

In his first school report, the head teacher wrote:

> Horatio is the most exceptional child I have ever had the fortune to come across. His abilities at mathematics and English are exceptional for a boy of only four and I am told he has a great love of nature. He is polite and courteous to teachers and pupils alike, and the dinner ladies inform me he eats all his vegetables. He is a perfect miniature gentleman, surrounded by frightful little nose pickers. If we could mold all our children like Horatio, we would be making the world a better place for generations to come. I am sure he will grow up to become an asset to our great nation.
> —Mr. Montague Smythe-Hogg, Headmaster

Horatio's great love of nature included a special interest in trees. On long woodland walks with his mother, he learned how to tell a beech tree by looking at its smooth trunk, or a sycamore by the shape of its leaves.

He loved his parents intensely, but when he was five his happiness vanished forever, and his life became marred by some very horrible things. Thirteen horrible things, if we are to be precise about it.

# The Thirteen Horrible Things That Happened in the Life of Professor Horatio Tanglewood before He Became Evil and Called Himself the Changemaker

1. At the age of five, on the windiest day of the year, Horatio witnessed his father die while chasing a picnic blanket over the edge of a cliff.

2. Two years after this most appalling event, Horatio and his mother hired an abandoned wooden house in Norway. On their return, Horatio's mother was considered completely insane after telling her family doctor that she and her son had witnessed Truth Pixies take part in a spickle-dancing competition in a forest near the village of Flåm.

3. At the same age, Horatio was sent to Blandford-on-Trent to live with foster parents, Mr. and Mrs. Twigg. Mr. and Mrs. Twigg lived in a house so tidy they didn't take the cover off their sofa, and spent all their time watching boring TV programs. They were very strict and made Horatio do all the vacuuming as well as all the washing up, and banned him from woodland walks and visits to his mother.

4. From the age of seven, Horatio never received a birth-

day card from anyone, so he decided to make his own and send them to himself. But when Mr. and Mrs. Twigg found them they called them "awful clutter" and put them in the trash. All he ever wanted was for someone to sing "Happy Birthday" to him, but no one ever did.

5. When Horatio was eleven he wrote a school essay called "How I Know That Pixies Are Real," which a teacher read aloud to the whole class. Everyone laughed, and the laughter kept echoing inside Horatio's brain forevermore.

6. The following year, Horatio was caught sucking his thumb in morning assembly. From then on, he was known as Horatio Thumbsucker the Pixie Lover.

7. When he was thirteen, he wet the bed on a school trip to York. His nickname was amended to Horatio Thumbsucker the Bed-wetting Pixie Lover.

8. Three years later he made his first trip to see his mother in the hospital, but she got confused and thought he was a pixie. She told him to go away after he refused to show her his spickle dancing.

9. Two days before his eighteenth birthday, his mother died in the hospital after choking on an overcooked Yorkshire pudding. At her funeral, Horatio vowed to the vicar (there was no one else there) that he would prove his mother had been right about what they had seen in the forest.

10. Only one week later, Mr. and Mrs. Twigg also died after their overheated television exploded during an episode of the popular show *Ooh, What a Lovely Clean House You've Got!* Horatio survived the explosion—he was sitting at a table doing his homework at the other end of the room. However, a shard of flying glass from the screen left a permanent scar underneath his left eye.

11. After studying Norse folklore at Christminster University and then gaining a professorship in the same subject, Horatio wrote a book called *On the Existence of Pixies.* One reviewer said that he would "rather drown in raw sewage than read another book from the pen of Horatio Tanglewood." That same reviewer fell down a loose manhole cover outside his home two days later. He drowned in raw sewage.

12. After being found with a screwdriver and a wrench at the scene of the crime, Horatio was forced to spend eleven years in Bleakmoor Prison, sharing a cell with a bodybuilding bank robber known as Mad Dexter the Muscle Flexer.

13. On leaving prison, Horatio moved to Norway, and bought the holiday home he and his mother had stayed in many years earlier. The childhood memories contained in the house made Horatio so sad that he stayed in bed for seven weeks, crying and sucking his thumb and screaming for his mother. And then one day, all of a

sudden, the tears ran out, and Horatio got out of bed and cycled to the village of Flåm. He was going to buy some groceries and then, once he returned, his plan was to head off to the forest and see the pixies and other wonderful creatures he knew awaited him.

# The Wagon

While Professor Horatio Tanglewood was writing his life story, explaining the truth behind the Changemaker, his most loyal huldre—Grentul—was watching a caloosh fight. But unlike the other huldre guards, he found little thrill in the sight of blood-soaked feathers and thrashing, flightless wings.

Of course, he never admitted this to anyone else. He could only imagine the ridicule he would get from the others, especially Vjpp. After all, a love of caloosh fighting was meant to be what made you a true huldre. The guards always talked of the grace of each fight. The skill and tactics of their favorite birds. But all this was a cover for bloodlust, and their hunger for cruelty and death.

He watched Vjpp now standing on the other side of the caloosh pit. He was clapping and cheering as one of the three-headed birds collapsed to the floor.

*"Vemp oda caloosh!"* Vjpp's eyes bulged with proud excitement as his favorite bird began pecking away at the other with all three of its beaks.

Grentul always found it strange how birds who were so peaceful when they were running free aboveground could become so violent toward one another after a few days of training underground. It wasn't that Grentul had any morals about such things. He didn't. It was just that he could find no pleasure in anything nowadays, not even violent sport. His only love was for the Changemaker. He was his life. His duty. As he was for all the huldre-folk. Protecting the forest from the Unchanged was the only thing that motivated him, and he liked to believe his sense of duty was greater than those of the other guards, even Vjpp.

He knew that one day the Changemaker would see the strength of his devotion, and reward him for it. It was this thought that prompted him to walk through the roaring crowd to the other side of the pit.

Once there, he leaned toward Vjpp. *"Ipp kensh,"* he told him, in an urgent whisper.

*It is time.*

The Snow Witch heard them first.

"They are coming," she told Martha. "Show them no sign of fear, for fear is a gift to them and you owe them no gifts."

The Tomtegubb and the two-headed troll woke up to the sound of Vjpp's laughter as he, along with Grentul and five other huldre guards, walked down the corridor toward them. They carried belts full of weapons and held flaming torches.

"This is it," said Troll-the-Right. "The next time we'll sleep is when we're dead. Dead! . . . Our bodies turned into stone.

Our spirits lost in the big black nothingness as though we'd never been born, as though we'd never known the simple pleasures of hurgleberry wine or rabbit casserole."

"You hate rabbit casserole," said Troll-the-Left. "And hurgleberry wine makes you sick."

Troll-the-Right scowled and made a grumbling sound. "No, it doesn't. I was only sick last time because *you* drank too much."

"I can't help it if we share the same stomach."

"Well, we won't share the same anything soon enough. Look, they're coming for us first."

Troll-the-Right was right. The huldre guards opened the cage and held out their swords.

"Don't do anything stupid," Troll-the-Right warned Troll-the-Left.

As Troll-the-Left currently had the blade of Vjpp's sword tickling his neck, he decided for once to take Troll-the-Right's advice, and so the two-headed troll was escorted peacefully down the corridor.

Next was the Tomtegubb, who cheerfully thanked the guards for opening the cage door for him.

"I can't wait for some fresh air," he told them, before humming his favorite section of "The Purple Trouser Song."

Then they opened the Snow Witch's door. The Snow Witch looked confused.

"Why now?" she asked Grentul. "Why after all this time

does he suddenly decide to sentence me to death, along with the others?"

She got no answer, or none she could understand, and so she walked out and said to Martha: "Remember. No fear, human child."

Martha nodded, but fear couldn't help but rise up inside her as Vjpp unlocked her door and walked toward her. He sheathed his sword and crouched down, bringing the fire of the torch near her face, causing Martha to cower from its heat. Vjpp's free hand stroked her cheek, brushing back until one of his claws was pointed delicately on her skin. He licked his lips with his blue tongue, as if Martha was a delicious meal set before him.

There had never been a human in huldre prison before, and so Martha was a kind of exotic prize.

Vjpp whispered strange words into Martha's ear. *"Venn op cunneef."*

Then another huldre addressed him. It was Grentul, who seemed to be hurrying Vjpp along.

Martha was pulled out of the cell and down the corridor with Vjpp's grip unnecessarily tight around her arm. They went up a dark staircase and out into fresh night air, where four white stallions and a wagon awaited them.

The wagon held a large cage, which already contained the Snow Witch, the Tomtegubb and the two-headed troll by the time Martha was thrown inside.

One of the huldre guards—the eldest, judging from

his wrinkled face and dry, tattered tail—climbed onto the wooden seat at the front of the wagon. He had a long whip, and used it to startle the horses into motion.

The other huldres walked by the sides of the cage, threatening their captives with torches if they got too close to the bars.

"*Oggup flimp!*" they kept shouting. "*Oggup flimp! Oggup flimp!*"

Martha sat cross-legged in the middle of the cage floor. The Tomtegubb sat next to her, humming happy tunes.

The Snow Witch placed herself down close to the front of the cage, away from everyone else. A gentle wind blew her white hair over her face, and she made no effort to pull it back.

Martha looked beyond her, past the wagon driver, at the four white horses in front. She could see, in the torch light, the thin scars on their backs, and she flinched every time she heard the whip.

Behind her, she could hear the two troll heads talking in gentle voices for a change.

"Are you scared?" Troll-the-Left asked.

"Yes," said Troll-the-Right. "I'm as scared as a rabbit."

"Me too," said Troll-the-Left, almost to his own surprise. "Me too."

Martha closed her eyes, and tried to imagine herself in her mum's arms. She remembered her warmth. Her smell. The little kiss she always planted on the top of Martha's head. A kiss-plant.

It was still there.

The love she used to feel passed from her mother. It would have taken more than a falling log to crush that. And she could still feel it now. The love from all those hugs, wrapped around her like a warm blanket, telling her everything was going to be all right. Telling her that even in the cruellest moments of life, love could never die.

# A Resting Place

Night fell quickly in the forest. Or rather, it *rose.*

As Samuel and Ibsen walked down the slope, it seemed as though they were heading down like divers into a lake, as if the night was something they could drown in. And with the darkness came the fear.

By day, the forest had been scary, but in the dark it was absolutely terrifying. Every crack of a twig or hoot of an owl caused Samuel to turn around and look for approaching trolls or other scary creatures. Every tree trunk slid out of the darkness as if to surprise him. Even the three-quarter moon seemed to be gasping in horror as it stared down at the boy and the dog below, walking in such a dangerous place after dark.

At least in daylight, Samuel had been able to see if creatures had a shadow or not. Now, in the dark, it was impossible to tell the good from the bad.

He looked at the ground, and could make out three-toed footprints. *Trolls.* He kept walking, and tried not to think too much about what would happen if he bumped into a troll. After all, the book had said trolls have no weakness at all, and the book would surely be right, as it was right about the Truth Pixie and all the other creatures.

(But of course, Samuel didn't know yet that you shouldn't believe *everything* you read in books.)

Fortunately, Samuel's instinct to walk down the hill had been correct. They came to a wide road with wagon tracks pressed into the earth and Samuel was certain it was the one the Truth Pixie had talked about. The one that would lead to the Changemaker.

"Here it is," Samuel said, feeling he needed to say something. "Here's the road."

He turned right along the road, and kept walking, and noticed Ibsen was beginning to get very tired. The dog's body seemed to be falling asleep as they walked. His tail drooped. His tongue hung out of the side of his mouth like a piece of ham. His paws grew heavier and heavier.

Samuel too was finding it hard.

"Stay awake," he kept telling himself.

But it was difficult. His eyelids had become heavy weights that could only stay open with the greatest of effort. And his pixie sandals were beginning to rub uncomfortably against his aching feet.

*Well, maybe it wouldn't hurt if I had a nap,* he thought.

After all, it's probably safer to stay still in the dark than to move around. And if they had a little sleep, they would wake up feeling more refreshed and alert and would therefore have a better chance of finding Martha. With that thought in mind, he looked for a suitable hiding place where he could lay himself down.

He led Ibsen off the road and headed in among some pine trees. If they found one with a wide enough trunk, they would be able to lie down behind it and stay safely out of view.

So he walked over to the largest trunk he could find and lay down, holding the book to his chest like a hot water bottle. Ibsen curled up by his side and dozed off in seconds. Samuel found it more difficult. First he rested his head against the trunk, but it made the most hard and painful of pillows. Staring up at the night sky—a giant dot-to-dot drawing of glowing stars—he knew he wasn't going to fall asleep here.

Next he lowered his head and placed it on the ground, but the earth was hard too. And awkward, from all the pine needles. He closed his eyes and tried to sleep, but it was as much use as trying to catch up with a rainbow. Every time he seemed to get nearer, it slipped farther away.

He was exhausted, but too uncomfortable. And he kept thinking of something his dad had said after Samuel's first day of secondary school:

*Happiness is everywhere, son, you just have to know where to look for it.*

His dad had been wrong. Where was the happiness in this forest? There was nothing but fear and cruelty and loneliness. And pine needles.

*This is no good. I'll never fall asleep lying here.*

He stood up and brushed away the pine needles from his cheek. Everywhere he looked, it was the same. Hard trees and hard ground. It was as if the whole forest had been designed to stop him from sleeping.

He walked away from Ibsen, in a kind of daze between sleep and wakefulness, forgetting he was in the most dangerous part of the forest. Then, when he was just about to try the ground once again, he tripped over something. Or, more precisely, *onto* something.

Something soft. Like a large furry pillow. Or stomach.

"My berries!"

The creature Samuel had fallen on was clearly startled to be woken up from its berry-related dream.

Samuel panicked.

"I'm sorry," he said, reaching for the book that had slid down the other side of the creature's belly. "I'm sorry . . . I was just . . . I was looking for . . ."

"Somewhere to sleep?"

"Yes."

"You can sleep here," said the creature, with a yawn. "You can sleep on my belly. I'm sure it must be the comfiest thing around here."

Samuel couldn't see the creature's face very well. It was just dark fur leaning against a darker trunk. But his voice was warm and welcoming and sounded rather like a drink of hot chocolate (if a drink of hot chocolate had a voice).

"I think I might . . . find my own place to sleep." Samuel

didn't know what to do. If he ran straight away, the creature might chase him. But if he stayed still . . .

"Berries," said the creature, who already seemed halfway back to its dream.

Samuel turned himself on his side, so his right cheek was against the soft fur. The creature was right. Their surely couldn't be anything comfier than its belly around here.

*So warm.*

*So soft.*

The gentle rise and fall of the creature's breathing had a hypnotic effect. And the smell of his fur seemed to be the smell of sleep itself, as if it sweated dreams the way people sweat off their food.

"Don't sleep," Samuel said to himself, knowing that the creature could be dangerous. Knowing it might have no shadow. Knowing he should go back to Ibsen. "Don't . . . sleep."

However, tiredness was winning the battle, tugging down his eyelids and switching off the lights in his mind.

But before his eyes closed fully, he looked at the open book on the ground beside him. The moonlit page read:

## THE SLEMP

*The Slemp is a large and fur-covered creature who spends most of its life asleep. In most respects, the Slemp is bearlike in appearance, with round ears and soft fur all over its body, but its large protruding jaws are similar to those of a lion.*

*Due to its fat, comfortable stomach, the Slemp is viewed by weary travelers as a living pillow. In its waking moments, the Slemp encourages passersby to rest their heads on it, in a voice so warm and soothing it is almost impossible to resist.*

*But resist you should, for if you make the mistake of falling asleep on a Slemp, you are unlikely ever to wake up again. Slemps have extremely sensitive noses, and love the smell of dreams that wafts out of sleeping ears, which reminds them of luscious berries.*

*Not only do Slemps like the smell of dreams, they also like the taste of them. Even in their sleep they can bite the heads off their dreaming victims without even thinking. Sometimes it is one complete bite. Sometimes it is a series of nibbles, but the jaws are so fast and so strong that in either instance you wouldn't stand a chance of survival.*

*WEAKNESS: The Slemp is so tired it rarely has the strength to run after its victims.*

Samuel gulped. His body was now wide awake with fear. The fear intensified as one of the Slemp's giant paws fell across the top of the boy's pounding chest.

Pressing the paw away from him, Samuel slowly raised his head off the furry stomach.

"More berries," mumbled the Slemp as Samuel lowered the paw back down.

Samuel stood up. Started walking. Stopped.

*The book. You idiot, you forgot the book.*

He tiptoed back, picked the book up, his hands trembling with fear.

The Slemp growled, as Samuel was disturbing its sleep. The growl was so deep it seemed to come from the very center of the earth, and there was nothing hot chocolatey about the Slemp now.

In the space of a second, the Slemp sat up and snapped its wide jaws in the direction of Samuel's head. The Slemp's sharp teeth were in time to catch a few strands of Samuel's hair, but nothing else. Samuel had pulled back just in time, and was now running at Olympic speed away from the deadly creature. He turned around and saw that the Slemp was back asleep, and felt relieved. The feeling didn't last. A moment later he heard something.

At first it sounded like heavy rain, but then he recognized it from the night before. It was the sound of horses on the road. Heading his way.

Having ran closer toward the noise, Samuel now hid behind a tree that was near enough to the road for him to peep out and get a clear view. Already, in the distance, he could see them.

Flaming torches, like those he saw when the huldres caught the Tomtegubb. He waited until the flaming torches were close enough to help Samuel see the rest of them.

Four white horses, lined two by two, pulling a wagon. The wagon held some kind of cage, and there were huldres marching by the sides, carrying the torches. They had swords too, and other unidentifiable weapons attached to their belts.

When one of the huldres on the near side turned around to scan the trees, Samuel could see the creature's unblinking, wide-apart eyes.

He shot back behind the trunk. Then dared himself to look again a second later. Inside the flame-lit cage, he saw a woman with long white hair in a long white tunic with skin so pale it seemed to shine in the dark.

There was a round, barrel-shaped creature who was singing a faint song. Samuel recognized the Tomtegubb instantly as the one he and his aunt had seen leave the forest. Then at the other end of the cage he saw a large creature with two bearded heads.

*A troll,* thought Samuel with a shudder. *A real-life troll. Just like the one in the painting at Old Tor's shop.*

But it was the sight of the fourth prisoner, however, that really shocked Samuel.

This prisoner wasn't a witch, or a troll, but something far more familiar.

A ten-year-old girl, in a navy-blue dress, sitting down on the floor, with crossed legs and a face that didn't look happy or sad or anything at all.

He said her name in a gasp.

"*Martha.*"

He felt a total and complete joy surge through him.

*She's alive. Alive!*

"I'll save you." He whispered the promise. "I'll get you back."

He walked down the slope and waved his arms. Martha couldn't see him, so he walked a few steps closer and tried again.

Later he would realize that he should have waited, then followed at a safe distance behind. But that was later, and this was now.

A guard turned around. The same guard who had scanned the trees before. This time Samuel was spotted. Orders were shouted in a strange language, then two of the guards jumped down from the wagon and began to race up the hill toward him.

# The Open Door

Ibsen had woken to the sound of hooves on hard ground. Samuel wasn't there. Ibsen followed his scent trail all the way to the spot where the boy was now standing, the spot where the guards were now running toward.

Ibsen barked behind Samuel, to tell him to get moving, but for a moment Samuel stayed exactly as he was. If he got captured, then he would be with Martha again and that was what he wanted, wasn't it?

*No.*

It would be easier to rescue Martha if he stayed free. If the huldres caught him, they would both end up dead.

So Samuel ran.

Fast.

His pixie sandals hardly touched the ground as he chased after Ibsen's tail, jumping rabbits and dodging trees, hopping over pinecones. He looked behind.

The huldres were getting closer. One pulled a dagger from his belt and sent it spinning through the air toward Samuel. It landed by his feet.

Samuel thought about picking it up, but it would take too

long. He kept running, ferns and bracken whipping his legs as he shot past.

They sped by the Slemp, who was still sleeping.

Ibsen galloped farther up the hill. Samuel followed, his chest burning with every uphill step.

The slope got less steep, then leveled out. Ahead, through the trees, there were stone houses in a crooked line, with fenced-off rabbit enclosures behind each one.

"Ibsen!"

The dog ran between two of the enclosures and around to the front of the second house. He ran under an outside table and in through the open front door.

Samuel glimpsed the curve of Ibsen's tail just as it disappeared inside.

Glancing behind, he realized the two huldres hadn't yet made it up the hill. If he went through the open door, they wouldn't see him.

A knife was resting on the outside table. It was stained with fresh blood.

He picked it up and went inside the stone house, shutting the door behind him. And that is when he felt a metal thud on the back of his head, causing his mind to swirl into darkness.

# A Troll's House

The first thing Samuel was aware of was the pain.

His head was pounding with the worst headache of his life.

The second thing he was aware of was the softness beneath the pain. A pillow. He was lying on a bed.

*Where am I?*

For a moment he thought he was back at home. He thought that everything that had happened since Martha's birthday had been part of a horrendous nightmare.

He opened his eyelids. A blurred figure was leaning over the bed with two sparkling, maternal eyes looking down into his.

"Mum?" he said. "Mum? Is that you?"

As his vision sharpened into focus, the two maternal eyes became one, and the person he had thought was his mother turned out to be the ugliest-looking woman he had ever seen. In addition to having only one eye—positioned in the middle of her forehead—she had various other hideous features. Her black hair was wild and tatty, like a strange kind of plant. She had a bulbous red nose with hairs dangling out of her nostrils, and her mouth contained five wonky teeth, each as gray and desolate as old headstones in a graveyard.

"It's awake, Troll-Father!"

Her booming voice did nothing for Samuel's headache. Each word was a brick banging the inside of his skull.

*Trolls.*

"I'm coming, Troll-Mother."

A male troll of slightly less ugly appearance (if only because most of his face was covered with a beard) came into Samuel's view. He too had an eye socket in the middle of his forehead, but with no eye inside.

He held his hands out blindly over the bed, in the vague direction of Troll-Mother.

"All right, grabby fingers," she said. "Keep your beard on!"

Then something disgusting happened.

Troll-Mother dug her fingers into her eye socket and, after a little effort, pulled out her eyeball. After that, she passed the eye to her husband, who promptly squeezed it into the hole in his forehead.

"What is it?" Troll-Mother asked, wanting to know what kind of creature was lying in her bed.

Once the eyeball was in place, Troll-Father looked at Samuel, his jaw dropping in disbelief. "A human," he said. "A human boy."

"Oh," she said. "A human! A human boy!" Her voice suddenly changed, and she looked full of sorrow. "Oh . . . oh . . . I'm so sorry, sir . . . If I'd have known, sir, I'd never have hit you with my rabbit pan, sir! Oh, what must you think of me? Oh, I do apologize, sir. And for the house as well, sir. It is a terrible scruffy mess. If we'd known you was coming by, we'd have tidied the place up a bit. It's just that it's terrible hard to keep on top of things, what with only one eye between us all."

Samuel sat up and looked around. The whole house was packed into one room, and lit by fat candles. From the bed, he could see a stove and a dining table and another bed. Two troll children with single empty eye sockets were sitting on the floor and stroking Ibsen, who was lying down and staring straight at Samuel.

"You're trolls," said Samuel, in a terrified voice.

"We be that, sir," said Troll-Father, in a much more gentle voice than that of his wife.

"Are you . . . going to eat me?" Samuel asked, fear intensifying his headache.

Troll-Father looked confused. "Eat you, sir?"

"I thought trolls ate humans. I thought they boiled them in a pot. It says so in . . ."—Samuel looked around for his book and saw it lying by the front door, where it must have fallen when he had been knocked out by the saucepan—"in that book."

"Well, sir, we don't eat humans," said Troll-Father. "I can assure you of that. You don't want to believe in books, sir. They be normally full of lies."

Samuel saw troll shadows, flickering in the candlelight.

He remembered what the Truth Pixie had said. *The creatures with no shadows are the deadly ones. Those with shadows are harmless.*

"The only thing we cook in a pot be rabbits. Unless you've got long fluffy ears you're safe with us, sir," said Troll-Mother. "I be so sad for clouting you round the head like that, it's just you have to be careful, don't you not? With all this evil all about us. Anyway, we hid you well and true from those horrid creatures. They came and knocked on all the houses in the village, but we said we hadn't seen you, we did. I thought they was about to search us up and down and sideways, but I think they was in some kind of hurry. Must be taking prisoners."

*Prisoners.*

The image of Martha sitting in the cage flashed back into Samuel's mind.

"I've got to go," Samuel said. He tried to get up but the pain from the bump on his head pulled him back. "I've got to find my sister."

"Your sister?" Troll-Mother asked.

"She was in a cage. There was a wagon. It was those . . ."

"*Huldres.*" Troll-Father whispered the word, as if it was something that could do evil if spoken aloud.

"Yes, they've got her. They're taking her to . . ."

He tried to remember the name of the overlord of the forest. *The Rainmaker? The Changemaster?*

Troll-Father suddenly seemed to regret having the eye. He

didn't know where to look. It was then that Samuel realized the book really might have gotten it wrong about the trolls.

"They'll be taking her to the Changemaker," said Troll-Mother.

As soon as she said "Changemaker," two gasps rose out of the eyeless boy and girl on the floor.

The little troll girl nearly cried, but no tears could stream from her empty eye socket.

"Don't be scared, Troll-Daughter," said Troll-Father.

"Be the Changemaker coming to get us?" the boy asked.

"No, Troll-Son," said Troll-Father.

"He will if you don't eat all your casserole," said Troll-Mother.

There was a silence, and Samuel tried to sit farther up in the bed.

"Can I see the human?" Troll-Son asked.

"Me! Me! Me!" said Troll-Daughter. She shot both her hands in the air like she knew the answer to something.

Troll-Mother went red with embarrassment.

"I must be saying sorry for my children," she said. "They not be clean and polite like you, sir. They be horrible little things, the both of them. They have no idea how to behave."

Samuel wondered why her children made her so cross, as they seemed perfectly normal to him.

"Oh well," sighed Troll-Mother. "I suppose they'll want to have a look at you. Troll-Father, give them the eye."

Troll-Father unplugged the eyeball from its socket and tapped his son on the shoulder. Troll-Son blindly felt for the eyeball and, after he eventually found it resting in his father's palm, squeezed it into his forehead.

"Hello," said Samuel.

"Hello," said Troll-Son, who—now that his parents couldn't see him—was picking his nose. "I be Troll-Son."

"I'm Samuel," said Samuel. "Samuel Blink."

"Samuel Blink," said Troll-Son, in clear admiration. He tried the exotic name over and over on his tongue. "Samuel Blink. Samuel Blink. Samuel Blink. Samuel . . ."

"Forgive my son, sir," said Troll-Father. "We be only humble trolls. We're not used to fancy names like that. We're not worthy of them, you see."

"Troll-Son, stop picking your nose!" said Troll-Mother, though how she knew where her son's fingers were Samuel had no idea. "Now, give the eye to your sister before you be shaming yourself any more."

The boy troll wiped his grubby finger on his even grubbier tunic, then pulled the eye out of his forehead, making a kind of sucking sound as he did so. Troll-Son tried to give the eyeball to his sister, but the little girl—who must have been no older than six years old—couldn't find her brother's hands.

"Where it be?" said Troll-Daughter. "Where it be? Where it be?" And she kept opening and closing her hands, saying over and over, "Where it be? Where it be? Where it be?"

Samuel watched as Troll-Mother went red with embarrassment again. "I am being so ever so sorry, sir," she said, walking blindly past her husband toward her children. "They are troll children, with no manners at all."

"It's okay," said Samuel.

But just then, just as the little girl's fingers found the eyeball, both children received a slap on the back of the head from their mother, who knew the heights of her children well enough to make sure she hit the right spot.

"Behave yourselves! You useless little pixies!" she shouted as she whacked them. (To call someone a pixie was the biggest insult a troll could give.)

"There's no need of hitting them," said Troll-Father, wincing his eye socket as if it was he who was being hit. "They can't see what they be doing."

"No, but the human can. What in Shadow Forest must he be thinking?" And she whacked her children again, only this time she swung a little bit too fast and knocked the eyeball out of Troll-Daughter's fingers.

"I lost it! I lost it! I lost it!"

Samuel watched in horror as the eyeball flew through the air. It landed on the bed, and rolled across the sheets until it rested a centimeter away from his left hand, from where it looked straight up at him. Staring.

Just staring.

Well, what else could an eyeball do?

# The Truth about Humans

The four blind trolls started clamoring about, their hands feeling the bed and down on the floor, desperately hunting for the missing eye.

"See what you've done!" said Troll-Mother crossly, although neither of the two children she was speaking to could *see* what they'd done at all. "Fancy! What you must be looking like! In front of the human!"

"Now, now," said Troll-Father, in a calming voice. "There's no point in getting all hipperty. It will be here somewhere, it will."

Samuel wondered why no one asked him where the eyeball might be, especially as he was the only one who could see anything.

"It's . . . er . . . here," he said. "It's by my hand."

"Oh," said Troll-Father, embarrassed. "Would you possibly maybe just if you wouldn't mind perhaps possibly maybe . . . pick it up for us?"

"HONESTLY! HOW CAN YOU ASK A HUMAN TO DO SUCH A DISGUSTING THING! HAVE YOU NO SHAME?" boomed Troll-Mother, who was now very hipperty indeed.

She looked like she was going to start whacking her husband, and Samuel had seen enough violence for one day.

"It's okay," he said. "I'll . . . er . . . pick it up."

Samuel looked at the slimy eyeball, with its thin red veins around the green iris. He lifted his hand but was scared to touch it.

*"What are you staring at?"* He mumbled the question under his breath to the eyeball.

When his hand was near enough he closed his own eyes tight shut, because somehow it made it all seem less disgusting if he couldn't see what he was actually doing.

"There," he said, picking it up. "I've got it. Who shall I give it to?"

"Well, I think it be Troll-Daughter's turn to—" said Troll-Father timidly, but he was interrupted by his wife.

"I think it's probably best to give it back to me, sir," said Troll-Mother.

She moved toward the bed and Samuel handed her the eyeball, which she forced back into place in the center of her forehead, blinking a few times until it felt just right.

"What a helpful human!" she said. "I be so sorry that you had to see my children behave so awful badly."

"I didn't notice," said Samuel, looking at the two eyeless child trolls as they stood perfectly still and quiet once again.

"Now, now, that is very kind, but most untrue," said Troll-Mother. "That is just your human manners shining out. They be most horrid. Most horrid. Not clean and polite like you, sir. Not like you at all."

"They not be *that* bad," insisted Troll-Father.

"You are too soft with them, that's the trouble," said Troll-Mother. "When I was a youngster my father would whip me for two hours, just for scratching my eyehole. These two little rotters only get to see the whipping post two times a month, and even then it is only for ten lashes. Ten lashes! What use that be?"

Samuel gulped. Maybe it was better to have no parents at all than troll parents. Even Aunt Eda didn't seem very strict compared to Troll-Mother.

"Now, why don't you stay for some supper? I've already skinned the rabbit. It will be ready in no time . . ." She smiled at the thought of having a human stay for supper. "The villagers will be so jealous! A real-life human!"

Samuel looked at the floor, and tried not to look too disgusted at the sight of the trolls' three-toed feet. "I need to find my sister," he said, but Troll-Mother didn't seem to be listening. She just went into the kitchen and began chopping the skinned rabbit with the bloody knife Samuel had carried into the house.

While his children tormented Ibsen, Troll-Father found the bed, and sat down near Samuel's legs.

He offered a meek smile. "She's always dreamed of having a human come to visit," he said. "I think she just wants to make up for clouting you around the head with that flenking great saucepan."

"I know," said Samuel. "It's very kind, really. But I have to go and find my sister. I have to get back to the road."

Troll-Father closed his eye socket. "If you don't mind me saying, sir. It's probably not a good idea you going to the Changemaker."

"But I have to rescue my sister."

Troll-Father sighed a heavy sigh. "Nobody who be sent to the Changemaker ever comes back, if you understand me, sir. He be . . . very dangerous, sir. He has turned the forest into a very bad place. That is why we trolls never go out in the daylight. We've got to protect our shadows, see." Troll-Father believed what he was saying. He didn't know that the Changemaker and the Shadow Witch couldn't steal troll shadows because of their heaviness. In fact, troll shadows are a lot heavier than troll brains, which might explain why Troll-Father had never worked it out. But the next thing he told Samuel was perfectly true. "If the Changemaker gets your shadow, you're doomed, like them huldre-folk. They're slaves to him. They didn't used to be like that. They used to be nice, gentle fellows, so they did, sir. Living peaceful in a village near the border."

Samuel remembered the deserted village and the skull with the wide-apart eyes.

"But I *have* to find her. I have to try. She's . . . she's all I've got."

Troll-Father looked sad, and slowly nodded. "Very well, but you don't want to take the road. It will take far too long. I will tell you a shortcut that will take you to the Still Tree. That is the tree the Changemaker be living in. I haven't been there for years. Not since the Changemaker came and made all these laws . . . I've never seen him myself, sir. No. He just sends his huldres or his witch servant to do his dirty works round here . . . I would be going with you, but I've got my family to look after, you see, sir. I don't want to end up like our neighbors. They were two trolls in the same body. Troll-the-Left and Troll-the-Right, they called them. One night they headed out of the troll territory and tried to escape the forest, but they got captured by the huldres . . . I can't let anything like that happen to me. I can't leave my family, sir. I'm most awfully sorry, sir."

"It's okay," Samuel said. "I understand."

So Troll-Father told Samuel the shortcut, which was: "Head away from the road on the narrow path that leads out of Trollhelm. Keep going until you reach an open plain. This is not the clearing, but you must cross it to get there. Travel through the plain to the woods on the other side. You will see a path. This path be leading directly to the Changemaker's clearing . . . But before you set off, you and your dog should eat. You'll go a lot slower on an empty stomach, you will. A bit of food will help that aching head, sir. Come on, sir. I'll be helping you out of bed. Troll-Mother, can I have the eye while I help Samuel Blink out of bed?"

And so it was that Samuel came to eat rabbit casserole with the troll family. He had never eaten rabbit before, and didn't particularly like it very much, but he was hungry and would need all the strength he could get if he was to face the Change-maker. He found it weird eating such a big meal in the middle of the night, but he tried to be as polite as he could.

"Would you like some hurgleberry wine, sir?" Troll-Mother asked, pouring herself and Troll-Father a goblet of purple wine.

"No, thank you," Samuel said.

"You don't mind if we be having some, do you?"

"No. Of course not."

Troll-Mother shook her head. "Such good manners you humans be having."

During their mealtime conversation, Samuel corrected a few of the trolls' beliefs about humans.

Troll-Father in particular looked increasingly disappointed as he discovered that:

1. Humans do NOT live to be eight hundred years old.
2. Humans do NOT have a belly button in their backs as well as their fronts. (Samuel had to lift up his sweater to prove this.)
3. Humans did NOT climb a big ladder and cut two holes in the sky for the sun and the moon to shine through.

4. Human babies do NOT know longer words than human grown-ups.

5. Humans do NOT all get along together in peace.

This last point saddened Troll-Father so much a tear ran down the middle of his face and dripped off the end of his nose.

"Do humans have wars?" Troll-Father asked.

"Yes," Samuel said.

Troll-Father shook his head in disbelief. "No. *No.* You are not like that. I can tell. Have you started any wars?"

Samuel laughed. "I am twelve years old. I'm only a child. Only the leaders of countries make those decisions. Prime ministers. Kings. Presidents."

There was a pause, and then Troll-Son asked: "Do humans got parents, Samuel Blink?"

"What sort of question is that!" Troll-Mother boomed. "That's a rude, hipperty question. I be so sorry, sir . . . Troll-Daughter, I hear you be scratching. Get your finger out of your eye socket, right now! Anyhow, I be so sorry, sir. You do not be answering him if you not want."

"It's okay," said Samuel. "Yes, they have parents."

"Do *you* got parents, Samuel Blink?"

"No. They're . . . dead."

There was a long, long silence. And then Troll-Father, who still had the eye, looked around the stone walls of his house.

"There is an old troll saying, sir: 'The present is a home built with the stones of the past.' "

"Oh," said Samuel, not knowing what Troll-Father was going on about, but pretending to all the same.

"It is all about how you look at things, sir. When you look at that wall over there, you probably be seeing a load of old stones."

Samuel looked at the wall and nodded, for that was indeed what he saw.

"Of course you do. But when I look at that wall, my heart fills with warmth for my dear father."

"Why?" asked Samuel. "Did he build it?"

"Not exactly," Troll-Father said. "Do you know what be happening when trolls die?"

"No," Samuel said.

"Their bodies slowly change shape and then be turning to stone," Troll-Father said matter-of-factly.

"Stone! Stone! Stone!" chanted Troll-Daughter.

Troll-Father pointed to another wall.

"They be my grandparents," he said. "And that wall behind me is my wife's mother." He smiled at some distant memory.

"She was the toughest stone to break into pieces!" Troll-Mother laughed. "As stubborn in death as in life she was, sir."

Samuel looked around at the four walls and felt a strange

chill travel through him, as if all the stones were watching the conversation.

"Trolls have always lived inside their families," said Troll-Father, after taking a sip of his wine. "Ever since time began. What are you meant to do—be burying them in the ground?" Troll-Father laughed, as if that was the most ridiculous idea he had ever come up with.

"That is what humans do," Samuel said. He tried not to think of his parents' wooden coffins lowering into the earth.

"Oh. Sorry. I didn't realize."

"It's okay."

Troll-Father tapped the side of his head. "But they are in here, aren't they?"

Samuel nodded.

"Well then, that is where you must be building a house. A house made of memories, for you to visit anytime you please."

The meal ended, and it was time for Samuel and Ibsen to leave.

"Good-bye," said Samuel, placing the book back under his arm. "And thank you. For the casserole. And everything."

"Good-bye," said Troll-Mother. "And be excusing my children, sir."

"Good-bye, Samuel Blink," said Troll-Son. "Samuel Blink. Samuel Blink."

"Bye bye bye bye," said Troll-Daughter.

"Be careful," said Troll-Father. "Please, be most ever so careful."

"Yes," said Samuel, looking to see all four members of the family wave him off. "I will."

Walking away from Trollhelm, Samuel thought about what Troll-Father had said.

*The present is a home built with the stones of the past.*

Maybe there was truth as well as comfort in those words. Maybe his parents were still alive, in a peculiar way, in the minds of Samuel and Martha. And maybe they always would be.

But it wasn't enough. As far as Samuel could see it, memories were only useful if they could be shared. And Martha was the only person in the world he had left to share them with.

If he never rescued Martha, he knew he would be truly alone.

# The Flaking Moon

Martha hadn't seen her brother.

Like the other prisoners, she had no idea why the wagon had stopped moving or why two of the guards had run up the hill. And when, a little later, an empty-handed Vjpp and Grentul came back to the wagon, Martha thought nothing of it.

"Perhaps they were practicing a song for us," suggested the Tomtegubb. "A surprise song that they didn't want us to hear."

"It's a nice thought," said Troll-the-Left. "But somehow I doubt it."

With a crack of the wagon driver's whip, the horses were off again, faster than before. The huldres were anxious to make up lost ground. They knew the Changemaker would be expecting them, and they knew they had to be back home, safely belowground, before sunrise.

The Snow Witch lay down on the floor of the cage and closed her eyes. She was frowning, deep in concentration. Whispered words left her lips, so soft they blended with the breeze.

"What are you doing?" asked Troll-the-Left, shaking her with his right hand. "You're making yourself ill."

"Leave her," said Troll-the-Right. "She knows what she is doing."

"Look!" The Tomtegubb was pointing at the air in front of his eyes.

A snowflake danced sideways on the breeze, before floating out of the other side of the cage. Martha and the other creatures watched as the snow began to fall all around them, getting heavier and heavier until the ground was a white carpet.

"The moon is very flaky tonight," said the Tomtegubb. Like all Tomtegubbs, he believed that snow was made of moon flakes. "Isn't it pretty?"

He began to sing:

*"Moon flake, moon flake, what do you see?*
*Floating from the sky to me?"*

"It's her," said Troll-the-Left. "She's making it happen."

"Look," said Troll-the-Right. "Look at her face."

Everyone looked at the Snow Witch's face. The lines in her skin were getting deeper. Her thin lips were getting even thinner. The hair that went down to her ankles was spreading across the cage floor.

"She's getting older every moment," said the Tomtegubb. "She can hardly breathe."

"It's a spell," said Troll-the-Left. "She's casting a spell. She's making it snow."

"She's flaking the moon!"

Martha looked at the flakes melting into the huldres' flaming torches. Then she looked at the ground outside.

The snow was ankle deep now, and the guards were getting worried.

"*Enna oder kullook?*"

"*Nit fijoo. Nit fijoo!*"

As the snow got deeper, the horses that were pulling the cage were finding it increasingly hard work. The wagon driver kept whipping the animals harder and harder, but it was no good. Being whipped on the back didn't give them any more strength in their legs.

"*Obkenoot!*" Grentul's cry prompted all the huldres to start pushing the wagon.

The Snow Witch's frown had become a grimace. She was in tremendous pain as the spell sucked the last years out of her body.

It was a blizzard now. There was as much snow as there was air in between.

"We should stop her," said Troll-the-Left.

"Leave her," said Troll-the-Right.

"She's in pain."

"She knows what she's doing."

Martha felt the Snow Witch's white hair tickle her ankles as it kept on growing. She looked at the aging witch and saw her fingernails lengthening so fast they stretched out of the cage. Martha moved over toward the Snow Witch and crouched down in front of her. She shook her head.

The Snow Witch coughed, and whispered an answer. "My winter had already come. Your summer is still waiting. Let it be, human child."

Martha shook her head again.

"You will escape," said the Snow Witch. "You will find your words. Leave me. It is better this way."

Martha looked out of the cage and saw the huldres struggling to lift their legs out of the knee-deep snow. She looked in front and saw the horses struggling to keep pulling the carriage.

Snow was everywhere. It was in the troll's two beards. It was making the Tomtegubb look like a large snowball. It was getting stuck behind the huldres' ears and up their scrunched-up noses and decorated their caloosh-skin clothes.

Then it finally worked.

The wagon, and the cage it carried, came to a halt. At first the horses were blamed, and the wagon driver's whip punished their backs. But then Grentul noticed the wheels were stuck because the snow had risen above the axle, and was continuing to rise.

"*Nit da enna kullook,*" he said as he watched the thick snow extinguish the flaming torches. "*Enna kullook!*"

He caught sight of the Snow Witch's long nails growing fast out of the cage.

"*Odduck felk!*"

His order was swiftly followed and Vjpp and another guard entered the cage, threw Martha aside, and started shaking the Snow Witch.

But it was too late.

The spell was complete.

And the Snow Witch, lying under a shroud of white snow and white hair, was dead.

# The Stubborn Spoon

Farther south in the forest, Aunt Eda was sitting at the Truth Pixie's table, with a bowl of gorgeous yellow soup tickling her nostrils. Outside the window, snow was falling heavily. It was the middle of the night, but Aunt Eda had promised herself not to sleep until she found Samuel and Martha. She'd also told herself not to stop walking, but that was before she had caught a heavenly smell wafting through the air. A smell so tantalizing, it made Aunt Eda think of nothing else. The smell was the Truth Pixie's Hewlip soup, which he always kept on the stove overnight, just in case anyone should be passing.

Aunt Eda had, of course, read *The Creatures of Shadow Forest,* including the page about Truth Pixies. But she couldn't remember precisely what it had said. Or she didn't want to. You see, Aunt Eda had gone a day and half a night without eating and now she would have found anything tasty, let alone a soup that was designed to hypnotize people with its smell.

Before she picked up her spoon, she decided to say something nice to the chef, who was still rubbing the sleep out of his eyes.

"I must tell you, I haff eaten lots of soups in my time. Reindeer soups, cod soups, beetroot soups. Lots of different soups. But I haff neffer smelled a soup like this."

The Truth Pixie nodded nervously. He did not care about nice words. The only thing he cared about was the sight of exploding heads. It had been so long! For months he had kept this soup on the stove, hoping to tempt passersby. And he had been so close earlier this evening. Now, at last, it was finally going to happen.

He watched, with an extreme sense of giddiness, as Aunt Eda picked up the silver spoon and lifted it slowly toward her bowl.

"You will like my soup very much," the Truth Pixie said, rubbing his hands together.

"Yes," said Aunt Eda. "I'm sure I will."

But then, just as she lowered her spoon to sink it into the steaming and deadly soup, something strange happened. The spoon stopped in midair. She tried to press it farther toward the soup, but it was no good. It was like trying to join the wrong ends of two very strong magnets together.

"How strange," Aunt Eda said, and not for the first time that day.

Ever since she had entered the forest, strange things had been happening. For example, she had nearly fallen into a caloosh trap, but had managed to hold on to her javelin that had lodged across the width of the hole, and then pull herself up and out with the greatest of ease.

"How strange," Aunt Eda had said, before continuing her journey.

Then there was the encounter with the Flying Skullpecker. Now, for those of you who don't know, a Flying Skullpecker is the most dangerous kind of bird you could ever hope to meet.

They had once been straightforward woodpeckers, but when Professor Tanglewood transformed the creatures, he changed the forest's two woodpeckers as well. Once the Shadow Witch had stolen their shadows, he told her to make their beaks strong enough to peck through human heads. When Aunt Eda saw one of them flying with its large, sharp beak pointed toward her, she tried to run away. The bird eventually caught up, and landed on Aunt Eda's bun. Its beak quickly began to peck her head, but Aunt Eda didn't feel a thing.

When Aunt Eda grabbed hold of the bird, she saw that its sharp yellow beak had bent and broken, no longer able to cause harm. She let the bird go and felt her head, which had no injuries at all.

"How strange," Aunt Eda had said again.

And now she was faced with a bowl of soup that didn't want to be eaten. Or a spoon that didn't want to go near the bowl.

She leaned forward over the Truth Pixie's table and tried again. This time, the spoon slid left and hit the table.

"What are you doing?" the Truth Pixie asked. "Why aren't you eating my soup? My special soup?"

"I don't know. I'm . . . *trying*." Aunt Eda was now standing up, thrusting the spoon toward the soup and not getting any closer. "But this spoon is so stubborn."

She placed the spoon down, and tried to use her hands, but just as she was about to grab the bowl, it slid across the table. When she reached out to touch it just to check she wasn't imagining things, the bowl flew through the window that the Truth Pixie always kept open for people to smell his cooking.

"Oh no," the Truth Pixie said. "You're a witch."

"A *witch*?" Aunt Eda was appalled at the pixie's rudeness. "I most certainly—"

And then it dawned on her. The bracelet she was wearing. The one with the pewter disc. She looked at it. She looked at the engraving. HEK.

"Look, I've got no shadow," the Truth Pixie said, backing away. "You can't do anything to me. Another witch already stole it."

"Oh," Aunt Eda said. "Oh . . . oh . . . oh . . ."

She remembered how easily she'd climbed out of the hole. She remembered the Skullpecker's broken beak. And now it made sense. The magical bracelet was protecting her from danger. And if that was true, danger must have been inside the soup.

"You were trying . . . to poison me." Aunt Eda spoke the words as the memory reached her. The memory of the page she had once read in Professor Tanglewood's book. "Weren't you?" She bent down and stared at the little creature with eyes so sharp they could have cut through even the greatest lie. But, of course, the Truth Pixie's mouth couldn't squeeze out small lies, let alone great big ones.

"Nnnn—yes!"

He went on to tell her what he had told Samuel. About his unstoppable truth telling, about the Shadow Witch, and the Changemaker, and how the Truth Pixie couldn't help his murderous ways.

"Haff you seen any human children?" Aunt Eda asked, caring little for the pixie's excuses.

"Yes, I saw a boy."

"Not a girl?"

"No. A boy. A boy with a nice and juicy head."

Aunt Eda gasped in horror. "Did he try the soup?"

"No, but he tried my sandals." He sighed wearily. "No shadow, no sandals, and no exploding heads. My life is empty!"

Aunt Eda looked at the pixie's bare feet, and felt relieved. Not that she knew how sandals were going to protect Samuel in such a dangerous forest.

"You are a ferry dangerous little fellow, aren't you?" said Aunt Eda. "Ferry dangerous indeed. Now, what if a little girl came walking past your house. What would you do?"

"I would give her my soup." The Truth Pixie slapped himself very hard on the face, but he could not stop telling the truth. "My poisonous soup."

Aunt Eda looked at her javelin, and wondered if she should skewer the pixie's little heart.

"Is there any way I could stop you?" she said. "From your murderous ways?"

The Truth Pixie held his hand tight over his mouth, but then blurted out: "You could lock me in the cupboard! That cupboard there. You could lock me in and turn the key."

Aunt Eda considered. "Are you telling me the truth?"

The Truth Pixie sighed. "The truth is all I can tell."

"I must go," she told the Truth Pixie as she pushed him in the cupboard. "You will tell me where the human boy went and then I will go."

And the Truth Pixie gave her directions as Aunt Eda turned the key. Then she picked up her javelin, and went out into the snow, which was fast becoming a blizzard. Aunt Eda was worried this might slow her down, but it didn't. In fact, the snow didn't even touch her. As it fell, it parted like a curtain, leaving a clear dry path for Aunt Eda to follow. A straight black line on the sloping white ground, which seemed to be leading her where she wanted to go.

"How strange," said Aunt Eda, rubbing her bracelet. "How ferry strange."

# The Triumphant Tomtegubb
# (and the Heroic Human)

While Martha stared at the dead Snow Witch, the other prisoners were noticing something else.

"Look," said Troll-the-Left, nodding toward the open cage door. "There's our escape."

"Are you out of your ugly head?" asked Troll-the-Right. "The door's only open because they're standing right by it. We'd get caught straightaway. And have you seen their weapons?"

The huldres' weapons were indeed pretty terrifying. Each huldre guard carried on his belt one small throwing ax, one sword, one tongue stretcher and two daggers.

"We're going to be killed if we stay here. At least if we escape, we've got a chance," said Troll-the-Left. "Look, their torches were put out by the snow. It will be harder for them to find us in the dark."

The Tomtegubb jumped to his feet. "Come on, human! Let's go!"

Vjpp turned around and saw the prisoners heading toward the open door. *"Fregg vemper,"* he hissed as he struggled through the snow.

All the huldres were now aware of the possible escape.

"Now!" Troll-the-Left said, overruling his right side. "Let's go now!"

But his command came too late.

Vjpp and a really tall huldre were now completely blocking the doorway—Vjpp holding a dagger, the other a sword.

"*Ober jann oggipdiff,*" Vjpp said. His blue tongue was licking his lips at the idea of using his weapon, ready to taste violence.

No one knew what to do. They didn't understand the huldre's words, but they understood his dagger.

Troll-the-Left placed a protective arm in front of Martha.

"See," said Troll-the-Right. "I told you it was a bad idea."

"Just shut your ugly face, will you?" said Troll-the-Left.

"Come on," said the Tomtegubb. "Let's look on the bright side."

While everyone was trying to find the bright side of a situation that was made only of very dark sides, something happened.

Vjpp moved closer. Close enough for Troll-the-Left to strike out and knock the dagger out of his hand and pick the huldre up by his throat.

"Watch out!" Troll-the-Right shouted, gesturing toward the really tall huldre crunching over the snowy cage floor with his sword.

But this time it was the Tomtegubb who lent a hand—or rather, foot—as he tripped the massive huldre up, sending him flying into the snow.

"Let's go!"

Everyone followed Troll-the-Left's orders and charged out of the cage door, where the other huldres—including the old wagon driver—were waiting.

Swords and daggers came toward them.

Grentul sent an ax flying through the air, spinning its way between the two troll heads.

*"Psst, under here."*

Martha turned around and saw that while the two-headed troll was being attacked, the Tomtegubb was pointing under the wagon.

"Come on," he said. "Hide!"

But Martha kept perfectly still, standing in the snow, until the Tomtegubb grabbed her hand and pulled her under. They stayed there for a while and watched Troll-the-Left reach into the cage and grab the ax that had just been thrown at him.

He then began to swing it around, slicing through the crisp night air.

"Not so flenking tough now, are you?" he shouted.

"This is a bad idea," said Troll-the-Right. "Why can't we just—"

Troll-the-Right never got to finish his question. His head was sliced neatly off by Vjpp's sword and landed right in front of Martha.

"NO!" Troll-the-Left was in despair, and swung the ax in wild revenge, killing the wagon driver, then grabbing his sword. Within moments, he had sliced the life out of four more huldres, so only Grentul and Vjpp remained.

"The horses," whispered the Tomtegubb to Martha as the bloody spectacle continued. "Let's go to the horses."

The Tomtegubb then started crawling on his elbows under the wagon. Martha followed, keeping her head as low as possible in the narrow distance between the freezing snow and the wooden panels she could feel touching the back of her head.

Once he was out in the open, the Tomtegubb unfastened two stallions.

"Get on," he said, making a stirrup out of his hands.

She climbed on one of the horses' backs, and the Tomtegubb clambered onto the seat of the wagon, to jump onto the other horse he had unfastened. The horse winced as the fat creature landed on his back and kicked him into motion.

"Come on," the Tomtegubb said, turning back to Martha. "What are you waiting for? Let's go."

Martha was a good horse rider, but she had never ridden a horse that didn't have a saddle. The other reason she didn't kick the horse into gear was that she was worried about Troll-the-Left.

"Come on!" The Tomtegubb's cry caused Grentul to turn and look at the two escaping convicts.

"*Pijook ediss,*" said Grentul. "*Enna bikk.*"

"*Enna bikk!*" agreed Vjpp.

The two huldres turned away from Troll-the-Left and ran toward the front of the carriage. Realizing that they were more interested in a human than a troll, Martha kicked the large white stallion toward a gallop.

She followed the Tomtegubb's horse, holding on to the mane and using it as reins. Turning around, she saw two huldres on two horses chasing after her in the dark, galloping through the snowy landscape.

"Faster!" the Tomtegubb shouted, realizing the huldres were rapidly approaching. "As fast as you can!"

Martha leaned forward, so her arms were holding on to the horse's neck. She did not kick her legs into the creature's sides again or threaten it with any more whipping, but simply patted the horse and blew warm breath onto its skin.

The horse responded to softness much better than to hardness, and instantly galloped faster. Soon Martha was neck and neck with the Tomtegubb.

"To the trees," said the Tomtegubb, with a massive smile on his face. "Stick with me, human girl."

He turned to look behind him and his smile fell like a stone at the sight of a fast-approaching ax. "Watch out!"

Martha directed the horse so that the ax flew past and landed in the snow.

"Whoo-hoo!" the Tomtegubb said, enjoying himself once again. "This feels amazing, doesn't it?"

Martha said nothing.

"Now," said the Tomtegubb, over the sound of hooves pounding snow. "Stay close . . . I'll lead."

His horse went off the road, and through the trees that stood like vertical shadows in the night. Martha sat herself up a bit, to look behind. The huldres were showing no sign of giving up, their cruel faces fixed firmly on hers.

"Isn't this the best game?" the Tomtegubb asked her.

But if this was a game, it was a very strange and dangerous one. And it was still impossible to say who was going to win, as the huldres remained exactly the same distance behind.

No closer.

No farther away.

Two more axes whizzed past, but they thudded into tree trunks, and even though the huldres held their swords in the air, there wasn't much they could do with them until they got nearer.

As the chase went on, Martha started to feel a oneness with the horse she was riding. The rhythm of the hooves matching the rhythm of her heart.

"Keep going!" the Tomtegubb shouted. "Run them into the sun!"

At first Martha didn't know what the Tomtegubb was going on about. After all, the sky was still dark.

But then they reached an open plain stretching before them like a large sheet of white paper. She could now see a faint line of purple on the horizon. As the snow melted into the earth, night was slowly melting into day.

She didn't understand why this was important, but she did notice that the two huldres were gaining ground. She noticed also that there seemed to be a new desperate urgency in their voices.

"*Felooka felooka!*" Grentul shouted, and turned his horse back toward the cover of the trees.

"*Bastipool!*" Vjpp kept going, thinking of nothing but the delicious cruelty he was going to inflict on the human.

The purple was joined by orange now, pushing the night sky up toward the stars.

"Any time now," said the Tomtegubb, with a singful voice.

Vjpp galloped alongside Martha's horse. He swiped his sword and Martha ducked just before it sliced her in two.

The Tomtegubb looked up at the brightening sky. "Any . . . time . . . *now* . . ."

Right then, just as the Tomtegubb was muttering the word *now,* something happened to Vjpp.

He evaporated.

The first light of day had caused his flesh to vaporize, leaving his skeleton to clatter off the horse. Martha turned to see the huldre's skull, with its wide-apart eye sockets, staring up at her from the snow.

"Whoa there," said the Tomtegubb to his horse, who was more than happy to slow down. The horse that carried Martha did the same.

"That was a close one, wasn't it?"

Martha nodded.

"Where do you want to go now?"

Martha said nothing, but the Tomtegubb knew the answer. "You want to go home," he said. "Back to the Outer World."

Martha nodded. If Samuel was still alive, he would have surely headed back.

"I will lead the way," said the Tomtegubb, turning his horse. "I will take you as far as I can, and then tell you how to get back."

Martha felt a great relief, and wanted to thank the creature.

"I might write a song about our adventure," said the Tomtegubb, fiddling with his golden whiskers. "Yes . . . It will be a long song. Even longer than 'The Purple Trouser Song.' Now, what shall I call it? 'The Lucky Escape'? Or maybe 'Galloping to Glory'? What about 'The Triumphant Tomtegubb and the Heroic Human'? No, that's too long. Maybe I could just call it 'The Triumphant Tomtegubb' and then mention the 'Heroic Human' in the verse . . . Oh, all right, I'll mention it in the chorus. But it's hard to find things that rhyme with *human* . . . Now, before we decide the words, we really ought to get working on a tune . . ."

Martha felt something happen to her face. Her cheeks lifted, and her mouth widened. She was *smiling,* and it felt good.

The Tomtegubb saw the smile but decided not to comment on it. Instead, he started humming different melodies, and the horses slowly carried him and Martha back toward the trees.

As Samuel and Ibsen had just begun to follow Troll-Father's shortcut, it had started to snow. Broad, white snowflakes fell around them like feathers. Within moments, it had become a blizzard. Ibsen kept his mouth open, to catch the flakes on his tongue, while Samuel found shelter under a tree.

The snow was so heavy that there was no use trying to walk any farther until it stopped. So Samuel sat himself down on the patch of sheltered ground and, as there were no pine needles, found it a lot comfier than before. Ibsen curled up beside him, and within no time they had drifted asleep.

They were still asleep when the snow stopped, and when a two-headed troll walked past on the nearby path. One of the heads had been chopped off and was being carried under an arm, but was still alive. And still very cross. The two heads were so busy arguing they didn't even notice the dog and the human boy under the tree.

"I told you we shouldn't have tried to escape," said Troll-the-Right as the purple blood dripped from his neck. "I told you, but you didn't listen."

"Would you just stop moaning? Just for a second? If you'd had it your way, we'd be lumps of stone by now."

"If I'd have had my way, we'd have never been locked up in the first place. Why was it me? Why did they slice *my* head off? That's what I don't understand. Where's the justice in that? It wasn't my idea to escape. It wasn't my idea to pick up the ax."

"It could have been worse, that's all I'm saying," said Troll-the-Left.

"Oh, right. Worse. Sure. Could you tell me something worse than having to be carried around by a great, ugly, stupid flenking idiot like you until the end of time?"

Samuel's half-asleep eyes opened to see Troll-the-Left squat down and place the head of Troll-the-Right on the snowy ground, and then walk off toward Trollhelm.

"Hey! *Hey!*" Troll-the-Right's head shouted. "What are you doing? You can't leave me here! Come back! . . . Hey! Get back here! . . . I'm . . . I'm . . . I'm sorry . . . I didn't mean to call you ugly . . . or stupid . . . or a flenking idiot . . . hey, come back!"

# Grentul's Reward

Grentul pulled his horse back just in time. He waited under the shade and saw Vjpp become a skeleton, his skull and rib cage clattering together as they hit the ground.

He looked around, desperate. Where was the nearest caloosh hole? If he stayed aboveground any longer, even in shade, he would die. Light was filtering through the canopy of leaves, lending the forest its terrifying daytime colors.

He felt the light pressing down on him, like a drowning man feeling the full weight of the ocean.

Then he saw it. A familiar circle of earth that he knew was a caloosh trap. He dismounted and ran toward it, out of the safe darkness, and felt the light burn his gray blood, ready to dissolve his body.

He reached the circle just in time and down he fell, onto feathers. He called for help. Help came.

Other huldres wanted to know what happened. Their questions tore at his head like angry wolves. He didn't answer. He just kept running through underground tunnels, heading always in the same direction.

North.

Eventually the tunnels became smaller, less well presented. These tunnels he was now entering were hardly ever used. They provided a connecting route to the Changemaker that could only be used during the greatest of emergencies. Normally the Changemaker wanted them to travel to him aboveground, under the cover of night, so they could police the forest along the route.

But if ever there was an emergency, then this was it. Huldre guards had died. Prisoners had just escaped. Two humans were loose in the forest.

He kept running through the unlit, unpopulated tunnels until he was finally there, right under the Still Tree. He felt for the ladder, and climbed up. After about twenty steps, he rose up through the latch door and into the darkest chamber of the tree palace.

He rang a bell, and waited. A few moments later Professor Tanglewood entered the windowless room. He was in a bad mood, because it was the day before his birthday, and he knew no one cared.

"Shadow Witch!" he called, having seen the huldre in the candlelight.

"I am here, master." The witch emerged from her chamber. Dark vapors left her mouth, then drew back inside.

"*Enna klemp oder flimp tee, Jangoborff,*" said Grentul nervously.

The Shadow Witch closed her eyes and mumbled her usual translation spell. The huldre spoke again but was this time understood.

"I have brought some news for you, Changemaker. About the prisoner."

"Is it bad news that you bring?"

"Yes, Changemaker. It is."

"Tell me."

"There was a snowstorm. The wagon got stuck . . . in the snow."

The Shadow Witch looked worried. "A snowstorm?"

"Silence," Professor Tanglewood commanded her. And then, to Grentul: "Go on."

"The wagon . . . got stuck . . . and . . ."

Like a wheel in the snow, the huldre was finding it hard to continue.

"Go on," said the Professor.

"It got stuck and . . . and . . . we noticed the Snow Witch was mumbling something, over and over. A prayer. A curse. At first we didn't know what. So we . . . opened the cage door. And we went inside to try and stop the Snow Witch . . . to stop her magic . . . and that is when they escaped and attacked us, killing five of the guards."

The Shadow Witch looked confused. "My sister? Why was she there?"

"Quiet!" barked the Professor.

"I don't understand," said the Shadow Witch. "Those

that are brought here are killed. You said my sister could be spared."

"Silence!" boomed the Professor.

"You were going to have me kill my own sister," said the Shadow Witch quietly as the realization took hold.

The Professor flapped her words away. "Silence, you witch. Silence!"

He turned back to the huldre. "Who? Who escaped?" asked the Professor. His voice was calm.

Too calm.

"The prisoners . . . A Tomtegubb, a two-headed troll and the human girl."

"The human girl? What human girl?"

The huldre grimaced, as though in pain. But why was he so worried? His master would reward his honesty. Surely he would now understand the strength of Grentul's devotion.

"The girl who fell down the hole. Yesterday."

"Yesterday? Are there any other humans?"

"Yes," he said. "Yes . . . a boy."

"A boy?" The Professor turned to the Shadow Witch, with a look in his eyes that seemed to require a response. The Shadow Witch said nothing. Her mind was somewhere else, lost in a snowstorm.

"Yes," said Grentul.

"Was he in the cage? Did he escape?"

"No . . . no, Changemaker. We passed him. By the side of the path. We went after him but he got away."

"Away? Two humans. Running free in the forest. This is the news you come to tell me?"

"Yes, master." Grentul allowed himself a slight, nervous smile. Surely now the Professor was about to reward him for carrying this news so far underground.

The Shadow Witch dared break her order of silence. "My sister. The Snow Witch. Did she escape as well?"

"No," said Grentul proudly. "She's dead."

The word paralyzed the old witch for a moment. Then black tears clouded her eyes and fell down her cheeks. The tears went unnoticed by the Professor, who still had more questions.

"Where did you last see the humans?"

"The girl rode off with the Tomtegubb. We lost her on the plain."

"And the boy?"

"He ran toward Trollhelm."

"Well told," said the Professor.

The huldre looked relieved. "Thank you, Changemaker."

Professor Tanglewood looked at his reflection in a mirror. He turned, his face flickering in the candlelight.

"Almost well told enough to let you live."

"Master? I thought—"

The Professor turned to the Shadow Witch, and told her: "Finish him. Do it. It is my order."

The Shadow Witch hesitated, but then obeyed. She was still thinking of her sister as she blew the dark vapors toward

Grentul. They surrounded him like a cloud, and he began to choke.

The Professor smiled, and took a closer look. "That really is quite a cough you've got there . . . Not enough air, that's the problem. All those years living under the ground, walking through those tunnels. Never seeing sunlight . . . But you can remember it, can't you? You can remember the golden days, chanting your hymns to the sun. The warm light on your face. The happy times when you could look down and see your own shadow, stretched across the grass. When the sun was something you worshipped, not something you feared."

It felt to Grentul like he was choking as much on words as shadows. As the words kept digging deeper, Grentul remembered the last tender moments before the Shadow Witch had arrived in the village. His mother making dinner at the log stove, laying four places at the table, then going outside to see the two ravens that had landed outside the house.

"Do you remember, Shadow Witch? Do you remember?" asked the Changemaker. "The shadows fled to you like lost children."

He was closer to the huldre now. Standing over him as the sun-fearing creature cowered at his feet, choking inside the shade that hung like a mist around him.

"If you get to live your life again, huldre, which I doubt very much, I give you one piece of advice. Save a witch's life. If you save a witch from the clutches of death, you own her life much like I own yours. Anything you wish for, she can make reality."

The Professor laughed, and turned around to see the Shadow Witch. He noticed her black tears.

"Why are you crying?"

"It is for nothing, master," said the Shadow Witch.

"If it is for your sister, then you are right, for death is nothing. Nothing at all." He laughed again as the huldre choked below him. "Your tears are too late, Shadow Witch. I have tested the love you held for your sister, and it was no match for your servitude . . . Keep going! More shadows! He's still alive."

The huldre held on to his own neck, struggling for air as more black vapors swirled around him.

Professor Tanglewood stopped laughing and tried to look serious. "Don't think this is any easier for me, huldre, than it is for that witch. Today I can taste the full burden of my role. I am not evil. Understand that. I am the Protector of the Forest. If you could read my new book, you would understand. If I hadn't made changes, the forest would be a safe place for humans. And what do you think would happen then? It would be swamped with tourists. Day-trippers. Or they'd have taken you all away and locked you in a zoo. Or a science laboratory. And before long, they'd chop the forest to the ground."

More shadows blew over the huldre.

"Please . . ."—choke—". . . please . . ."

"There have to be sacrifices for the greater good. Yours is an honorable death. You die for the forest. Take pride in that. Take pride . . ."

Grentul could see nothing but blackness. As a suffocating pain filled his body, he held on to one last remembrance. Sitting outdoors with his mother as she made one of her sun carvings, watching the wood peel back and drop onto the grass. Her soft gentle face, lost in concentration.

"Mother," he said, or tried to, as the last remnants of life were sucked from him.

The Shadow Witch inhaled the shadows back inside her as she stood watching the dead huldre heaped on the ground. His blank, blinkless eyes. The motionless tail, curled in a kind of question mark.

Her sad thoughts broke off with another order from her master.

"Shadow Witch," he said. "The two humans are still in the forest. If they are still alive, take their shadows. Change them, in accord with my policy. Together, Shadow Witch, you and me, we must protect the forest from the Outer World. Now go! Find them!"

Professor Tanglewood watched the Shadow Witch fly away, becoming a dot, then disappearing completely into the sky. He closed his eyes, and smiled sadly, as he thought of how different it had been, in the beginning, when he first met the Shadow Witch.

# How Professor Tanglewood
# Met the Shadow Witch

By the time he arrived in Norway, it can be safely said that Professor Horatio Tanglewood was already thoroughly evil. He enjoyed being nasty in the way other people enjoy a game of tennis or a nice peanut-butter sandwich.

However, he still had a very tiny piece of goodness left inside him, which was evident on his first day in the country when he was cycling back from Flåm. When he reached his driveway a very important event happened, although Professor Tanglewood didn't realize its importance at the time.

He saw a cat dangling from the roof. It was a black cat, clinging desperately on to the gutter. Another cat—a white cat—was meowing up from the grass as if to say, "Hold on! Hold on! A man with a bicycle is coming to save you!"

A memory came to him, from the foggy reaches of his mind. He remembered seeing the two cats before, a long time ago, when he had holidayed here with his mother.

"Such beautiful darlings, aren't they, Horatio?" his mother had said as she had tickled the white cat's neck.

"Yes, Mummy," he had told her. "Yes, Mummy; yes, they are."

He mouthed the words again as he halted his bicycle. Suddenly he felt like he was someone else—not Professor Tanglewood the evil murderer, but seven-year-old Horatio, the boy who still loved the world and the creatures it contained.

Within no time at all, he was off his bicycle and galloping inside the house. He climbed the stairs three at a time and opened his bedroom window.

"Here, kitty; here, kitty; it's all right," he said as he stretched his arms as far as they would reach and grabbed hold of the cat's neck.

Horatio looked at the collar. He saw the protective Hek bracelet that had given the Shadow Witch enough strength to hold on to the roof for over an hour.

"Hek," he read aloud. "Who would name a cat after a witch? Unless, of course . . . you *are* a witch."

The black cat ran downstairs and out the open door, where it joined the white cat in running toward the trees.

The mystery wasn't solved until Professor Tanglewood explored the forest the following day and found the pixies and other creatures he and his mother had once seen all those years ago.

He suddenly realized that he no longer needed the Outer World.

*How does that world compare to this?* he wondered.

He suddenly realized he could start a new life in this wonderful forest.

He met friendly huldres, learned the art of spickle dancing, ate gorgeous Truth Pixie soup, and enjoyed comfy naps lying on the belly of a large furry creature called a Slemp. But what Professor Tanglewood enjoyed most was that there were no humans whatsoever. All he had was a world of wonderful food, beautiful music, and peaceful sleep. He enjoyed the most perfect air, the clearest drinking water and the kind of scenery that only belongs in happy dreams.

In short, the Professor had discovered paradise, and his happiness was about to intensify. One night, while he sat talking about sun worship with an old huldre, he came across two beautiful women.

They were almost identical, except one was dark and one was fair.

"Hello," he said. "I'm Professor Horatio Tanglewood. You may have heard of me. I'm quite important."

"Hello," said the fair woman, who breathed a cloud of frosty breath. "I'm the Snow Witch. This is my sister, the Shadow Witch."

"Hello," said the other, whose words rose out of shadows. "You saved my life."

The Professor was entranced. "Did I?"

"I was the cat who nearly fell to her death."

"Oh," said the Professor. "Oh yes. Of course. I remember."

The Shadow Witch nodded. She lifted up her wrist to reveal a black bracelet, with a pewter disc hanging from it. He noticed a similar one, but white, on the wrist of the Snow Witch.

"You saved my sister's life," said the Snow Witch, her pale face melting into a smile. "You are a kind and wonderful man. Not like some humans we hear about. The ones who chop down forests and attack nature. That is why we were there, you see. That is why my sister was on the roof. We keep a lookout, to make sure the forest stays safe."

Professor Tanglewood was, by this point, most intrigued. He turned to the Shadow Witch, who was, if anything, the more beautiful of the two. "So," he said. "I am a hero. I saved your life. What *exactly* does that mean?"

"There is a code of honor for forest witches that we have always followed," said the Shadow Witch. "The Hek Code. One part of that code says that if someone saves a witch's life, they can ask the witch to cast spells on their behalf."

Professor Tanglewood nodded, as if this was the most normal thing he had ever heard in his life.

"So, what spells can you cast?" he asked the Shadow Witch, raising his eyebrow in a way that he was convinced made him look exceptionally handsome.

"Any spell at all. So long as it affects the forest. I cannot work magic in the Outer World, but anything inside the forest, I can change."

"You saved the right witch," said the Snow Witch. "Her powers are much stronger than mine. I can conjure the snow and make a frost, and do a few other weather spells, but a Shadow Witch is really the best kind of witch. She can change anything that casts a shadow."

"Most interesting," said the Professor. "Most interesting indeed."

The Professor's first wish was for a home. A wooden palace, perched in the branches of the largest tree in the forest.

His second wish was for a pen and paper, which the Shadow Witch conjured out of an old caloosh feather and a pine tree.

"Now that I am your master," he said, "we really need to make sure those stupid villagers stay out of the forest for good."

"But, master," said the Shadow Witch, "my powers are only strong inside the forest."

The Professor nodded. "I know. I wasn't talking about you. I was talking about me."

The Professor had decided to cast a spell of his own. He would write about the place where he lived, which he now named Shadow Forest in honor of the beautiful witch he had just met.

In that book, he managed to transform all that was wonderful about the forest into something that was terrifying. The Truth Pixie's soup became poison. The comfortable, pillow-bellied Slemp became an eater of dreams. And the sun-loving huldre-folk became underground creatures who worked for an evil being called the Changemaker, whom the Professor had made up. Of course, to make it realistic, the Professor gave each creature a weakness. After all, how would he have been able to leave the forest and publish the book if there wasn't any chance of escape? The huldres, for instance, exploded in daylight. The Truth Pixie couldn't tell lies. And so on.

Then, once it was written, he headed back to the Outer World to publish his book, sell his house (to a newly married couple—a javelin thrower and a ski-jumper) and wait for the reviews to arrive. They were all bad, of course, but this time Professor Tanglewood wasn't bothered. All that mattered was that the superstitious villagers of Flåm believed every word. They did, as the book only served to confirm their own nightmares. The local bookshop ordered a thousand copies and sold out in a week.

That the Professor then returned to the forest and never came back would have only added more power to his book, and fear into those who read it. Then, a few months after, he decided to make the creatures even more convincing.

He asked for the Shadow Witch to turn him into a troll so he could go and steal goats in the Outer World.

"If the goats on the field were stolen by a troll, then they would know for sure my book was real and never dare to enter the forest," he told the Shadow Witch.

"Yes, master, but—"

And then, as the Professor was looking at the Shadow Witch, he noticed something. "You look rather ugly today, Shadow Witch," he said. "Are you getting wrinkles?"

The Shadow Witch looked sad. "Yes, master; yes, I am. Every time I use my magic, I get older. That is how witches age. It takes so much out of us, you see."

"Oh well, Shadow Witch. You're going to get even older and uglier, aren't you? Now, turn me into a troll. No buts. That is my command, Shadow Witch."

And so it was. The Professor was turned into a troll and he went and stole a goat. And the next night he stole another. And so it went on.

Every goat he stole he roasted over a fire and ate all by himself, until he made himself sick.

But his plan backfired . . . In fact, the goat stealing became the very reason why someone decided to enter the forest.

That's right, it was Uncle Henrik.

He left Aunt Eda and followed the three-toed footprints all the way back to the clearing. He knocked on the door of the Still Tree, expecting a troll to answer, but of course he got a human instead. And then he asked the Professor to give him his goats back.

The Professor viewed Uncle Henrik with interest. He was very stubborn, even by human standards. Rather like a foolish dog.

And then the Professor had another idea. He commanded the Shadow Witch to make sure the man could never talk about the forest to anyone in the Outer World.

"But, Professor . . ." said Uncle Henrik. "I won't tell anyone about the forest. I don't care about it."

"Don't care! Don't *care*! It is paradise."

"I already have my paradise. On the other side of the forest. I have my wife."

The Professor was not a stupid man. He knew that a tiny goat farm was not paradise, and was determined not to let this human have the chance to tell others about the wonders of the forest.

"Shadow Witch. Do as I command."

It was done.

And Uncle Henrik could never speak of the forest again.

# The Saddest Sight the
# Shadow Witch Had Ever Seen

The Shadow Witch flew over the forest as a raven, scanning the ground for signs of the two human children. She flew over the Truth Pixie's small cabin and remembered the happy time she and her sister had once spent there, enjoying his wonderful soup. She remembered too the less happy second visit, when she had returned with her master and stolen the creature's shadow.

Of course, she had never wanted to turn the Professor's book, *The Creatures of Shadow Forest,* into reality. In fact, she had argued with him:

"But, master, it will destroy everything you love. Everything you want to protect. And it will bring great danger. You will be placing your life at risk."

"Not if you make me the most terrifying creature of all," said the Professor. "Make them scared of me. The one who changed their lives. Let them know me as . . . the Changemaker. Infect that name with terror. Do you understand?"

"Yes, master."

"Then do as I command. Steal shadows and then make the changes I ask for. All of them."

Of course, there were a few problems. Certain creatures couldn't be changed.

The Tomtegubbs, for instance, cast no shadow. And the trolls' shadows were too heavy to be stolen. So these Unchanged creatures became enemies of the Changemaker. That is, of Professor Tanglewood, although the Professor never let the creatures know his real name.

If the Unchanged were ever caught outside their own regions or trying to escape, the huldres placed them in prison. Then they might be sent to the Professor, who would command the Shadow Witch to kill them.

Another problem had been the Snow Witch, who made a blizzard that lasted for days, making it more difficult to change all the creatures. The Professor ordered the Shadow Witch to steal her sister's protective Hek bracelet, then rob her of her powers. After this was done, the Snow Witch was sent to huldre prison, never to return.

Now, years later, as the Shadow Witch flew over the forest, she remembered the appalling deeds she had done in order to fulfill her master's command. Such terrible things.

She scanned the ground but there was no sign of the humans.

Maybe they had escaped. The thought consoled her, but she knew it was unrealistic. The chances of two human children escaping the forest alive were close to none.

She swooped lower, and followed the main road from above. Gliding down through the air, she could see the tracks of the wagon that had carried the human girl. And the Snow Witch.

When she reached the empty cage, her raven feet landed on one of the top bars. She saw the huldres' skeletons, lying outside on the ground. Inside, she could see no sign of the human girl. There was nothing but some drops of troll blood and the last remnants of snow.

The snow was only on one side of the cage, and in the form of a mound. Body-shaped. Instantly, the Shadow Witch knew she was looking at her dead sister.

She flew down inside, and landed in a shallow puddle of icy water.

*Sister. I am sorry. I never meant to weaken you. Forgive me.*

The melting crystals of snow struck her as the saddest sight she had ever seen.

She flew away, her heart heavy with the order she knew she had to follow. Her eyes searched between the trees, and across the open plain, but there was no sign of the humans. Then, after half a day of looking, she saw something.

At first it was just two dark, slow-moving specks heading south through a wide path in the woods.

When she got closer, the specks became a human girl and a Tomtegubb riding on white horses. She landed in front of them and shocked them into a stop as she turned back into a witch.

# The Changes

"Get off!" the Tomtegubb shouted to Martha. "Get off the horse and find some shade! Hide your shadow!"

The Shadow Witch tried to shut the Tomtegubb up with a silence spell, but she had absolutely no power over him. Tomtegubbs, despite their very solid bodies, have no shadow whatsoever, not even in the broadest daylight. In fact, they have a kind of reverse shadow, leaving the ground beneath their feet even lighter than it would be otherwise. They had never been able to be controlled by the Shadow Witch, as they never had a shadow to steal.

"Get off!" he told Martha again.

But it was too late. Martha had dismounted from the horse, but before she could find shade, the Shadow Witch had almost finished her spell.

Martha stared at the ground and watched as her shadow detached itself from her feet and rose up from the ground in a dark vapor, before it was sucked inside the Shadow Witch's mouth.

"I am sorry, human child," said the Shadow Witch.

The Shadow Witch turned herself back into a raven and

flew away. The Tomtegubb turned to Martha and, for once, looked less than happy. "Oh no," he told her. "You're going to change."

And he was right.

Martha felt her dress tighten and sink into her as though it was a second skin. She felt itchy all over, and watched as blue feathers—the same color as her dress—sprouted out of her arms. This was such a strange sight that she hardly realized she was shrinking at the same time.

For once, the Tomtegubb was speechless. But in his head he couldn't help working on the final verse of "The Triumphant Tomtegubb and the Heroic Human.'

*"And then something happened that was quite absurd—*
*The human sprouted wings and became a bird."*

Martha spread her wings and flew up into the air, finding it as easy as walking. It was as if she had known how to fly all her life, but no one had ever given her the wings she needed to find out.

*"The songless bird flew high in the air,*
*While the Tomtegubb just stopped to stare."*

Martha flew over the forest and, finding the Shadow Witch, decided to follow her. In the hope she might be changed back to being a human.

The Shadow Witch caught sight of a familiar dog's tail sticking out from beneath a tree and swooped down to get a closer look. Martha followed, not realizing she was heading straight to the tree her brother was sleeping under. She landed on one of the branches, while the raven landed away from the shade, and turned back to the Shadow Witch's true form.

Ibsen awoke, and growled.

"So," said the Shadow Witch to the elkhound. "We meet again."

Ibsen barked, to wake Samuel, and moved out from under the shade.

"Ibsen, what's the matter?" Samuel asked.

Ibsen ran and jumped high into the air, with his growling jaws heading for the Shadow Witch's neck. Samuel opened his eyes and saw the old woman with long black hair and a long black tunic who breathed black vapors as she spoke.

"Still," said the Shadow Witch. The dog duly froze in the air, as static as a photo. "Sleep." The spell caused Ibsen to fall, and land softly. He was already deep in sleep as he touched the ground.

"Hey! What have you done to my dog?"

Martha waited for Samuel to become a bird but he didn't. The Shadow Witch knew that birds all understand one another, and she knew that the two children talking to each other, even as birds, would be against her master's wishes.

So she had to think of an animal of the land, not the air. And one hopped along the path, just at that moment.

"Please," said Samuel, standing up. "Don't hurt me. I'm only in the forest to find my sister."

Samuel ran out from under the shade of the tree, his shadow stretching before him in the morning sun. Then he had a sudden feeling of lightness as he ran straight over the shadow, as if it was a black rug on the ground. He watched it rise into dark vapors that floated back toward the Shadow Witch.

Not knowing what to do, he pulled the book out from under his sweater and held it between him and the witch to try to block her magic. It was no good. The witch closed her eyes, and spoke words that crept inside Samuel's ears like insects, making his head feel itchy from the inside. Soon his whole body itched.

He dropped his book and felt his face. Soft fur was growing on his chin, his cheeks, his forehead. His clothes were all disappearing into fur. And then he noticed his ears begin to change shape, stretching high over his head.

"I'm sorry . . . We didn't mean to enter the forest . . ."

His mouth, his tongue and his teeth were changing as he spoke.

"Please, I won't—"

Before he had time to finish his sentence, the transformation was complete. Samuel the human had become something else.

Not a bird, like his sister, but a rabbit.

"I must leave you," said the Shadow Witch as a black tear rolled down her wrinkled cheek. She became a raven again and flew back to her master, leaving the rabbit and the blue-feathered bird to fend for themselves.

# Inside the Sack

Samuel the rabbit tried to wake Ibsen.

"Ibsen! Wake up! Wake up!"

It was no good.

Either Ibsen couldn't understand rabbit language, or he was so deep in sleep he wouldn't have heard anything anyway.

The blue-feathered bird was still sitting on the branch. Still watching.

"What do you want?"

The bird didn't answer.

Samuel tried Ibsen again. "Wake up! We've got to find Martha. We've got to go to the Changemaker."

Of course, Samuel didn't have a clue what he was going to do when he *got* to the Changemaker. What match was a rabbit going to be for a creature who terrified a whole forest? And even if his sister was still alive, how was she going to recognize him?

All he knew was that he had to keep trying to find her no matter what. So he tried to wake Ibsen one last time and then set off, hopping down the path, with the blue-feathered bird landing on branches in front of him, watching his every move.

Before long, he was completely lost. The afternoon turned into evening, and the forest became bathed in orange light. Trees loomed for miles above him, casting shadows that seemed to stretch forever.

It grew dark.

The infinite shadows disappeared under the blanket of night. Rabbits ran past him, looking desperate. They were all headed in the opposite direction.

One stopped in front of him.

"They're coming. They're coming!" she told him.

"Who are coming?"

The rabbit had no time to answer. She hopped toward the undergrowth while Samuel turned and watched her fluffy tail bounce away into the distance.

Then his newly sensitive ears heard something. Something behind him, getting closer. It sounded like a stampede of elephants, but when he turned around he discovered it was in fact a stampede of giants, running in a line toward him.

*Oh no,* thought Samuel as he realized he was totally exposed.

He started to hop toward the ferns and high grass where the other rabbit had headed. But Samuel was too slow, as he still hadn't got used to having his back legs bunched up by his sides.

"Come on! You can make it!"

*Who was that? Where had that voice come from?*

And then he saw a pair of eyes in the grass. It was the rabbit who had told him "they're coming." She was now giving encouragement from her hiding place.

"Hop! Use your legs!"

"I can't," Samuel said. "I'm not used to it!"

"You're thinking too much. Stop thinking! As soon as you stop thinking, it will come naturally."

Samuel couldn't stop thinking. He tried and he tried, but his brain was working far quicker than his body.

"Push down on the ground. Thump that earth! That's it! That's—"

Just as Samuel was starting to get the hang of hopping like a proper rabbit, something tugged him by the ears high in the air.

"Agh! Get off! Get off my ears!"

He was pulled upward, feeling sick as he watched the ground shoot away from him at incredible speed.

"Help! Please! Get off me!"

He was hanging in the air face to face with the giant who held him.

*No. It couldn't be.*

The huge eye, perched directly above the enormous red bulbous nose, stared in wonder at the furry creature in his hand.

"We be having a fine one here, Troll-Mother," he said.

"A right tasty specimen, I reckon. He'll bubble up real good, this one will."

Samuel could see the three eyeless members of the troll family behind, holding on to one another's dirty clothes. They passed the rabbit sack down the line toward Troll-Father.

"No!" Samuel said, the furry skin above his eyes stretching back to the point of pain. "No! It's me! Samuel! The human boy! You liked me. You gave me directions. You gave me rab . . . food."

But it was no good. Troll-Father might have understood the fear in Samuel's eyes, but as far as he was concerned, it was fear belonging to just another rabbit, not the human boy who had run into their house.

"Right, into the sack with you."

The next thing Samuel knew he was dropping through the air and into blackness.

"Aaaaaaagh!"

He landed on the rough woven fabric and tried to get his balance, but the sack was bouncing on Troll-Father's back as he walked. A tiny hole let in the light of distant stars.

The trolls marched on, but found no more rabbits. Samuel's heart thumped fast inside him, and his furry skin itched with fear. He remembered the knife he had held, soaked with rabbit blood.

Amid such bleak thoughts, something else grew inside his mind. A feeling that, whatever happened, things might still be all right. This was the most ridiculous feeling he had ever had in his life.

After all, he was a rabbit. He was trapped in a sack. He was intended for a casserole.

But like the distant stars that kept shining through the hole in the rough weave of the sack, this feeling of hope stayed with him. After all, he'd survived evil huldres, murderous pixies and a deadly Slemp. And he'd done this by concentrating on what really mattered—finding Martha.

So in his mind, he kept saying his sister's name. Just her.

Just Martha.

*Martha.*

Until there was nothing else.

# The Servants of Thubula

After a length of time—somewhere between a second and forever—Samuel was pulled out of the sack by his ears and roughly thrown into the pen with the other rabbits.

"Please!" Samuel called after Troll-Father. "This is a mistake! It's me! Me! The human boy!"

Troll-Father wasn't listening. Samuel pressed his face into the crisscross pattern of wire as he watched Troll-Father direct his eyeless family through their crooked door. "Left. Left. Right a bit. Left. That's it. Straight through. Be minding your feet, Troll-Daughter. There you go."

The door closed, along with Samuel's hope. Turning around, he saw about thirty other rabbits in the opposite corner of the pen.

Samuel hopped over and, as he got closer, heard a low and solemn voice.

"Oh, Thubula, we thank you for letting our brother travel safely to your green field, with its endless supply of carrots . . ."

The gray old rabbit that faced the other rabbits stopped

talking, and looked at the new arrival to the pen. The others all turned to stare.

"Sorry," Samuel said. "Carry on."

The old rabbit carried on with what he was saying.

Samuel quietly left the huddled rabbits and hopped around the perimeter of the fence. Yesterday he would have been able to step over it with ease, but now it was ten times his height.

He tried to lift his front feet and slot them through the fence in order to start climbing, but it was no good. He kept on getting trapped in the wire mesh.

Then the voice of the old rabbit was right behind him, up close.

"My name is Gray-Tail. I am the Spiritual Advisor for our community. I am here to welcome you to the . . . What are you doing?"

"I'm escaping," Samuel said, pulling a foot free of the wire. He didn't turn around.

"And why in the name of Thubula would you want to do that?"

"Because I'm not a rabbit. I'm a human. I'm a boy called Samuel. I went into the forest to find my sister, but now I have fur and . . . these ears . . . and . . . I've got to escape."

Samuel's nose began to twitch really slowly. At first he wondered what was happening, but then he realized this must be how rabbits cry.

"There is nothing to fear," said the old rabbit.

"What's a human, Daddy?" Samuel turned to see a bunny looking up at Gray-Tail.

"A human is a rabbit from the other side of the forest. Don't worry, bunnies. Humans are just like us, only maybe a little more confused."

"I've got to escape," Samuel said.

"Escape?" The word rippled through the rabbits like a pebble falling into water.

"It's dangerous. It's important to get out," Samuel said. "You should all try and get out."

The rabbits all laughed at the same time. It was only Gray-Tail whose whiskers didn't move at all.

"Some rabbits want to leave when they first arrive," he said. "That is normal. But I will educate you about the Truth the way I have educated the others."

"The Truth?"

"Yes," said Gray-Tail. "The Truth. Because I have a feeling you might believe in the rumors."

"Rumors?" asked Samuel.

"The rumors that often go around the forest—about our captors. Some say they are trolls who skin us and chop off our heads and cook us in casseroles."

When Gray-Tail said the words *chop* and *cook,* more waves of laughter filled the pen.

"But that's true," said Samuel, his words drowning in the commotion.

"The truth is we are lucky," said Gray-Tail. "We are the Chosen."

"The Chosen," said the other rabbits all at once, in a tone of reverence.

Samuel couldn't believe what he was hearing. "The Chosen?"

"We were brought here by the Servants of Thubula."

*"The Servants of Thubula?"*

"All the rabbits here are very lucky indeed," explained Gray-Tail. "They have been chosen by the servants of Thubula to enter the Green Field on the other side of the cottage."

"They're not servants of Thubula," said Samuel. "They're trolls."

Gray-Tail wasn't listening.

"They will bring us to the Green Field of Thubula. A beautiful paradise where rabbits roam free, with no need to hide in warrens," said Gray-Tail. "It is a magical place where old rabbits become young again and no rabbit ever dies."

"No," said Samuel. "The place on the other side of the cottage is the exact opposite of that. The only thing that waits for you on the other side of that cottage is certain death. There is no Green Field of Thubula!"

A few bunnies began to cry, and the adults kept saying over and over: "Shame! Shame! Shame!"

Gray-Tail whispered in Samuel's ear. "Don't upset the bunnies. No one will forgive you if you upset the bunnies."

The rabbits were surrounding Samuel from every angle now, moving closer.

"Shame! Shame! Shame!"

Samuel wondered, for a moment, if the angry rabbits could be more dangerous than the trolls. But Gray-Tail stopped the advancing mob by raising his ears and commanding: "Quiet."

A short silence followed.

Then he said: "Leave him. He is a human. They are the most ignorant type of rabbit. Leave us to talk, and I will educate him of Thubula and His plan to prepare us for the Green Field."

Samuel watched as the mob of angry rabbits moved away from him, comforting their bunnies as they did so. "No, no, he didn't mean it," he overheard one parent saying. "There are no trolls. Don't worry."

The old rabbit's eyes fixed on the new arrival in front of him.

"Two nights ago we lost one of our most dear friends, Flicker-Nose," he said. "A young rabbit, in his prime. They came in the night, and took him away from us. Now what is it better to believe? That he's been killed and skinned and cooked and then digested inside a troll's stomach? Or that he's been chosen by Thubula's servants to live a happy life in a rabbit's paradise on the other side of that cottage?"

Samuel didn't know the answer, so he kept quiet. And

then a dreadful thought came to him, arriving with an echo of Gray-Tail's words.

*Two nights ago . . . cooked and digested . . .*

The rabbit he had eaten in the casserole had been Flicker-Nose. Samuel felt sick, and wondered if it made him a cannibal.

Gray-Tail pointed his nose toward the happy crowd of rabbits and bouncing bunnies. "Look at them. Look at the peaceful and content community we have here. You aren't going to change that with your frightening stories, do you understand me?"

Samuel made one final plea. "If we don't work together, we're all going to die."

"No rabbit lives forever," said Gray-Tail. "Just ask my aching bones. The question is, do we live happily or miserably in the meantime?"

Gray-Tail didn't wait for an answer. He just turned and hopped his slow body back over to the other rabbits.

Samuel knew he was on his own now. He looked toward the rising sun, and the bird on the fence lost in its glare. *Why is it following me?* he wondered. *What does it want?* Samuel didn't know and right now he had bigger things to think about. He moved closer toward the wire, passing through the grid of shadows. And then, when he was as close to freedom as he could possibly get, he started to dig.

# Digging the Tunnel

"He's mad!"

"What a weird style of digging!"

"Why would he want to escape?"

"What in the name of Thubula is he doing?"

Samuel tried to ignore the other rabbits as he dug his tunnel. They sat around him, laughing and passing comment, as if it was a kind of theater. The only rabbit who didn't laugh at Samuel was Gray-Tail, who sat in silence for the whole day.

As Samuel dug deeper, the voices became more distant. His front legs were aching but he kept going, determined to get as far as he could before nightfall. All day he dug and dug and dug, the earth above him sprinkling down onto his fur and into his eyes.

He longed to have his human arms back, or his human legs that could have so easily strode over the fence, but he made do with what he had. And what he had was determination. No matter how much soil went in his eyes, and no matter how scared he got of the dark closed space of the tunnel, his paws kept on digging.

All the time he only had one thought, and that thought was *I have to escape.*

At one point, the blue-feathered bird flew in and stood there watching him.

"Go away," said Samuel.

The bird said nothing. It just stayed with its blinkless eyes staring in the dark.

"Go away. You're blocking the light."

The bird did as it was told, and Samuel kept on digging. He was dizzy with hunger. His eyes were stinging from the crumbling soil. His tiny heart was beating so hard he could feel blood pulse against his skull. If that wasn't enough, his skin itched from the combination of fur and sweat.

Eventually, he had to stop. The pain in his paws and legs was too much.

"Five minutes," he told himself, although now he was a rabbit he had no idea how to keep track of time.

There was a noise behind him.

He turned his head and saw soil falling like rain.

*Oh no. This can't be happening.*

He tried to turn his whole body around, but the tunnel was too narrow. As he struggled to maneuver himself, he made the situation a lot worse.

A cloud of earth covered his fur and filled his lungs—the tunnel behind him was collapsing.

"Help! Help! Somebody!" But his voice was blocked by a wall of earth.

*This is it,* thought Samuel. *I'm going to be buried alive. This is the end.*

But it wasn't. The earth stopped falling just before it reached Samuel's hind legs. He was trapped under the ground with earth all around him like a coffin.

*Coffin.*

The word stuck in his brain as he started to dig, forward and upward, with new energy.

Earth could fall down on him at any moment, making him one more dead rabbit in a world of dead rabbits. He dug uphill, no longer caring which side of the fence he came out on. Panic had given him more energy, but he was finding it harder and harder to breathe.

At school, he had been able to hold his breath for whole lengths of the swimming pool and pick plastic bricks up underwater. But now he was a rabbit he couldn't hold his breath at all.

Just as he was about to run out of air completely, the earth fell down on him and everything was darkness.

*I am dead,* thought Samuel. *No. I am still thinking. I must still be alive.*

The earth felt light, not heavy on his head. He shook it off and blinked and found himself out in the open.

*It is nighttime. I must have been digging all day.*

He looked behind him and saw the other rabbits staring at him from behind the fence.

"He has betrayed Thubula!"

"He has refused paradise!"

"Shame on him!"

"Shame!"

At the end of the line of rabbits was Gray-Tail, saying nothing.

After all, what could the old rabbit say? Samuel had shown him that it was possible to escape before the—

"Aaaagh!"

Samuel was yanked high in the air by his ears. He recognized the grip instantly as that belonging to Troll-Father.

"No!" the rabbits shouted. "Pick me! Pick me! He's not worthy! He's not worthy of the Green Field!"

But Troll-Father begged to differ. "Nearly got away there, didn't you?" He held Samuel up in front of him as he walked around to the other side of the cottage. "Don't think you'll be escaping now, though, furry fellow. Not unless you be digging a tunnel out of our stomachs!"

# The Miracle

By the time they reached the wooden bench, Samuel's ears felt like they were about to tear off. He saw the brilliant white moon reflected in the metal knife, and became fully aware of what was about to happen.

The booming voice of Troll-Father miles above him: "Troll-Mother, I've got him ready. He'll skin good, this one will."

The door opened, and Troll-Mother walked blindly toward the bench. "Where he be hiding, then?" she asked, her hands out in front of her, the fingers opening and closing like dangerous plants.

Troll-Father placed Samuel on the table, with a heavy hand fixing him in place. Samuel's rabbit face stared up at him from the blade of the massive knife.

"Ah yes, he be there . . . *he be there . . .*" said Troll-Mother, her fingers reaching his fur. She pressed deeper, to feel the life she was about to take. *"He be there."*

Samuel could hardly believe that these were the same trolls who had been so kind two nights ago.

"It's me," Samuel said. "It's me. I'm not a rabbit. I'm a

human. A human. I know I look like a rabbit, but I'm not one. I just changed. Please . . ."

It was useless, of course.

They couldn't hear him. Trolls may understand humans and humans may understand trolls, but neither understand rabbits.

He tried to work out how long he had left. Troll-Mother had to put in her eye, and sharpen her knife and then . . . well, that was all she had to do. However long these two jobs were going to take was the precise length of the rest of Samuel's life.

Something flew over Samuel's head. A tiny dot, reflected in the cold metal in front of his face.

*What was that?* he wondered.

Before he had time to think, he heard Troll-Mother's voice again.

"Give me the eye. Let me see the little beauty. Come on, pass it over, you useless lump."

"All right," said Troll-Father, sticking his finger into his eye socket.

Samuel heard a wet clicking sound as the eye was pulled out.

"Right, Troll-Mother, there you be. There's the—"

Troll-Father's words were replaced by the sound of fluttering wings. And just at that exact moment his hand, as well as Troll-Mother's, left Samuel's back. Samuel looked up and saw what was happening.

And so, what *was* happening?

A miracle, that's what.

Just as Troll-Father was passing the eyeball over to his wife, a bird flew right in front of his face. It was the bird that had been following Samuel. The one with blue feathers who had flown into the tunnel.

"Agh, get off! Who's there?" Troll-Father said as the feathers flapped in his face.

Then Samuel saw the eye slip out of his hand and drop onto the bench, in front of him, rolling straight toward the edge.

"I've dropped it," Troll-Father said. "I've dropped the eye . . . There was a bird—"

Troll-Mother started screaming. "You stupid flenking idiot! Find it! You hairy lump! Find it!"

"All right," said Troll-Father. "Don't be getting hipperty." His hands landed on the table, searching for the eye. They were about to reach it when the bird flew down and picked it up in its clawed feet, before flying off high in the air.

"Well?" Troll-Mother asked. "Have you found it?"

"I'm . . . er . . . it's here somewhere."

While Troll-Father searched for the eye, Troll-Mother searched for Samuel.

"Come here, rabbit," she said as her hands moved like crabs across the bench. "Where are you? Come here, fur-brain . . . come to Troll-Mother . . ."

Samuel hopped as fast as he could away from the hands

heading his way. After three hops he was at the edge, staring down at the ground below.

"Jump," he told himself. "Jump. Do it."

A finger touched his fur. Samuel closed his eyes. He remembered his dad taking him up to the high dive at the swimming pool. He hadn't dared jump. Now, though, he had no choice. He had to be brave, like a hero.

He closed his eyes and hopped out into the empty air. It seemed ages before he hit the ground.

*Thud.*

The landing hurt, but he could still hop. Which he did, as fast as he possibly could, away from the blind trolls, who kept feeling on the bench for their missing rabbit and eyeball.

Samuel hopped around to the other side of the cottage, and saw the bird fly toward the rabbit enclosure.

If his eyes had been stronger, he would have been able to see that same bird letting the eyeball drop directly into the hole Samuel had dug his way out of earlier that day, giving it an almost perfect view of the shining stars and the brilliant white moon above.

# Part III

# The Elkhound's Return

Professor Tanglewood had been writing a birthday card to himself when the Shadow Witch flew to him, and brought him news.

"Well? Is it done?" Professor Tanglewood studied the Shadow Witch, but she wasn't looking into his eyes. He began to worry that she hadn't found the human children.

"Yes, master. The humans have been changed."

"Into what, if I may ask?" The Professor was clearly relieved, and his question had an almost happy playfulness about it.

"Into a bird. And a rabbit."

"A rabbit!" The Professor looked startled at the thought. "Who? The boy or the girl?"

"The boy, master."

"A stroke of genius. What a fantastic birthday present for me. He will never survive."

She was looking straight at him now, but he couldn't read her expression. Studying her too dark eyes was like staring down two bottomless wells.

"He was with someone," she said.

"The boy?"

"Yes. He was with a dog."

"A dog? What type of dog?"

"An elkhound."

Professor Tanglewood's eyes widened in disbelief. *"No."*

The Shadow Witch suddenly looked worried, and regretted giving this information. "Master, I don't thi—"

The Professor raised his hand, to silence her. He took a deep breath, as if the news was something that needed to be inhaled in order to be fully understood. "He must have told them."

"Master?" The Shadow Witch didn't understand.

"The elkhound must have brought them into the forest."

"But, master, it makes no sense. Why would he want to do that? Why would he want to return? Why would he put the children's lives in danger? And how can a *dog* tell a human anything?"

The Professor flapped away the Shadow Witch's questions as if they were annoying flies. "Our policy is no longer enough. We must reconsider what we are to do with humans who enter the forest."

"Master, if we transform the humans into animals, the forest will always be—"

"Safe? How can you say that when you know that is no longer the case. We transform a human into a dog and what happens? The dog brings more humans into the forest?"

"Master, we don't know . . ."

"Silence! You are not here to question me. You are here to obey me. I saved your life. I *saved* your *life*. The Hek Code. You do remember the Hek Code, don't you?"

"Yes, master. Of course. I am a witch. The code is what I am."

He stood up from his desk: "Very well. Then you must do as I command."

"Master, what is it that you command?"

"I want you to find the human children and kill them. Both of them. The girl as well as the boy."

There was a pause—a long pause—and the Shadow Witch said: "Yes, I understand."

The Professor shook his head. "No."

"Master?"

He was looking at her, and saw something new inside those dark, gleaming eyes. Something he didn't trust.

"Give me your Hek bracelet."

"My Hek bracelet, master? Are you going out of the clearing? Is that why you need it? To protect you."

"Yes," lied the Professor. "Now. I command you."

The Shadow Witch reluctantly slipped the bracelet off her gray wrist and handed it over to her master.

"Now, give me your powers," he demanded.

"Master?" She had heard, but she did not understand.

"I command you to give me your powers."

"But, master, my powers are a burden you do not want." She looked at the birthday card he was writing to himself, and felt a deep hatred for her master.

Professor Tanglewood took a deep breath and closed his eyes. "Give. Me. Your. Powers."

The Shadow Witch thought of her sister, melting in the cage, and found a new strength inside her.

"Master, I can't."

The Professor opened his eyes, and looked at the Shadow Witch as if she was someone new. "You can't? You *can't*? What about the Hek Code? It is inscribed into the essence of your being. My order is your command."

"Master, there is something even more powerful than the Hek Code. Something that has been buried, but which has now risen once again inside me."

The Professor gasped in disbelief. "Pray, tell me. What is this deep and powerful thing?"

The Shadow Witch paused, as if hardly believing her own resistance. "The love I have for my sister."

"Your sister is dead."

She nodded. "I know. But the love lives stronger than ever before."

"I don't understand. What has your sister got to do with anything."

The Shadow Witch cried more black tears. "I have done terrible things in your name. Terrible things. I have turned paradise into a nightmare. And I can't do it anymore. I can't give you my powers . . . I'm sorry."

Her head dropped when she finished talking, as if the words had been keeping it upright. She turned, walked past the pickled heads and out of the room. She kept walking through the windowless chamber, passing the skeleton of the last huldre she had been forced to kill, and headed toward the door of the tree house. She was so lost in miserable thoughts that she did not hear the Professor creep across the floor, unsheathe the huldre's sword and pull it back through the air ready to deliver the fatal strike.

"I am sorry too," he said, before pushing the blade through her body and back out. Black blood dripped from the sword.

The Shadow Witch found strength enough to turn around.

*"Why?"* she whispered.

Following the word, shadows left her mouth in vapors. Professor Tanglewood understood the shadows were the source of her magic and so pressed his mouth against her dying lips, and felt a new and dark power enter his body. All the shadows of every changed creature—including Samuel and Martha—were now drawn into him. He could control them all. And do exactly what he wanted.

"Now I truly am something to be feared," he said as his skin changed from pink to gray. "I am a true Change-maker."

The Shadow Witch collapsed into his arms, and he held her there for a moment, in the windowless room. Waiting as the dark vapors he had inhaled began to take over every part of him.

# The Boy Who Just about Knew He Was Samuel

The blue-feathered bird was hard to keep track of. It was dark, and from Samuel's distance, it didn't look either blue or feathered. It was just a small dark dot vanishing into a dark and windy night.

Samuel kept hopping, aware of the blind trolls behind him still groping around for their eyeball.

"Shame!"

"Shame!"

"Shame!"

"Shame!"

He ignored the chants of the rabbits, but there was something else bothering him. The ground seemed to be tilting forward. He looked around, but none of the rabbits seemed to notice.

"What's happening?" he asked the rabbits. "The ground's moving. Can't you feel it?"

Of course, the ground wasn't really tilting. What had happened was that the Professor—or rather, the being the Professor had become—was using his new powers to draw Samuel back to his shadow. A shadow that was now contained, along with all the others, inside the Professor's body.

The effect for Samuel, though, was of gravity shifting ninety degrees, turning the flat ground into a vertical cliff face. A cliff face with trees sticking out of it.

His body dropped.

"Aaaaaaaaaaaaaaaaaaaaagh!" He twitched really fast, which is how rabbits scream. Fortunately (if such a word can be used), the spell made sure that Samuel would avoid colliding into any trees. On and on he fell, sliding down upward slopes, flying over each descent, skimming over the open plain that the Troll-Father had told him about. The sensation of falling was so strong that he was unaware that he was also changing back from a rabbit to his normal self.

"Aaaaaaaaaaaaaaaaaaaaagh!"

The scream came out of his mouth now, not as a series of fast twitches, and it lasted right until he reached the clearing. Once he was there, the ground lay back down and gravity stood back up and Samuel skidded to a complete stop.

He was a boy again. A human. His skin no longer itched with fur.

He lifted up his head. In the distance, he could see a small fire. Behind the fire was a huge tree, with a wooden palace perched in its branches. The tree seemed too still, even for a tree, its branches completely unaffected by the wind.

# The Sister Bird

"Changemaker!" Samuel shouted toward the Still Tree. "Where's my sister?"

A gray figure stepped out of the wooden palace and turned into a raven. He flew toward Samuel, landing in his natural form a few yards in front of him.

Samuel noticed how strange the figure looked. Like a man who lived in a world of no colors. His skin wasn't pink or yellow or brown like human skin, but various shades of gray. Indeed, it wasn't possible to think of Professor Tanglewood as a human anymore. Consumed by shadows, he had at last turned into his own invention, the sinister overlord known to all the forest—and Samuel—as the Changemaker.

His lips were dry and black as if they were made of thin pieces of charcoal. That shadowy darkness was in his eyes too, and under them, blackening the vertical scar on his face.

It wasn't his looks that made the Changemaker so terrifying, however. It was the way he made Samuel feel as he walked nearer.

Weak. Confused. A stranger in his own, shadowless body.

"Who am I?" Samuel mumbled to himself. "I am Samuel. Remember. Samuel. *Samuel.* Sam-uel?"

His own name sounded foreign to him, as if it belonged to someone else.

"Hello, Samuel." A black vapor left the Changemaker's lips as he spoke, and went up his nostrils.

"You . . . are . . . the . . . Change . . ." Samuel found it a strange effort to speak, as if the words were heavy things to be carried.

"I'm so glad you could join me. It's my birthday, you know."

Samuel felt like he was about to faint, but he kept himself together enough to say: "My sister . . ."

The Changemaker looked irritated that Samuel hadn't acknowledged his birthday.

"Your sister. Yes? What about her?"

"She . . . where . . . she . . ."

"I'm sorry. You're not speaking any sense. What is it with young humans nowadays? Where's their grasp of language? All right. I'll make an educated guess. You want to know the whereabouts of your silent sibling. Am I right?"

Samuel didn't have any idea if this was what he wanted to know. It was as though his mind had been stolen along with his shadow. In fact, his mind was so lost that he no longer felt scared. (You might think this was a good thing, but there is only one thing worse than feeling scared, and that is feeling nothing at all.)

"Well," said the Changemaker. "There she is. Up there in the tree. Can you see her?"

Samuel looked but couldn't see anything.

"Look closer . . ."

Samuel strained his eyes and saw a dot at the end of the branch that stuck out higher and farther than any other. A bird. Why was his sister a bird?

A single memory entered the desert of Samuel's brain. A memory of the bird that had saved him from the trolls when he had been a rabbit.

"I don't know why you would care," said the Changemaker. "What use is a songless bird? It's about as good as a body without a shadow . . . or a child without their—" He stopped, and a look of sadness fell across his gray face. "Never mind. Don't worry about your sister. If she wants to be up the tree, let her stay there." He called up to Martha: "Say hello to your brother. Say hello . . . Oh, silly me. How can a bird say hello?"

The Changemaker closed his eyes as his cracked lips began chanting some kind of spell. When he was finished, Martha was suddenly transformed from a bird to her original form. A ten-year-old girl in a navy-blue dress stuck on the highest branch of the tree.

Samuel looked and could see what was happening, but his mind was too weak to know what to do or why to do it. Even if he had thought of something, it would have been too late. The thin branch could hold a tiny bird much easier than it could a human, and gave up trying.

Martha fell, down and down and down, her dress making the most hopeless of parachutes. But inches before she hit the ground, her body froze in the air. Then she sat up as if she was lying on an invisible bed and placed her feet on the ground.

"Come, children," said the Changemaker. "Let me tell you a story."

Samuel noticed something speed past his head, flying through the air. At first he thought it was another bird, but when he saw it stop in the air and float down into the Changemaker's hands, he realized that it was in fact a book.

"*The Creatures of Shadow Forest*," said the Changemaker, catching the book and then giving it imaginary reviews. "A towering masterpiece. A most extraordinary achievement. Professor Tanglewood has excelled himself with this work of jaw-dropping genius. I can't *wait* for his autobiography."

He beckoned Martha and Samuel toward him, and they walked over, as if pulled by some invisible thread.

"Have you read his book?" The Changemaker leaned his gray face toward Samuel. "What did you think of it? Tell me. Did you like it? Speak! Speak! Speak!"

"I . . . don't . . . I . . ."

"Mmm. Not sure? Maybe you need to read it a little more closely. What do you think?"

"I . . . er . . . I . . ."

"Squeak! Squeak! Squeak!"

On that final "squeak," Samuel shrank down to the ground and found himself turned into a small, white mouse.

The Changemaker picked him up by his tail and placed him inside the open book.

"I am now going to tell you a story," said the Changemaker. "It is a true story. It is the story behind the story these pages have to tell. And when it is over, you will be over too. Your sister will watch as I close the book and squash your little mouse guts inside these pages. Blood and ink—it is much the same, you know . . . Oh, what an exciting birthday this is going to be!"

He then told Samuel and Martha the story of his life. He told them everything. About his childhood. His forgotten birthdays. His time in prison. On and on, reciting extracts from his autobiography as well as *The Creatures of Shadow Forest,* unaware of the time.

It was morning now. Pink light softened the forest, casting long shadows.

The fire had died.

"Since then, I have had to—how shall I put it?—*relieve* the Shadow Witch of her duties, and take matters into my own hands," the Changemaker said, with a heavy sigh, as he reached the end of his story. "And whatever is going to happen next, one thing is certain. No one will ever leave the forest alive."

# Inside the Book

The gray and evil creature closed his eyes and blew Samuel's shadow toward him, which was in the shape of a mouse now. Once Samuel had it back, he also had his fear, as he became fully aware of what was happening to him.

The Changemaker began to close the pages of the book with Samuel inside. He did it very slowly, savoring every moment, as though it was the last mouthful of a very tasty meal.

Samuel saw the other page coming down toward him, and he could see the word he was going to be squashed into as the shadow of the paper rose over him. The word was:

*terror*

He tried to run to the edge, but the Changemaker tilted the book upward so that Samuel slid back to the middle.

What was going to happen to his sister after he died? What cruel game was going to be in store for her?

He felt the page on his back, beginning to press down.

"Martha," he squeaked, knowing she couldn't hear him but still having to say it. "Martha, I—"

He stopped. The pressure on his back was too much. This was it.

The end.

But then he heard something.

Something soft and beautiful, that almost canceled out the pain.

And just at that moment, the book stopped right where it was. He was alive. Squashed, but alive. And the sound—the *singing*—kept going, in a soft and slow voice that seemed strangely familiar.

"*Happy . . . birthday to you . . .*"

The whole forest had gone silent just to listen.

"*Happy birthday to you . . .*"

Then Samuel turned to his sister, who seemed a giant to him.

"Martha. You're singing."

He watched Martha's mouth open and close around the words, and could see her looking directly at the Change-maker.

"*Happy birthday to . . . Horatio . . .*"

The weight lessened off Samuel's back as the being who had once been Professor Horatio Tanglewood began to cry shadowy tears. That was all he had ever wanted, to hear someone sing that song to him, and now it was really happening.

"*Happy birthday to you.*"

When Martha stopped singing she seemed as surprised as Samuel by her rediscovered voice. The book went limp in the Changemaker's hands and Samuel slid down the page, fell through the air and landed in a puddle, where he then swam to safety.

"Happy birthday . . . to *me*," said the Changemaker, drying his eyes. "Happy birthday to *me*. That is the most beautiful thing I ever heard. Did you mean it? Did you really mean it? Is that how powerful my story was? That you understood everything I have done?"

"Yes," said Martha, looking at her brother as he crawled out of the puddle.

Martha still didn't have her shadow, and the singing had taken everything she had left out of her. The only thought she had space or energy for was the thought of her brother, and all the trouble she had gotten him into by running into the forest.

In a rare moment, the man who the Changemaker used to be overruled the monster he had become, and it was inside that moment that he returned Samuel to his human self and released Martha's shadow.

"Samuel," she said, her voice still sounding as fresh and delicate as the morning dew. "I'm sorry." She had found words again, when they were needed most, and so long as she was alive, she wasn't going to lose them.

The Professor looked at the two children, and as he looked he grew more than a little jealous of the love the siblings had for each other.

"Oh no," he said. "I'm a fool. A fool. She doesn't care about my birthday. Nobody cares about my birthday. Nobody has ever cared." He remembered how his foster parents, Mr. and Mrs. Twigg, had forbidden him from having any birthday cards and, through some twist of logic, suddenly became determined to destroy both Samuel and Martha in the most horrible way possible.

He closed his eyes, and began to work his terrible magic.

"Let there be dark," he said as he began to inhale the long tree shadows that stretched across the clearing. And the more he inhaled, the more power he felt, and he drew shade from farther into the forest.

A black, swirling fog crept over the ground and covered Samuel and Martha. They both couldn't see anything in the darkness, and struggled for breath. If the fog had stayed around them, they would have choked to death, but the Changemaker wanted to watch an even more entertaining kind of end.

After all, it was his birthday.

So the shadows went straight past Samuel and Martha, and were sucked inside the former professor, whose body suffered a kind of fit trying to contain them.

"Oh, Shadow Witch," he whispered. "Why did you never want power like this?"

Samuel looked at his sister.

"Run!" he shouted. "Run!"

He grabbed her hand and they started to race across the clearing, but after only a few steps they realized something. Something that made their hearts pound in terror and their eyes bulge in disbelief.

It wasn't just that they were heading toward the trees.

The trees were heading toward *them*.

# The Waking Forest

The sight was scarcely believable.

An army of trees, with their twisting and misshapen wooden limbs, moving over the earth toward Samuel and Martha. Branches moving independently of the wind. Roots pulling themselves out of the ground like feet from shoes.

The sounds were as terrifying as the sight.

The terrible creak of bending wood.

The hideous whisper of churning earth.

The pounding heartbeat of two terrified children.

Samuel and Martha stopped running and froze in horror. The natural order had been reversed: humans rooted by fear; free-moving trees heading their way.

Of course, their free movement was an illusion. The trees *were* in motion, but their was nothing free about it. Having gained possession of the shadows, the being who was once Professor Horatio Tanglewood was guiding the forest with the kind of hand movements a conductor would use to lead an orchestra.

"What do we do?" Martha asked.

Closer and closer came the trees, branches stretching forward, twigs reaching out like fingers.

"Turn back," said Samuel, pulling his sister's hand as he started heading away from the trees.

But it was too late. The trees were too close now—close enough for a root from the nearest tree to coil itself around Martha's ankle.

"Sam-uaaagh!" she screamed as the tree pulled her away from her brother's hand.

But there was nothing Samuel could do, as he was about to become the victim of another tree. A branch swooped down and wrapped around his waist before raising him high in the air.

Up he soared, his body folded forward over the branch as the ground dropped away from him. He could see the Changemaker, laughing clouds of black vapor as he conducted the trees. And Martha, trapped close to the trunk of another, its roots and branches around her like the arms of an overprotective parent.

"Marth-aaaaaaaagh!"

Samuel felt two sensations. The feeling of rising too fast, and the feeling of being gripped too tight around his middle. But two sensations became one as the branch suddenly released Samuel, throwing him higher still.

His arms windmilled through the air, desperately trying to find something to hold on to.

The tree had thrown him outward as well as upward, and

he was soaring over what was left of the clearing. He waited to hit the ground and die, but he didn't. Instead, he fell into the soft branches of another tree. Or rather, the branches of another tree had reached out and caught him.

Again, he was held by the waist and thrown back into the air.

If he had been able to have a clear thought amid all the sensation his body was feeling, Samuel would have realized what was happening. He would have realized that the Changemaker was orchestrating a game of catch, with Samuel filling the role of the ball.

Back and forth he was flung, from tree to tree, while his sister was being slowly squeezed to death down below him.

"Let's hope no one's a butterfingers." The Changemaker's laugh echoed through the clearing.

"Stop!" Martha shouted as the branches tightened around her legs, her chest, her neck. "Please." The shout had weakened to a choke. "Stop."

She watched in desperation as the two trees throwing Samuel began to pull him in separate directions. The game of catch became a game of tug-of-war as Samuel's role switched from ball to rope.

He had never know pain could reach such intensity. The agony was everywhere, taking over his whole body—his shoulders, his knees, his wrists, his ankles—as the two trees pulled farther and farther apart, testing the strength of his bones.

"Now, children, I am afraid we must say good-bye,"

said the Changemaker. He raised his hands, ready to make the final instruction for the trees to follow. The instruction that would tear Samuel in two and tighten the stranglehold around Martha's neck.

The Changemaker closed his eyes.

He hummed "Happy Birthday."

He savored the delicious power he felt inside him. Power over the species that he had once belonged to. The species that had bullied him at school, and called him names, and sent him to prison, and never let him celebrate his birthday.

He opened his eyes.

"Now, children, it is time—as they say—to die."

And that is when they saw it.

Both of them.

Their eyes were squinting against the pain, but still they saw it.

A small straight line soaring high through the air, toward the Changemaker. Some kind of spear.

He turned around, following the children's eyes. And he was just in time to catch sight of the javelin before it hit him, but too late to stop it from entering his body.

"No!" he screamed, black blood spilling over his hands as he clutched the weapon that pierced his chest and back. As he screamed, shadows left his body from his mouth and headed back toward the forest. He fell to the ground.

Samuel glimpsed someone at the far edge of the clearing. It was Aunt Eda with Ibsen by her side.

After that, everything was swallowed in choking darkness as shadows flew back to the trees, the plants, and all the creatures they had once belonged to.

Inside that darkness, the branches let go of Martha's neck and body, and the roots crawled away and tucked themselves back under the earth they had emerged from.

At the same time, the two trees that had been pulling Samuel stopped their game of tug-of-war, and Samuel clung on to the wood that had been wrapped around his waist. When the darkness ended, Samuel dropped down from the low branch and landed softly.

He went over and hugged his sister as Aunt Eda and Ibsen ran toward them.

But then they heard something.

"Help!" It was Aunt Eda.

As she had run past him, the Changemaker had reached out and grabbed hold of her ankle, and a new cloud of shadows emerged from his mouth. Aunt Eda and Ibsen choked, trapped inside the cloud.

Samuel and Martha ran to help.

"Stay back," said Samuel, to his sister. "I know what to do."

He approached the cloud of shadows and held his breath, digging his hand in his pocket. Before the Changemaker knew what Samuel was doing, the boy had dropped a Hewlip leaf into his mouth.

"Oh no," said the Changemaker as he exhaled the last of the shadows.

"This isn't how it's meant to—"

"Run away," Samuel told Aunt Eda, Martha and Ibsen.

And they did. They ran away, and didn't turn back when they heard the dreadful splatter of the Professor-turned-Changemaker exploding behind them. A noise that sounded, to Samuel, like a triumph and a tragedy all at once.

# The Return of Uncle Henrik

"Martha! Samuel!"

Aunt Eda held her arms out like she had done at the airport, but this time even Samuel welcomed the hug. He held her close, and felt something he hadn't felt since his parents died. A feeling of being filled up, right to the very top, like lemonade in a glass. He didn't know exactly what this feeling was, but he guessed it was being loved.

"You followed us," he said. "You came to save us."

Aunt Eda planted kisses on both their heads, and tried not to cry. "Well, yes, what else was I to do? Now, now, now, you must tell me, are you both all right?"

"Yes," said Samuel.

"Yes," said Martha, and it was that long-awaited yes that brought a tear to Aunt Eda's eye.

"Oh, children, I have been so worried about both of you."

"I'm sorry," Martha said.

Aunt Eda waved the sorry away. "No, Martha, you did not know what was in the forest. It isn't your fault."

Samuel turned to look at the javelin sticking out of the

ground. The Hewlip leaf had been so powerful that there were no visible remains of the Changemaker at all. "How did you get here?" he asked his aunt.

"I had a bracelet. A witch's bracelet," she said as she showed him the cloth band and pewter disc attached to her wrist. "It was ferry useful. It protected me. And then I found Ibsen by the side of a path. He led me here."

Martha thought about the Snow Witch, and remembered what she told her about the bracelet. She wondered if it was the same one. But then she wondered something else.

"Where is he now?" she asked. "Where's Ibsen?"

"Oh no," said Aunt Eda, looking around for her dog. "Oh no. Ibsen? Ibsen? Where are you? Where are . . ." Then she gasped. Her eyes widened in disbelief. "No. No, it can't . . . no . . . I'm seeing things . . . no . . ."

There was a tall man walking toward her, smiling softly.

Samuel looked at the man and recognized him from the photographs. The ones he had seen in the attic, of the Olympian standing triumphant on a ski slope. The beard. The smile. The eyes. He looked older and grayer, but it was definitely him.

"*Uncle Henrik.*" The name fell out of Samuel's mouth as a whisper.

Uncle Henrik said something in Norwegian to Aunt Eda, who was still openmouthed in shock. Then he turned to the children and spoke.

"Hello, Martha. Hello, Samuel." He had a gentle accent

that melted his words the way toast melts butter. "Yes, it is me. I am your uncle Henrik."

"Where haff you been?" said Aunt Eda, feeling his face to make sure it was true. "Haff you been hiding in this terrible forest? Did I do something wrong?"

"No. You did nothing wrong. And I haven't been hiding. I have been with you the whole time. By your side."

Aunt Eda didn't understand.

Uncle Henrik pointed to the javelin and to the space where the Changemaker had been. "He let me leave the forest. But he changed me. All those years ago. He turned me into an elkhound. I was transformed, but I was still me. I still kept my promise. I came back for you."

"*Ibsen,*" she said.

Uncle Henrik wiped the tear from her cheek. "I have never left your side all these years."

"All these years," echoed Aunt Eda, unable to hide the sadness in her voice.

They held the moment, and then Uncle Henrik said to Samuel, "Thank you for the cheese, by the way. It wasn't as nice as the 'Gold Medal,' but it was tasty all the same. And not as deadly as Truth Pixie soup."

"Oh," said Samuel, embarrassed as he remembered how rude he'd once been to the dog. "That's all right."

Aunt Eda was going to say something else when she noticed a distant sound. A sound that hadn't been heard in the forest for many years.

Uncle Henrik had heard it too, a strange but musical chanting. "I know that sound," he said. "I heard it years ago. When I came into the forest before. It is the sound of huldres worshipping the sun. They must all be back in their village."

Martha gasped in horror. *"Huldres?"*

Aunt Eda was confused. "But huldres don't come out in the sun."

"They used to," said Uncle Henrik. "Before the changes."

Samuel looked around at the trees that lined the clearing. They didn't look evil or menacing anymore. They looked calm and peaceful and exactly the way trees should look. And then he saw a shape in the air. A raven, flying toward them.

The bird landed and turned into a beautiful woman. *The Shadow Witch.* She walked over toward them with her long, dark hair floating on the breeze. "The forest is at peace again," she told them, breathing in through her nose as if the peace had a smell. "And I am young again, back to how I was before my dark deeds made me old and ugly. Everything is back to what it once was. It is a happy place once more. A paradise."

Then the Shadow Witch looked at Martha. "Thank you," she said.

"What for?"

"For saving my life."

Martha looked confused, so the Shadow Witch explained. "If you hadn't walked into the forest, I would still be his servant." And then she spoke louder, so everyone could hear. "All of you, you have saved me. And you have saved the forest. My sister's death was not in vain. The Professor is dead. All his evil wishes will be reversed. And it is to you I owe my powers now. If you stay in the forest, you need never grow old. You need never die."

"The forest will be a paradise again," said Uncle Henrik.

And then they began to think about what paradise might mean.

"We could liff in peace and eat Truth Pixie soup and it wouldn't hurt us," said Aunt Eda, whose mouth watered at the thought.

"We could listen to songs all day long," said Martha, who knew the Tomtegubb could sing wherever he wanted now.

"And we could sleep on a Slemp every night," added Samuel, who was still rather tired. He noticed a tattered book lying on the ground near where the Professor had died. *The Creatures of Shadow Forest*. The book that had nearly squashed Samuel to death.

"Well, everyone," said Uncle Henrik. "What shall we do?"

Aunt Eda considered. "Paradise is not a place," she said. "If I am with you, all of you, I will be ferry happy whereffer I am." Aunt Eda looked at the two children. "Samuel? Martha? Do *you* think we should stay in the forest?"

Samuel turned to his sister. "Martha," he said. "What do you want to do?"

Martha frowned, as if thinking about a very hard sum. A sum that measured the value of singing Tomtegubbs against other things.

"I want to go home," she said eventually.

"Me too," said Samuel.

"Home?" Aunt Eda wasn't sure which home they meant.

"With you," said Samuel. "And Uncle Henrik."

"Home, where you have to go to school?" Aunt Eda asked. "Where you have to eat smelly brown cheese?"

This was a good point, and Samuel considered it for a while.

He remembered what his dad told him. *You can find happiness anywhere, son, if you look hard enough.* It might be harder to find happiness among a foreign school and breakfasts of brown cheese than in a magical forest, but he was willing to try.

"Yes," said Samuel. "Home."

And so it was that they began their journey home, passing spickle-dancing pixies, harmless woodpeckers, sleeping Slemps and singing Tomtegubbs. They walked softly through Trollhelm, and by the stone house where the Troll family Samuel had known were inside asleep, still unaware that the forest outside had been changed.

They walked through the huldre village, where smiling creatures had returned and were carving sun sculptures out of wood and chanting their hymns to the sun. Samuel knew, in that moment, that huldres would never appear in his nightmares again.

"Now," said Aunt Eda as they approached the edge of the forest. "Are you sure you want to leave the forest behind. Because when we are back in the outside world we will want to keep this a secret. We can be happy to live near such a magical place, but it might be best not to tell anyone. Do we all understand?"

"Yes," said Uncle Henrik, Samuel and Martha all at once, like people saying a prayer in church. "We understand."

Then they hesitated, just for a moment, before stepping out from the shade of those final pine trees. And there it was—the white wooden house, the driveway, the washing line. In the distance they could see the fjord, and the mountains, and the road leading to Flåm. Aunt Eda slipped the bracelet from her wrist and placed it in her pocket, not knowing if she would ever need it again.

Martha smiled when she saw the house and placed her hand inside her brother's. It felt as natural as the grass beneath their feet.

"So," said Uncle Henrik in his melted-butter voice. "Here we are again."

As they walked down the grass slope, Samuel gently squeezed his sister's hand, and she gently squeezed it back.

*This is it. This is our home.*

As he had that thought, Samuel looked up to the sky and saw a raven flying high above. The raven circled in the air and waited for the four of them to reach the house. It stayed there, flapping its wings, as Aunt Eda opened the door and led everyone inside. Samuel waited for a moment, on the doorstep, and cast one final glance at the bird. To any other eyes, it could have been the most natural sight. Just a bird flying near a perfectly ordinary forest.

Samuel smiled.

He knew it was the Shadow Witch, watching them safely home.


## THE END

(Which was really just a beginning.)

TURN THE PAGE FOR A PREVIEW OF THE
NEXT NOVEL STARRING SAMUEL BLINK,

# Samuel Blink
## and the
# Runaway Troll

# Uncle Henrik's Funny Turn

Samuel Blink was lying on the ground, pulling clutches of grass out with his fingers, as if it was the green hair of some rather evil and large-headed monster.

He was bored, you see. Totally, utterly, brain-numbingly bored. Not that he absolutely minded being bored. No. On the scale of "Worst Things to Be," being bored was nowhere near the top. It was certainly not as bad as many of the other things he had been this summer. Like being frightened out of his skin, or feeling so sad he could hardly breathe.

But still, if only his stuff had arrived from England. Or if Aunt Eda and Uncle Henrik had a TV. Or a computer. Or a book that wasn't written in Norwegian. If only there was somewhere exciting he could go.

True, it looked *nice* around here. Just by tilting his head left, away from the white wooden house, he could see the still waters of the fjord and, farther in the distance, the vast rugged triangle that was Mount Myrdal. But nice as it was, you can't play with a view. You can only look at it. And as it was, according to Uncle Henrik, three months away from the start of the skiing season, it was going to be quite a while before it offered some genuine fun.

Of course, there was one place he could see that could offer something exciting. It was the pine forest right in front of him, that began where Aunt Eda and Uncle Henrik's land ended, right at the top of the grassy slope. But he wasn't allowed in there.

"We still haff to be careful," Aunt Eda had told him and his sister, Martha. "If we don't effer cause trouble with the forest, the forest won't effer cause trouble with us."

"But the forest's safe, now," he'd said.

"Well, we don't know," she said. "Not for sure."

This was true, of course, There were still a lot of unknown things about the forest, like whether all the trolls who lived there were good or just some of them. And this type of question could do something to lessen the boredom of an afternoon, but not quite as much as seeing a troll face-to-face.

He was just about to pull a particularly large clutch of grass when he heard the faint sound of the telephone ring in the house. A few minutes later his aunt was calling him from the door.

"Samuel!" she said. "I haff to tell you something. And what are you doing on the grass? You are far too close to the forest."

Samuel sighed, and pulled himself up to walk over to his aunt. She was quite a stern woman, in some ways, and certainly looked it with her hair tied in her bun and her buttoned up cardigan and her tight mouth and prickly chin. But she was a good and kind woman too, who was only really guilty of worrying a bit too much.

"That was Fru Sturdsen on the phone," she said, once Samuel was in the hallway and taking off his shoes. He noticed Martha was in the kitchen, talking to Uncle Henrik at seven hundred miles an hour as he prepared roast elk and cowberry jam for supper.

It was funny. After their parents died, Martha hadn't said a word for weeks, but now you couldn't shut her up. It was as though all those unspoken words had been saved up like money in a bank and she was spending them at every opportunity. And all she would talk about was the same thing—the time she spent in Shadow Forest.

". . . and so . . ." she was saying, ". . . when I was in the underground prison with the Snow Witch I met this two-headed tro—"

"*Martha*," said Aunt Eda, sharply, as she overheard. "I think we haff heard enough of this conversation. Perhaps we shall talk about something else. Like how you are feeling about your new school? And remember, when you start school you must not mention Shadow Forest. I know it is ferry exciting to liff next to a forest full of such strange creatures, but we must not effer tell anyone about it. This is ferry important, because as I say Fru Sturdsen has been on the phone and—"

"What kind of a name is Fru?" said Samuel, frowning at the name as if it had an unpleasant smell.

"It's not a name, it's a term of address. *Fru* means 'Mrs.' in Norwegian. *Herr* means 'Mister' and *Fru* means 'Mrs.' So I am talking about *Mrs.* Sturdsen. Your new teacher."

Samuel's heart sank. How was he ever going to fit in at a new school if he didn't know the language?

"What did she want?" Samuel asked.

"Well, she telephoned to say how ferry excited she is to haff two new children starting her school tomorrow. And she also said it would be a good idea if you wrote about what you did in your holidays. They do it after effery summer apparently."

Samuel rolled his eyes. "Homework before we even start?"

He had already thought schools in Norway sounded strange, with ten-year-olds like his sister being in the same class as twelve-year-olds such as him. But having to do homework *before* term began—that was even worse.

"Apparently, yes," said Aunt Eda. "Homework before you start."

Uncle Henrik stopped crushing cowberries for a moment. "I remember when I was at school," he said, his gentle face broadening into a smile. "Every summer I used to make sure I did something interesting just so I had something to write about."

"Yes," said Aunt Eda briskly. "Well, I haff to say that is

not the same problem we face here, is it, Henrik? Quite the contrary in fact. I am worried that there is rather too much for them to say."

"What's the big deal?" Samuel said. "Everyone thinks there are weird creatures in the forest. That's why they're too scared to visit it."

"They're scared because they don't know for sure," she said. "And if they know Henrik is back after all those years he was meant to be missing in the forest, then efferyone will want answers. So we must pretend we know nothing, and you must not write anything about the creatures of the forest. And tomorrow, when you are both at school and people find out where you liff, you must not try and impress them with stories about the forest."

"Hey," said Martha, blushing. "Why's everyone looking at me?"

"Because you've got an unstoppable mouth," said Samuel.

"No, I—"

"Listen," said Aunt Eda, raising her hand to stop an argument. "It's going to be difficult for all of us. But you must pretend you haffn't effer seen Uncle Henrik. Well, not until we decide what we are going to do. And they must not know about trolls and pixies and so forth. What do you think Magnus Myklebust would do if he found out we had seen such things?"

"Who's Magnus Myklebust?" asked Martha, stealing a

pickled onion from a jar she had opened in the kitchen.

Aunt Eda and Uncle Henrik shared a glance, and Samuel noticed there was something strange about this glance, but he couldn't work out what it was.

"Mr. Myklebust is a man I used to know before I went to the forest," said Uncle Henrik in a slow voice, as if each word was precious and breakable and needed to be let out as carefully as porcelain teacups from a chest. "I met him after I retired from ski jumping and moved to Flåm with Eda."

"Not anymore," said Aunt Eda, shaking her head. "No. Definitely not anymore."

"What's so special about him?" said Samuel, staring at the empty dog basket.

Aunt Eda laughed. "Beleef me, there is nothing ferry special about him. But he is not ferry nice. Not ferry nice at all. And he has neffer liked your uncle ferry much."

"Why not?" said Martha, taking another pickled onion.

"It is a long story. And you haff your homework to do. But anyway, the point is that if he found out about the forest, he would want to chop it down and make money out of it. If he wasn't so scared of what might be in the forest, then he would do it right now. He already owns half of Flåm. Ski lodges, holiday homes. He is the richest man in the willage. And he has always been wanting to know about the forest. So if he found out, we would be in trouble. There are local laws about this kind of thing. Laws that go back hundreds of years, to the time of King Håkon the Good, the first Christian king of Norway. Laws about knowledge of efil creatures. Laws that no one has bothered to update. We must be ferry careful." Her attention switched as she noticed Martha pinching another pickled onion.

"Now, Martha, that's enough nibbling. You won't be able to eat your elk. Honestly, what is it with you and pickles?"

Martha shrugged. "They're tasty," she said. Indeed, for Martha, this was the very best thing about Norway. There were pickles everywhere. Pickled berries, pickled nuts, pickled onions, pickled cucumbers, pickled cornichons. And she was eating them at every given opportunity.

"Right, well, when you do your homework, you must not say anything about the creatures that liff in the forest. And when you go to school, you must not say that your uncle has come back. That is ferry important."

Samuel leaned back as far as he could on the rocking chair, supporting himself on tiptoes. "So . . . you want us to lie?"

Aunt Eda closed her eyes, tight, as if someone had just flicked water on her face. "Well, it is not really *lying*, it is just not telling the whole truth."

Samuel nodded, and rocked forward on the chair. "Yep. Thought so. Lying."

Aunt Eda was getting flustered. "No, it's . . . could you just *sit* still."

As soon as she said the word *sit* in such a sharp way, a rather remarkable thing happened. Uncle Henrik dropped his chopping knife and sat down on his heels, with his hands on the floor. His tongue was hanging out of the side of his mouth, and he was panting, as if doing an impression of a dog. But if it was an impression, it was a very good one, and Uncle Henrik's eyes showed no sign of a joke. Indeed, Uncle Henrik's eyes showed no sign of Uncle Henrik. It was as though he was in some kind of a trance and had momentarily forgotten he was a human being.

But Aunt Eda didn't seem to look too bothered. She just rolled her eyes as if it was a perfectly normal occurrence.

"What's happening to Uncle Henrik?" asked Martha, so confused that she stopped crunching on her pickle.

"Is he all right?" added Samuel, getting back off the rocking chair.

"Yes, yes," said Aunt Eda, through a sigh. "He had a couple of these turns yesterday."

"Turns?" said Samuel. He remembered how his mum had used to say his granddad had "funny turns." But Samuel was pretty sure granddad's variety of funny turn never involved sitting on all fours on the kitchen floor, panting like a dog.

"Before you woke up, I haff found Henrik lying in the dog basket," said Aunt Eda. And as she said the word *basket*, Uncle Henrik cocked his head to one side and gave her a look of canine bemusement, before charging through the house on all fours. Martha squealed as he nearly ran her over and Samuel jumped out of the rocking chair to get out of his way. But Uncle Henrik flew past the rocking chair and ended up in the dog basket, where he lay down. Obviously, he was rather too big for the basket, and seemed most awkward in there, with his head leaning over the side and his legs sticking out. Yet, despite his clear discomfort, he still found time to lick the back of his hands, as though they were paws needing a wash.

"Henrik!" shouted Aunt Eda. "Henrik! Snap out of it! You are not a dog! Henrik Krohg get out of that basket immediately. Henrik? Henrik? Can you hear me?"

And Samuel and Martha watched as Uncle Henrik's eyes fluttered, as though he was waking up from a bad dream.

"Oh," he said, wearily, as he pushed himself to an upright, thoroughly more human position. He blushed, as he realized Samuel and Martha were watching the whole thing. "It's happened again, hasn't it? I thought I was still a—"

"Yes," said Aunt Eda, stroking his arm. "But don't worry. You're back with us now. Everything's going to be fine. I'm sure. Yes, everything's going to be fine."

# Roast Elk and Cowberry Jam

Samuel stared at his plate of roast elk and cowberry jam and wondered if he would ever get used to Uncle Henrik's food. Seriously, who would think of putting meat and jam on the same plate? If his mum and dad hadn't died, he and Martha would be still in England, eating normal food. And then, after eating the normal food, he would have gone upstairs and done something equally normal like play on his computer or watch TV or read a book or ride his bike to Joseph's house. Joseph was his best friend. Or had been. How could he expect someone to stay best friends with him if he was in a different country?

"Come on," said Aunt Eda, noticing Samuel hadn't lifted up his fork. "It will get cold."

So Samuel began to eat his meal, which didn't taste anywhere near as bad as he had imagined. And neither he nor his sister brought up the subject of Uncle Henrik's funny turn. They didn't want to embarrass Uncle Henrik any more than he already was, because they liked him very much. He had a more gentle manner than Aunt Eda. You wouldn't think they would go well together, but—rather like roast elk and cowberry jam—they somehow made a good combination.

"So," said Samuel, "if we're not meant to talk about the forest, why don't we talk about ski jumping? Why don't you put your medal downstairs, where everyone can see it?"

You see, Uncle Henrik had been a ski jumper in his youth, and a rather good one, coming in second in the Olympics.

Uncle Henrik laughed quietly, and shook his head. "No, I don't think so. It can stay in the attic, I think . . . And anyway, who would see it?"

This was a good point. After all, no one except the postman ever came around, and for the last two days even he hadn't come by, and so Aunt Eda had been collecting letters from the post office in Flåm.

"*We* could see it," said Samuel. "And it would be cool to have it on the wall." *Better than all those rubbish paintings of mountains,* he thought, but didn't say this out loud.

Martha swallowed a large mouthful of elk and decided it had been a while since she'd said anything. "What did it feel like, when you used to jump? Were you scared? I was *so* scared when I was in the huldres' cage traveling through Shadow Forest."

"Yes," said Uncle Henrik. "I was sometimes very scared indeed. But sometimes a bit of fear isn't a bad thing. It is how we find out who we are, and what we are made of. You stand at the top of a ski-jump tower, like the one that is on Mount Myrdal, and you are on your own and there is no one you can rely on but yourself. I tell you, it is the best feeling in the world."

"Oh, children, you should haff seen him," said Aunt Eda. "Flying through the air! It—"

She was interrupted by the telephone, and went to answer it. Everyone stopped to watch as Aunt Eda's face began to look cross and frightened all at once. Even though she was speaking in Norwegian, it was clear to Samuel and Martha that it wasn't a welcome call.

"Yes . . . Magnus, is that you? . . . You heard what? . . . Oh, what nonsense! . . . Don't be ridiculous . . . I can assure you that no such thing happened . . . no . . . absolutely not . . . now, I suggest that a busy man like yourself could do better than listen to silly gossip . . . now, I must go . . . *morna*, Magnus. *Morna*."

Her hand trembled as she put down the receiver.

"Who was that?" asked Martha.

"Mr. Myklebust," said Aunt Eda. "The man I told you about. The man who wants to destroy the forest. And possibly us too."

Uncle Henrik's normally calm face creased with worry. "What on earth did he want?"

"Well, he's heard a story from Johannes. The postman. About what happened three days ago."

Samuel was confused. "What *did* happen three days

ago?"

Aunt Eda and Uncle Henrik looked at each other, and Henrik's cheeks became the same color as the cowberry jam on his plate. "It's all right, Eda," he said. "I'll tell them."

Then he took a deep breath, as if he was standing once again on top of that ski-jump tower and told Samuel and Martha what had happened.

"I had another 'funny turn,' as your aunt put it. I heard the letters go into the letter box and I lost myself completely. I ran on all fours and ran to the door and I . . . I . . . I bit Johannes. I bit his hand and then he pulled it out and I kept . . . I kept barking . . . like a . . . well, like a dog . . . I wasn't aware of it at the time . . . it was like I went to sleep and became something else for a few seconds and then when I woke up I was staring out of the window at the postman's face. And of course, once I saw him I ran upstairs again to hide, but I suppose it must have been too late."

Samuel and Martha sat there and nodded as if this was a perfectly normal piece of information. They knew that as well as being a goat farmer and a ski jumper in his life, Uncle Henrik had also spent many years as a dog. Yes, a real life lamppost-wetting, flea-scratching, postman-biting dog.

"No," said Aunt Eda. "It is not too late. Not at all. Mr. Myklebust knows nothing. Nothing at all. Not for certain. We haff to be careful, that is all. Henrik, you must not go out of the house. And when you are downstairs, we must draw the curtains. And children, we do not do anything that puts ourselves in efen more of a situation. You must not think about going back to the forest. We must forget it efen exists. And if you effer see anything leef the forest, then you must tell me or your uncle straightaway. This is ferry important. You remember what I always say, don't you?"

Martha and Samuel looked at each other, and recited Aunt Eda's favorite saying word for word. "If we don't effer cause trouble with the forest, the forest won't effer cause trouble with us."

Aunt Eda frowned. "Why do you say 'effer,' I don't speak like that. I say 'effer,' not 'effer,' thank you ferry much."

And Martha nudged Samuel, and Samuel laughed and the laughter was contagious because pretty soon it had spread to Martha and then to Uncle Henrik, and eventually even Aunt Eda was laughing as well. And, for a considerable few moments, their laughter seemed to make all their worries about new schools and nosy phone calls disappear out of the house and float away on the clean mountain air.